*I wish I knew who they are. My enemies . . . .*

Kate keeps getting mysterious phone calls. About me? I am allowed to hear ordinary conversations like when she says she doesn't feel like playing golf or can't come to a committee meeting or doesn't want a new vacuum cleaner. When she gets these mysterious calls she closes the door of the room so I won't hear what she says. I could listen on the extension but when I think how good she is to me I put temptation behind me.

Kate is like a mother to me. Is my mother anything like that? If I love her how can I forget her? Could I ever forget Kate? *Sic transit Gloria mundi*. What makes that go through my mind all the time? Dr Greenspan says I'm a virgin. So I must be.

I hate lies . . . loathe and despise liars. Lies have surrounded me all my life . . . I can't remember what they were but know they existed. Worse: lately I've told lies and I know I will lie again and again and again when I have to.

## By Vera Caspary

(Select Bibliography of titles available in
The Murder Room)

### NOVELS

### SHORT STORIES

Vera Caspary, the acclaimed American writer of novels, plays, short stories and screenplays, was born in Chicago in 1899. She is perhaps best known for *Laura*, the 1942 novel that was made into a successful film in 1944. Her writing talent shone from a young age and, following the death of her father, her work became the primary source of income for Caspary and her mother.

A young woman when the Great Depression hit America, Caspary soon developed a keen interest in Socialist causes, and joined the Communist Party under a pseudonym. Although she soon left the party after becoming disillusioned, Caspary's leftist leanings would later come back to haunt her when she was greylisted from Hollywood in the 1950s for Communist sympathies. Caspary spent this period of self-described 'purgatory' alternately in Europe and America with her husband, Igee Goldsmith, in order to find work.

After Igee's death in 1964, Caspary returned permanently to New York. She died in 1987 and is survived by a literary legacy of strong independent female characters.

# The Secret of Elizabeth

VERA CASPARY

An Orion Paperback

This edition published in 2022 by
The Orion Publishing Group Ltd
Carmelite House, 50 Victoria Embankment
London EC4Y 0DZ

An Hachette UK Company

3 5 7 9 10 8 6 4 2

A CIP catalogue record for this book is available from the British Library.

ISBN mmp: 978 1 4719 2090 5
ISBN ebook: 978 1 4719 1891 9

Typeset by Input Data Services Ltd, Somerset

Printed in the UK by Clays Ltd, Elcograf S.p.A.

MIX
Paper from
responsible sources
FSC® C104740

www.orionbooks.co.uk

# The Secret of
# Elizabeth

# Chapter One
# The Mystery
## Introduced by Chauncey Greenleaf

1

As I am to become, later, an actor in the drama, I had better introduce myself at once and, begging your indulgence, explain my impassioned interest in the mystery of Elizabeth X. Since boyhood the thriller as literature has been to me the source, not only of study, but of unceasing pleasure. As the son of a woman famous as the author of detective and murder stories, I had in earlier years cherished the idea of becoming a writer in that field. My Ph.D was earned with a dissertation on *The Significance of Mystery in the Literature of the XIXth Century*, and I have since published two monographs on related subjects. But I have long known that I lack the imagination necessary for the creation of suspenseful literature; indeed I find it difficult to create violent situations, to wallow in gore or to contemplate the carnal realism demanded by readers of contemporary fiction.

The opening chapters of the mystery were related to me on an early train (8.04 am local from Westport, express from South Norwalk to New York). Long before we reached Grand Central Station, I sensed the impending excitement of a true mystery, and have since seen it develop into a drama as

1

remarkable and as convoluted as the tales of that grand old master, Wilkie Collins. What a stew he would have concocted of its ingredients; how his fantasy would have larded the dish with juicy morsels of suspense, spiced it with savoury hints and conjectures, added the luscious fruits of hope and the acid taste of horror. As I am not so gifted, I shall have to present the story as it developed.

I hope the reader will not be put off by prose which my ex-wife, in a moment of spite said, redundantly, made me sound like an old antique. At that time, barely thirty and sensitive, I took her criticism so to heart that in the following nineteen years I failed in various attempts to write in the style of fashionable young authors. In other ways I am thoroughly modern, so much so in fact that certain colleagues as well as relations and New England neighbours consider me radical. Now, in telling this tale, I shall retreat happily to my 'XIXth Century' mentors.

As I said, I was on the early train, had settled in a seat beside a window, and was deep in the *Times* when a new passenger seated himself beside me. From Westport to South Norwalk we observed the early commuter's rule of silence. It was only after the train had started again that he addressed me.

'Good morning, Professor.'

Engrossed in an account of corruption in the nation's capital, I did not bother to lower my paper, but merely grunted a greeting.

My elbow was jogged. 'See that fellow over there?' I lowered my *Times* and recognised my neighbour, Allan Royce.

'Which fellow?'

As usual the early train had become crowded at South Norwalk. A number of passengers stood in the aisles, clinging to the backs of seats to preserve their balance as the train joggled and jittered along. Royce nodded towards a young chap with undisciplined red hair and predatory eyes.

'I've noticed him before. He usually takes the 8.43,' I said. 'May I ask why you are interested?'

'He's been snooping around my house for a couple of nights. He drives a Triumph, two-seater convertible.'

'Probably a student of architecture,' I ventured. It was not uncommon for the breed to drive up our lane to view the Royce house. Four years before, when the house was new, articles about its unique construction in architectural journals and popular magazines had brought students and sightseers swarming up our quiet lane. Whispering Hill Road is a *cul de sac* with only seven houses on its two miles, ending in Royce's property. My house, a quarter of a mile down the road, is its closest neighbour.

'He's not the only one who's been snooping in our neighbourhood,' I said. 'State Troopers have been passing and Pop has honoured the area with a number of visits.' Pop is the local nickname for our police chief whose initials stand for Percy Orville Potts.

Royce confirmed this with a scowl. 'Haven't you heard?'

I do not think he intended to tell the story in detail, but it was apparent that he needed to talk to someone worthy of his trust. He began with a lengthy and not altogether relevant account of his wife's disposition (indisposition would be a more accurate description). After nine years of frustration Kate Royce had given birth to a daughter. For five weeks she was an ecstatic mother, her life centring around the beautiful infant. One morning she found the child dead in its crib. (I am reminded of an entry in Mary Shelley's journal:

3

*Find my baby dead. Send for Hogg. Talk. A miserable day. In the evening read 'Fall of the Jesuits'.*) A dry dismissal of tragedy, but Mary had no doubt of her fertility while poor Kate Royce, having waited nine sterile years, despaired of ever having another child. She refused to return to her work as a social statistician, shunned society and gave herself to despair that verged on the suicidal.

It was in early September, the first Sunday after Labor Day, that Allan persuaded her to pull herself together and attend a party given by friends in Redding. He had hoped the company would divert her. Drinks, laughter and unrestrained conversation had quite the opposite effect. It was shortly after ten o'clock when Kate, using the trite excuse of a headache, asked her hostess's leave to depart.

It was a chill and windy night at the dark of the moon. To avoid the noise and glare of the highway, Allan chose a narrow road that wound through a dense wood. Kate seemed more than usually tense. Except for a brief answer to his question about her headache, she remained silent. Allan's attention was given to the road's rocks and hollows while his inner mind was fixed on the complexities of the next day's work in New York where he was supervising the erection of a sixty-floor condominium.

A sudden exclamation from Kate so startled him that he let the car jolt over a protruding rock. 'Look, Allan, look!'

Among the dense foliage a white shape moved like a spectre, indistinct at first, then clearly seen, hidden again by thick brush, and after the car had rounded a curve, its headlights picked out a girl in a white dress. His foot remained steady on the accelerator.

'Aren't you going to stop?' Kate demanded.

'What for?'

'Go back, dear, please go back.' Kate's tone was frantic. 'She may need help.'

Allan was unsure. City crime had crept into the country-side. Young women were said to carry guns. Better for a man to mind his own business in these parlous days. He turned his head and saw the girl stumbling blindly toward the car. Kate's pleas continued. 'You can't just leave a girl wandering in the woods at this time of night.'

Backing the car, Allan argued, 'What's she doing in the woods at this time of night? Probably stoned or drunk.'

'Maybe escaping from some brute who tried to rape her.'

'Don't be so romantic.' Although he doubted the wisdom of the act, he stopped beside the girl.

Kate jumped out. 'Can we give you a lift?'

The girl seemed startled, wary as an animal who has heard movement in the underbrush. Kate's hand fell gently upon the girl's bare arm. 'You needn't be afraid of us. We want to help you. Where do you want to go?'

There was no reply. The girl, clad in a white dress with arms and legs bare, shivered in the cool night air. She obeyed humbly when Allan told her to get into the back seat. 'Where are you going?' he asked, and was again re-warded with silence.

Allan started the car, for there was no sense in remaining in the woods and no way to go but forward. After a time Kate switched on the car light and turned to look at the passenger who had slipped down on the seat and was curled in a position that would have been extremely uncomfortable had she not been so deeply asleep that neither the jolting of the car nor the voices of her rescuers disturbed her.

'The poor child's exhausted.' In Kate's tone Allan

recognised the sweetness and firmness that had been absent since that evil day when she had found her baby dead in its crib.

At the next junction, Allan looked at cars approaching from both directions. 'Wouldn't you know? There's never a police car when you want one.'

'You wouldn't turn her over to the police!'

'What else can we do with her?' asked Allan querulously as he turned in the direction of Westport with the intention of dropping her off at the police station. Kate protested. 'You can't do that to her, she's sound asleep.'

'What's that got to do with it?'

'They'd book her for vagrancy or something, and she'd have a police record for the rest of her life. An innocent young girl.'

'What makes you think she's so innocent?'

Kate switched on the light again and looked in the back, but all she saw was a crumpled white dress and a mass of dark hair.

'What do you suggest doing with her?' Allan demanded.

'Isn't it obvious?' Kate waited for him to suggest what she had already decided. They were not two miles from Whispering Hill Road, but four miles from the centre of town.

'God knows who you'd be taking into your house.'

'She's not a criminal.'

'What makes you so sure?'

'The way she's sleeping. No one with a guilty conscience could sleep like that.'

'Do you suppose criminals lie awake all night contemplating felony?' scoffed Allan.

Some of the old grit and humour had been restored so that Kate was determined both to have her way and avoid a clash. 'Just till tomorrow, darling. When she wakes up and tells us where she lives, I'll drive her home. So please, dear, let's not wake her. You're strong enough to carry her in,' and to ensure against objections, she added, 'You've carried me and I'm much heavier.'

Allan could not forgo the gallant gesture. Kate hurried ahead to unlock the door so that Allan was free to carry the sleeping girl to the guest room. On the bed the girl stretched, whimpered and turned from the light. Dark spots and leaf stains on her dress, caked mud on her legs and arms, the tangles and bits of forest debris caught in her hair gave flagrant contrast to the spotless sheets.

Allan brushed a dead leaf off his jacket. 'Such filth to be brought into the house.'

'Sheets can be washed.' Kate drew the coverlet over the sleeping girl and stood beside the bed, looking down tenderly on the smudged face. Allan had undressed and brushed his teeth before she came to their bedroom. During the night he awakened to find himself alone in their king-sized bed. Presently Kate returned to confess that she had turned on a small lamp in the guest room. 'In case she wakes up and is frightened. At least she'd see she's not in a cell in the police station. And,' she added with a sheepish laugh, 'I left milk and cookies in case she's hungry. She's so pitifully thin.'

Allan could not but appreciate Kate's concern for the waif. He caressed and kissed her with the result that her old vitality was restored and both rejoiced in such love as they had not known for many months. Allan described the act as extraordinarily passionate. Both overslept the next morning so that Allan dressed hastily and left without breakfast in order to catch the early train.

As soon as the door closed behind him, Kate hurried to the guest room. The sleeping girl moaned and twisted on the bed. Tears stained her cheeks and the long dark lashes were damp. The bathroom door had been opened, the milk and cookies were consumed. Kate left quietly. Shortly before noon she returned to find the guest room unoccupied. A panel of the glass wall stood open. In the garden, as still as a tree trunk, stood the girl. Kate hurried out.

'Good morning,' she said. The girl seemed unaware of the intrusion. Kate moved closer, placing herself directly in front of the other so that their eyes met. The girl seemed not to see her, but to be aware only of some object far away. Her eyes were like an infant's, deep violet blue with milky blue-toned whites. With a pang Kate recalled the eyes of her dead baby. She made an attempt to speak unemotionally. 'How do you feel after that nice long sleep?'

The girl drew back, placed a hand over her heart as though to quiet its tumult. Tension increased. The slender body was shaken by tremors. Kate wondered how she could reassure the agitated creature who seemed like a doe or faun, uncertain of an enemy, wishing to flee but paralysed by terror. Rather than call attention to the obvious fear, Kate took a matter-of-fact tone. 'Aren't you hungry? Wouldn't you like some breakfast?'

Lips quivered, but no words came out. The girl was strange. Mute? Mad? A fugitive? Apprehension filled Kate's mind. With effort she shook off her misgivings. 'Come,' she extended her hand, 'we'll find something you like in the kitchen.'

Without taking the proffered hand, the girl followed Kate through the house to Allan Royce's famous modern kitchen. Sunlight poured through delicately tinted glass upon the floor of imported tiles, upon polished wood, gleaming copper and stainless steel. 'Sit down,' Kate indicated a small table in the corner window. 'What would you like? Eggs? Bacon? Cereal or perhaps . . .' she turned from the refrigerator to see the girl bent over the table, her head resting on crossed arms. As cheerily as she could manage, Kate went on, 'perhaps a sandwich. It's almost lunch-time. I've got some lovely cold roast beef. Or cheese.' She paused, recognising the start of irritation at the lack of response. Coming to stand beside her guest she was assaulted by the odours of dried earth, dead leaves and perspiration. Tact had become difficult, but she forced herself to speak kindly. 'Perhaps you'd like to clean up before you eat. A bath or shower . . .'

The girl sprang to life. 'Yes, please.' She skipped ahead of Kate to the guest room, jerked off the filthy dress and stood before her hostess naked and unashamed. At the bathroom door she paused and spoke: 'How did I get here?'

'We, my husband and I, found you wandering in the woods last night and brought you home.'

'Oh!'

'Don't you remember?'

'Thank you for your kindness.' The girl proceeded into the bathroom and shut the door.

Kate called to her that she was going to put the soiled dress into the machine with her washing. The girl shouted thanks through the closed door. From her own closet Kate took a shift of that faded blue denim favoured by the young. She was taller and heavier than the girl, but it was not necessary for the informal garment to fit precisely, and Kate added a leather sash to be tied around the slender waist as well as the required underwear.

When the girl reappeared, fresh from the shower, pale cheeks rosy, dark hair tied up in a towelling turban, she seemed quite unlike the waif in the woods. In the borrowed shift she moved with the proud carriage of a stylish young woman whose posture showed good health and good breeding. Nor was she the child the Royces had thought; no longer cringing or crouching, she showed a fully developed body, slimmer even than those emaciated nymphs who appear in advertisements on television.

She was, Kate reported when Allan telephoned, really quite good-looking.

'Who is she?' he asked.

'We haven't talked yet. She's having breakfast. She's got an appetite like a horse. A starved horse.'

'Well, find out where she lives and take her home if it's anywhere around there. And phone when you know anything. I'll be in the office.'

Kate poured herself a cup of coffee and joined the girl at the table in the window. 'Let's get acquainted. I'm Kate Royce, my husband's Allan, he's an architect. You may have heard of him. He did the Acme building and, oh, lots of others, and this house.'

'It's beautiful. I'd love to live in a house like this.'

'And what about you, dear?' Kate disliked showing curiosity or assuming it her right to ask questions.

The girl retreated into obstinate silence.

'Who are you?' After another silence, Kate's patience became strained. 'Can't you tell me? What are you afraid of?'

Shadowed lids closed over the lustrous eyes. Pale lips trembled. 'I don't know,' the girl said. 'I don't know who I am.' As though the confession lifted an unbearable burden, the girl relaxed, sank back in her chair and uttered a sigh that hinted at tragedy.

'You don't know your name?'

'Please believe me. I've been trying since I woke up and I can't remember. Not anything. It's weird.'

'Do you know where you live? Anywhere around here?'

'I don't know where here is. Where are we?'

'Westport, Connecticut. About five miles out of town.'

The girl nodded wearily. In the glass-enclosed corner she was the victim of harsh sunlight and tinted glass. Lilac shadows circled her eyes. Under frail flesh a blue vein throbbed. She sucked in her lips, drew a deep breath and beat the table with a taut fist. 'I don't know who I am nor where I live. I can't remember. It's a kind of sickness, I guess, mental sickness.' She uttered the phrase like a cry for help. 'There's a name for it. I can't remember that either.' The irony forced out a weak laugh.

'Amnesia.'

'Yes, amnesia. Please believe me.'

Behind the closed door of her bedroom Kate spoke to Allan who refused to believe that the girl was honestly suffering complete loss of memory. Kate, whose sympathy had been completely captured by the girl's bewilderment and sadness, pleaded with him to take pity on the poor creature.

'Better take her down to the police station,' Allan said.

'No, no, I can't. She's such a nice girl, educated and well bred. Wait till you hear her speak.' Kate was not sure whether the accent was English, the result of theatre training or acquired in a fashionable boarding school.

'You've got to make a report,' Allan argued. 'Her folks may be looking for her. If she's such a nice girl her family's probably frantic.'

'What would the police do with her, Allan? Put her in a cell?'

'It's your duty, Kate. How'd her people ever find her if it wasn't reported?'

'Oh, no,' sighed Kate. Nevertheless she promised that she would inform the police that a girl who could not give her name or address dwelt in the home of Mr and Mrs Allan Royce of Whispering Hill Road. She telephoned the station and spoke to Chief Inspector Potts.

\*

'And what happened? What did the police do about her?' I asked. The story had so grasped my attention that I had not noticed the passing of time nor the space we had travelled. Beyond the window darkness was relieved by the occasional lights of the Grand Central tunnel. The train jerked to a stop. Allan sprang up and moved towards the exit. I followed but was impeded by passengers pushing between us. I rudely shoved my way through the crowd so that, as we ascended the ramp, I was again close to Allan.

'What did the police do about the girl?' I asked again.

'Sorry,' he said, 'I'm late for an appointment.' He sprinted ahead. I kept behind, pushing and jostling, while I roared my demand for a continuation of the story, but was finally separated from him by a hurrying passenger, none other than the redheaded chap who had been seen snooping about the Royce house. Before I could catch him up, Allan leaped into a taxi. As I did not know which train he would travel on in the evening, I had to wait until the next day to hear a continuation of the story. You can be sure I was at the station early the next morning, watching every passenger arrive, hoping that Allan had not caught an earlier train. Just as the 8.04 pulled in, he raced along the platform and flung himself into the last car. I followed close behind.

## 2

Not all that I set down in this chronicle was related by Allan Royce on early morning trains. Much of it Kate told me afterwards, some was observed, and certain details, I confess, were born of my imagination and knowledge of the persons involved—but no more than is needed in order to give character to their actions and speech and to add a bit of sauce to the bare bones of reality. For my tendency to be romantic, I must ask forgiveness.

Allan had been nervous about the stranger in his home, had taken an earlier train than usual that evening and had been surprised to find Pop cosily established in the living room, a tall glass in hand. While not an intimate friend of the Royces, the chief of police was rather fond of Kate who had more than once, before she had given up her job, consulted him on matters concerned with juvenile crime in urban communities. Somewhat pompous, the Chief was a jovial fellow, good-natured with all but felons, and liked by all except those suspected of felony.

'I just told the little lady she's got nothing to worry about,' he informed Allan. 'In twenty-four hours, forty-eight at most, we'll know her name and address and licence number.'

The girl sat quite still, pressing herself into a corner of the couch as though she wished to make herself invisible. The change in her appearance amazed Allan. The waif he had carried to the guest room had turned out to be a handsome young woman. 'A little beauty,' he told me. 'Even old Pop was trying to make an impression.'

The Chief kept assuring her that she had nothing to fear. She had only to come to his office to be photographed and fingerprinted, and in a couple of days she would know her identity and probably recover her memory as well. 'What makes you so sure?' Allan had asked. Chief Potts held up his hand with the fingers spread apart. Pointing to their tips, he said, 'These. Infallible records of identity. In many states they're required on drivers' licences. Ought to be everywhere, ought to be a federal law. People in accidents, explosions, fires wouldn't be nameless victims. They could be identified in minutes unless, of course, they're burned to a crisp.' He laughed and looked to the others for laughter. There were no echoes. Kate refilled his glass. 'So by tomorrow evening we'll have the little lady's name and licence number.'

'Unless she hasn't got a driver's licence,' Allan said.

'Of course she's got a licence, everybody's got a licence except the indigent poor. And a young lady like her owns a car for sure. Been driving since she was old enough to get a junior licence, haven't you, dear?'

'I don't know.'

'Don't know!' The indulgent tone showed that the Chief considered loss of memory no more than a girlish whim. 'You drive a car just like you walk or eat or do anything natural.'

The girl offered an apologetic smile.

'Don't feel bad about it, little lady. Before you know it, you'll be remembering everything, maybe even stuff you'd rather not remember. Why, I wouldn't be surprised if tomorrow night you'd be safe at home with Mommy and Daddy.'

I write these words with distaste. Coarse language does not distress me so much as the use of baby talk by a grown man. And a police chief! I was further offended by Allan's report that the ageing dolt had declared that his Mommy would scold him if he was late for supper. He patted the girl's bare arm and once again told her she had nothing to fear with P. O. Potts taking care of her. She promised to report to his office the next morning to have fingerprints and her photograph taken.

'But please,' she said, 'don't let it get into the newspapers.'

As Allan accompanied him to the door, Potts repeated what Kate had told him about the girl's expensive dress and what he called her snob accent. It was his theory that she had lived or been staying at one of the big estates around Fairfield and had been kidnapped or assaulted. 'Raped, maybe. The shock could have caused this . . .' he tapped his forehead, 'this condition. Amnesia, it's called. Kate's got her to promise to see Dr Greenspan after I'm through with her.'

The next morning Kate drove her to the police station where the fingerprinting and photographing were done, her height, weight, colour of hair and eyes recorded. For convenience a name had to be given her.

'What name would you like?' asked Kate.

Blushes and silence suggested acute embarrassment.

The Chief tried to console her. 'It's a privilege, young lady. Most people don't get a chance to choose their names. They're thrust upon them.' Having gone through life as Percival Orville Potts, known by peers and underlings as Pop, he knew whereof he spoke.

'How about Elizabeth?' Kate spoke impulsively, not at the moment aware that she was suggesting the name of her dead baby.

'That's a nice name,' Pop said. 'You like it?'

'It's a beautiful name,' the girl said.

'You got to have a last name, too. To be filed under. What about Elizabeth Doe?'

'X,' the girl said with a trill of laughter. 'Elizabeth X. I bet you have no other Xs in your file.' The fancy delighted her. For the first time she showed the spirit and humour which were to enchant all who came to know her.

So it was Elizabeth X whose fingerprints, photograph and measurements were sent to the State Police, to the New York and Washington Bureaus of Missing Persons and the FBI: later, reported to other police departments and investigative agencies, always with the warning that the story and her picture were to be kept out of the newspapers. Not that Pop hasn't considered the advantage for himself.

'What advantage?' I wanted to know.

'He thinks she belongs to some wealthy family in Greenwich or Fairfield, or even Westchester, and that they'd appreciate avoiding a scandal. You get the idea?'

'I never thought of Pop as mercenary nor willing to indulge in illegal practice?'

Allan raised an eyebrow. 'Have you ever had a traffic ticket in this town?'

I disregarded the cynicism. 'He must be grateful to you for taking her off his hands. If you'd brought her directly to the station, what would he have done with her?'

'We don't mind keeping her with us. She's no bother. As a matter of fact, Katie's getting quite a kick out of it. She's livelier than she's been for months.'

'Has there been no clue to the girl's identity? Curious, isn't it?'

'Sure is. You'd think a girl like that would be missed by

someone. There must be a family somewhere. People who have reported missing daughters have been informed, but so far . . .' Allan paused to think about the curious situation while I glanced at the headlines of my *Times*. When he spoke again, he went off at a tangent. 'On Saturday morning just as I was about to leave for the club a couple arrived at the house; nice people, he's a broker and she's the do-gooder type. Hard to believe they'd have a daughter who made and placed the bomb that blew up a McDonald's in Queens. The picture of their daughter rather resembled Elizabeth. But they all look something alike in the photographs, all with serious eyes and long dark hair, you wouldn't believe any of them to be a criminal.'

'The young revolutionaries? You don't believe she's one of those,' I said with disapproval, for the story had, perhaps unreasonably, created a romantic image of a lost and lovely young woman. 'What do you mean by all of them looking alike? Are there so many young female criminals roaming the country?'

'Five, six, I'm not sure. The FBI agents have shown us pictures. Hard to believe, girls from good families, college graduates, wanted for bombings, bank robbery, even murder.'

'What times we live in. Has women's liberation come to this?'

'Elizabeth seems to think enemies are pursuing her. Not that she knows who they are, but she's terrified of someone or something. Kate says she talks a lot about these vague enemies.'

After the visit to the police station, Kate took Elizabeth to the office of Dr Greenspan who pronounced her health excellent except for undernourishment due, he believed, to the diet fads of modern young women who regard an ounce of normal flesh a deformity. There was no evidence of rape, but infinitely more startling was the fact that the girl was a virgin. Both Kate and Harvey Greenspan considered an unviolated hymen an anachronism in a girl whose exact age was undetermined, but who was certainly over twenty.

Dr Greenspan did not try to provoke Elizabeth to recall anything of her past. To Kate he expressed the belief that amnesia was due to shock, not physical violence, since there were no welts or bruises on her body but, he said, 'Something has hit her up here,' and touched his temple as seemed the habit of people in speaking of Elizabeth, 'or deep down in the underbelly of the unconscious.' A scrupulous practitioner, Greenspan fancied himself something of a psychologist, yet was not so unprofessional as to essay more than this superficial diagnosis.

The following day he telephoned to tell Kate that he had mentioned the case to Dr Phoebe Tisch. That the famous psychoanalyst had chosen to spend summer weekends among us was regarded as an honour in an area not unaccustomed to names renowned in the arts and professions. On rare occasions Dr Tisch consented to bless a neighbourhood gathering with her august presence, spoke to only a few selected guests, and drank two glasses of *Punt e Mes* (not a favourite aperitif among her neighbours but always provided by hostesses informed in advance of the famous doctor's taste). 'Phoebe . . .' Dr Greenspan used the given name in order to impress Kate with his intimacy with the celebrity, 'is interested in the case. She'd like to talk to the girl. She'll come to your house for cocktails on Sunday if you invite her.'

Kate was not enthusiastic. She had been subjected twice to Dr Tisch's company and considered the analyst something of a Gorgon. 'We ought to ask Elizabeth, oughtn't we? Isn't that part of the technique?'

'Dr Tisch won't treat her as a patient. There'll be no fee. There's a lot of controversy about amnesia. Phoebe believes that a talk with your girl might give her an insight into problems she intends to tackle in her next book.'

Kate talked the matter over with Allan, and since he approved she telephoned Dr Tisch's New York office with an invitation for the following Sunday. The invitation was accepted by a secretary who informed Mrs Royce that the doctor drank *Punt e Mes*. 'As if the whole neigh-bourhood didn't know,' sniffed Kate. 'I shall offer her sherry.'

The train stopped before either of us noticed that we had reached our destination. Passengers crowded the aisle, keeping us prisoners in our seats. 'In spite of trying to keep it under wraps, word's got around and we're having problems with snoopers,' said Allan, coming down heav-ily upon the word. The red-haired chap he'd pointed out the day before stood close by. Apparently he'd heard the remark for he turned to acknowledge his misdemeanour with an impudent salute. Allan gave no sign of having noticed.

# 3

Nothing is less fashionable today than maidenly virtue; it is a quality more to be scoffed at than admired. A virgin who has celebrated her twentieth birthday is considered by her elders as well as her peers as retarded or unattractive to the other sex. I admit to this failing in myself. Reared as I was among writers, radicals and advanced thinkers, I had lost my esteem for chastity before reaching puberty. My ex-wife had often, sometimes humorously, more often boastfully, spoken to me of pre-marital adventures. I was neither shocked nor jealous and, as the tales were repeated, not amused. On our wedding night my most memorable emotion was gratitude that I was not obliged to struggle against maidenly qualms.

I confess that I was somewhat put off by the news that Elizabeth was chaste. Imagination, seduced by intimations of mystery, was not inspired by an anachronism belonging to the age of corsets, yet curiosity would not be appeased until I had seen the nameless girl. On the pretext of bringing my neighbours a basket of pears from the Golden Champion tree planted by my father, I paid an unannounced call that Sunday afternoon.

'Why, Professor Greenleaf, what a surprise, a pleasant surprise,' exclaimed Kate Royce as she opened the door. 'At long last you honour us with a visit. How long has it been since we've seen you?'

'I see your husband on the train sometimes.'

'So he's told me and I've told him a dozen times to ask you to dinner.'

I handed her the basket; she kissed me. Although my upbringing was anything but formal, I have never become comfortable with this custom of greeting mere acquaintances with intimacy more appropriate to family and lovers. Since Kate is a fine-looking woman who uses a pleasant perfume, I enjoyed the greeting. 'If you'll do this whenever I visit you, I promise to come often.'

'It's a promise.' She led me into the living room. 'Allan's playing golf. What about a drink?'

'It's rather early.'

'Tea?'

'Nothing, thank you. I'll have a drink with you a bit later if I may stay a while.'

'Stay for supper. I've got a lovely ham in the oven.'

That I did not immediately respond to the invitation was due to disappointment. The mystery guest was not on view. A ball of yarn and an unfinished garment lay on one of the divans. Kate seated herself and began to knit. I mistakenly chose an armchair too low for comfort. The Royce's furniture had been designed for harmony with the style of the house which, in spite of the extravagant praise of architectural and decorating journals, I found no more inviting than a dentist's waiting room. Not wishing to show curiosity, I spoke to Kate about everything except the subject that most interested me. How splendid it was that my Golden Champions were so plentiful this year. How were her tomatoes? Was I also a victim of the heinous woodchuck who had deprived the Royces of the tenderest vegetables?

We were so passionately involved in plans for next spring's war on woodchucks, raccoons and rabbits, we were not immediately aware that Elizabeth had come into the room. The late afternoon sun, fallen low, cast a veil of gold on her dark hair and fair flesh as she stood facing the glass wall. Kate had said she was good looking, Allan had called her a little beauty; to my eyes, dazzled by the sunlight, her radiance seemed to transcend mere comeliness. In contrast to the lovely slenderness of the nymph was the bulk of a squat, lively woman who had entered with her. Kate introduced me to Dr Phoebe Tisch who graciously remembered that we had met before, and to Elizabeth who acknowledged my existence with an adorable smile.

Kate served drinks.

'Ah *Punt e Mes*,' cried the eminent psychoanalyst as though she had discovered a rare neurosis. 'I am so fond of it. What good fortune that you keep it on your bar.'

'We don't usually,' Kate was less than gracious, 'but knowing you would be here, my husband went out and bought it.'

'Very kind of him. Will any of you join me in this excellent drink? Elizabeth, do you like *Punt e Mes*?'

'I don't know.'

'Have you ever tried it?'

'I don't know.'

Dr Tisch turned to Kate with a significant glance as though her query had given proof of Elizabeth's lost memory. The drink had been poured and Elizabeth had taken a sip. Her lips puckered, her nose wrinkled with distaste. Dr Tisch missed the reaction. 'Do you like it, Elizabeth?' she asked in a clinical voice.

I had caught a glimmer of mischief in Elizabeth's eyes before she turned to Phoebe Tisch and pleased her by answering, 'It's delicious.'

'The unspoiled palate enjoys subtlety,' declared the doctor.

Kate raised her eyebrows. I knew what she was thinking since the same thought was in my mind. For all of her knowledge of the psyche, it was presumptuous of Dr Tisch to assume that the girl's palate was unspoiled. How did she know that Elizabeth was not an experienced consumer of aperitifs; unless the girl had inexplicably recalled the fact in the half-hour of private conversation with the doctor in

Allan's study? 'Have another,' she said when Elizabeth had drained the glass: poured it out herself and forced it on the girl.

'Thank you so much,' Elizabeth said sweetly.

Soon afterwards Dr Tisch left. Kate walked out with her, and remained for some time beside the car, engaged in conversation.

Alone with the girl, I found myself tongue-tied, mute, bereft of words. She made no effort at small talk. Disconcerting moments passed before I poured myself another whisky and moved to the divan where Elizabeth sat. 'Hello,' I said. She let out a small trill of laughter.

'You didn't like the drink?' I said.

'It tastes like medicine.'

'Then why did you say you liked it?'

'She wanted me to so very much.'

'Why were you so anxious to please her?'

'I like her. She's a nice lady.'

'A very distinguished analyst.'

'If she's so brilliant, she ought to know better than to wear a dirndl at her age.'

I laughed. Elizabeth was pleased and we were able to smile at each other.

'Do you think she can help you?' I said.

'Remembering?' Her laughter was of a different kind; the artificial gaiety expressing the shame or guilt of a flaw in personality. 'Dr Tisch says I don't want to remember. She says something that happened to me recently may have started it, but it's probably deeper than that, it may be my whole life I want to forget.' Dainty hands, folded in her lap, had grown tense. She laughed again, ruefully. 'She doesn't think it will last very long, amnesia is seldom permanent unless,

23

unless—' here she faltered and spoke with reluctance—'the patient is permanently—' She paused again and tapped her forehead.

'Let's talk about something else.'

'You're being tactful, thank you.' The radiant smile was again turned upon me. 'Everyone around here is very kind, so thoughtful. Don't you adore Kate?'

'I admire her.'

'She's been wonderful to me. A complete stranger, with nothing, nothing, no money, no clothes, no memory.' The humility of the words was denied by a sudden burst of gleeful energy which whirled her off the divan, danced her around the room and brought her back to sit closer to me. 'It's beautiful here, so beautiful, so much love and generosity, I've never known anything like it in my whole life.' She stopped again to question herself. 'What haven't I known? Isn't it ridiculous? How can I compare anything with what I can't remember?'

Her memory was lost but not her mind. She had the grace to regard her situation with humour, to recognise irony. These qualities fascinated me as much as the mystery. Had she been without charm, had her voice been harsh, her complexion flawed, her eyes small and set close together, her bones ill-sculptured, I doubt that I would have been so affected.

When Kate returned to the living room, I asked forgiveness for having failed to respond to her kind invitation, and told her that if it would cause no trouble I would happily share their dinner. At the table the conversation which, on the surface avoided the subject, could not but refer to Elizabeth's failed memory. Too often there were questions to which her only reply could be that she did not know;

whether, for instance, she played golf; where she had acquired that perfect French accent, if she had heard a certain pianist, what college she had attended. There were references which she recognised: the names of books and authors, composers and their works, historical figures and living celebrities, but she could not tell how nor when she had acquired the knowledge. She admitted ignorance with high, light, girlish giggles, self-conscious and naïve. Her laughter often seemed irrelevant, but turned against herself, was touching. I think now that it was her innocence I found most beguiling. In contradiction to Dr Tisch's assertion that she sought escape from shame or guilt, I believed her a perfect example of perfect purity. Without memory, she was without regrets, without remorse, free of sin. Without memory she was a babe gazing at the world with startled eyes, a child with an adult mind, she was Eve before the fall.

I confess that I wore out my welcome, staying until my hosts began to yawn and Elizabeth's lids lowered over the lustrous eyes. As the evening advanced, I became more and more enamoured of the winsome girl.

4

I came like a Greek bearing gifts, the reddest and ripest tomatoes in my garden, the largest squash, clusters of grapes whose blushes would have enhanced a Dutch fruit piece of the seventeenth century. Kate's thanks told me she was aware of the cause of the neighbourly generosity. She kept me talking at the door so that for a time I was afraid I would not be invited in. Then Allan, recognising my voice, called out an invitation to join him in a drink of the cider brandy he had bought from a local farmer. I was disappointed in not finding Elizabeth who had repaired to her room at the sound of the doorbell. She was exhausted, Kate said, after a brutal session with a pair of FBI agents.

'They asked a lot of questions she couldn't possibly answer and accused her of lying.' Kate had become fierce. 'They don't believe in the amnesia.'

'They're after one of those girl fugitives,' Allan said.

'Can you believe it, Chauncey?'

'They think she might be that Bennington girl . . . what's her name? . . . who took part in a bank robbery that killed a teller and wounded six . . .'

'Elizabeth couldn't kill a fly. She's as . . .' Kate washed down the rest of the sentence with a swig of cider brandy. Elizabeth had danced into the room.

'How nice to find you here, Mr Greenleaf. Your pears were super.'

'He's brought some magnificent grapes, and tomatoes and an obscene squash,' Kate said.

Elizabeth blessed me with a sparkling smile. 'Do you grow flowers, too?'

'His garden's fantastic,' Kate said. 'Are your dahlias out yet?'

'The late blooms are at their height now. Would you do me the honour of coming to see my garden?'

'I'd adore to,' Elizabeth said and, like a child, asked Kate's permission.

As I had no classes the next day, I suggested that I pick her up in the morning when the garden was at its best. Elizabeth said that Kate had pointed out my house when they drove down to the market that morning, and as it was only a step away she could come by herself. A half-mile step, I told her, but she laughed at the thought that this was not an easy walk. So she is accustomed to walking, I thought, and there floated through my mind a vision of her hiking beside me on my favourite trail. Other fancies flashed on the mental screen: Elizabeth admiring my Sheraton and Duncan Fyfe, Elizabeth preening before the baroque mirror, Elizabeth amused by the collection of old copper and iron pots hanging beside the kitchen fireplace, Elizabeth in my Victorian four-poster.

'Come for lunch. If the weather's like today's, we can eat in the garden. Is that all right?' I asked Kate who had not been included in the invitation.

With good reason I confess that I am a house-proud man. To me the famous Royce place, photographed and described in technical journals and home-making magazines, a mecca for architectural students and tourists who had thronged our lane when the house was new, is a monstrosity of glass and angles, glaring light and vulgar metal. My house is old and mellow, built at the turn of the Eighteenth Century, amended, revised, edited and enlarged with the royalties from my mother's novel, *The Dutch Silver Murders*, the greenhouse and gardens added with the proceeds from the sale to Hollywood of her *Grecian Urn Mystery*, the swimming pool put in with the greater profits of the book and play, *Paris Green*. I was up betimes that morning, set my house in order, drove to the village for delicacies, arranged bouquets and cooked a simple but splendid lunch. I was setting the table when I saw her in the lower garden, pausing to examine a blossom, to inhale a fragrance, to wonder at the variety and subtlety of coloration. She plucked a marigold, thrust it into the buttonhole of the oversized white shirt she wore over new blue jeans; jerked away from an aggressive bee, brushed a fallen leaf from her hair, all without knowing that her graceful movements were observed by a doting Pygmalion.

For she was to be my Galatea, my creation, the product of my education and experience as an educator. In a few students in the colleges where I have taught, I had found responsive young minds that I had hoped to mould to finer shapes, but have always been thwarted by the disciplines of the classroom and the formality of relations between teacher and pupil: and by the wilfulness of youth obstinately resisting all but the latest fads. In Elizabeth I recognised a mind quick and capable of concentration, a sharp wit, with freedom from the bonds of experience, the detritus of guilt, the shards of disappointment that harden the arteries of consciousness. It was not my desire to restore her memory, but rather to give her new life, establish new values, heighten awareness of truth and beauty. What a woman I would make of her, with what riches I would fill the empty vessel. The challenge set me on fire.

The doctor had guessed her age to be between twenty and twenty-five. I hoped it was the latter. A twenty-year-old girl would look upon a man of forty-nine as ancient, whereas at twenty-five she would have the sense to appreciate maturity. Before the afternoon was over I made the pleasing discovery that she admired not only my house, my garden, my cooking but myself, me, Chauncey John Greenleaf. She had asked about my work, my education, my small achievements. Hers was the admirable talent, so lacking in my ex-wife, of intent listening. Every trifling fact interested my Galatea; she asked intelligent questions. I was flattered when she remarked, wistfully, that she wished she could attend the University in New York and become my student.

'Private lessons might be preferable,' I said.

'It would be a waste of your time.'

'Enjoyment is no waste. Quite the contrary, it nourishes the spirit.'

I was overjoyed when she told me she was reading *Swann's Way*. Dr Tisch had recommended it as a stimulant to reveries that could arouse recollections of a patient's past. 'She said the association with things I thought while I was reading it might help my memory.'

'Has it?'

'No. Maybe in a way. I was reading in bed the other night and suddenly I had a kind of vision of a house.' She closed her eyes in the effort to recall the vision. Lest I disturb the mood, I remained silent. A bee settled on her bare arm, and moving gently, I brushed it off. Opening her eyes she stared at me as though she had lost all memory of the past hour. 'Do you know whose house it was?' I asked.

She shook her head so vigorously that the long dark tresses were tossed from side to side. 'Maybe it was a dream. I might have fallen asleep. Dr Tisch told me to write down my dreams, but usually I forget them as soon as I'm awake enough to pick up my pencil and pad.' She jerked away from the aggressive bee. 'Let's go inside before we're stung to death.'

We had been almost three hours at the lunch table and spent another happy hour in the library. I had to answer a number of questions about my mother and the books she had written. Whilst I cannot recommend them as literature, I believe the novels of Sarah Ellen Chauncey to be as good as any in her chosen field. I gave Elizabeth a copy of *The Chinese Tea Mystery* to read when Proust became too heavy. The delightful afternoon would have gone on longer had Kate not arrived, asking sarcastically if I meant to keep Elizabeth for dinner and the night.

Kate had become alarmingly possessive of the girl. On another occasion (I was now seeing Elizabeth almost every day) I warned her of the danger of allowing herself to become the target of an older woman's affection.

'Oh, it's nothing like that,' Elizabeth protested. 'Kate loves me as she'd love a child. She'll protect me if they come for me.'

Who were they? Elizabeth had spoken of 'them' a number of times, but when asked who it was that might come for her she took refuge in amnesia, saying she could not name the enemy but knew certainly that evil forces were on her trail. Tisch would have called this paranoia, as indeed she had, but I believed it to be the result of all those sessions with detectives and agents of the Federal Bureau of Investigation who insinuated, without making direct accusation, that she had shot policemen and civilians, robbed a bank, sold heroin on the street and made and placed bombs in public buildings. It was unbelievable, insane, impossible to believe that this lovely, this angelic girl, so naïve, so innocent, could have committed acts of infamy.

At the Queen Bee Supermarket I learned another, and to me alarming, angle of the mystery. In the aisle between the detergents and the breakfast cereals my shopping trolley collided with another which turned out to be Kate's. After conventional greetings, the usual conversation about health and weather and the price of coffee, Kate asked if I was familiar with the name of Gordon Hildebrandt.

'Of course,' I said. 'Isn't everyone?' The name had special significance for me as an old friend, a companion of Harvard days, occupied the Gordon Hildebrandt

Chair of Comparative Philosophy at the University of Texas.

'He phoned me yesterday to ask . . .'

'Hildebrandt? He's dead, died a few years ago.'

'Gordon Hildebrandt, Second,' Kate said.

'The son. Oh, of course. Wasn't there something about him in the papers recently?' I recalled vaguely some item of a sensational nature, the sort of news I seldom read but had noticed because the name had interested me since my old friend occupied the chair the elder Hildebrandt had endowed.

'He's always in the papers. Isn't he one of those oil millionaires or something?'

'Oil, wheat, banking, chain stores, probably many other profitable things. Why did he phone you?'

'About Elizabeth. He says he's her fiancé.'

'No!'

'Oh, yes, he seemed very sure. He told me not to let her leave before he gets here.'

'When's he coming?'

'In a few days. He said he'd have come immediately but he's got to stay in Fort Worth for a bit while his lawyers finalise—that was his word, Chauncey—finalise. Don't you detest people who *ise* words? He's very worried about her.'

'If he's so worried why doesn't he come sooner and let the contracts go unfinalised?'

'He said it was an important deal, international, and he was under an obligation to have the contracts ready when his associates arrive from Japan and Switzerland. He asked if there was an airport near here where he could land a private plane. I said I'd find out, and he told me not to bother, one of his secretaries would do it.'

'Have you mentioned this to Elizabeth? What was her reaction to his name?'

'He asked me not to say anything to her.'

'Why not?'

'He thinks the shock of seeing him might restore her memory. He's going to ask his analyst how to handle the situation.'

I had already begun to dislike Gordon Hildebrandt the Second. Since I distrust people who seek psychoanalytic counsel before making decisions, my prejudice was aggravated. To my mind Gordon the Second who had inherited oil wells and wheat lands and chain stores, etc., etc., etc. was a weak shilly-shallying creature utterly devoid of character. I have to admit that my opinion was compounded by jealousy of a man who could claim Elizabeth as his fiancée, and envy of the luxury he could provide. I hoped his international deal would fail, his plane . . . but no, my conscience forbade such vengeful reflections and I bade myself wait with fortitude to see what would happen with the arrival of the unwelcome millionaire.

*

A night or two later as I was leaving the theatre after seeing an inane film I met Elizabeth with that red-haired young man accused by Allan of snooping. She introduced us and each acknowledged having known the other's name. I invited them for a drink with me at a nearby bar. Pressed close together at a table designed for pygmies, Richard Shannon courteously said he had heard great things about Professor Greenleaf from several reporters who had been my students, and I returned the compliment by saying that I had seen his name signed to a series of articles in *The Weekly*, a journal I read only because a former student, now an assistant editor, sent me a complimentary subscription.

'You didn't tell me you write for magazines,' said Elizabeth.

'Didn't I? I guess I forgot to mention it.' He sounded a bit vague and looked troubled.

'How unusual,' I remarked. 'The young writers I know, and I have a wide acquaintance, try to impress pretty girls with their importance as writers.'

'Why didn't you tell me?' persisted Elizabeth, and turning to me, said, 'He told me he was a detective.'

Under freckled skin a blush spread.

'A more impressive profession,' I teased. 'Is it true or were you pulling her leg?'

'I happen to be working on a case.' The blush deepened, its carmine giving contrast to the copper tone of the freckles.

'Have you joined an agency? Or is it a freelance experiment connected with a story you're writing?' As I reconsider the scene at this late date, I find it necessary to confess that my taunts were born of jealousy of the younger man.

'I can't talk about it,' he said, and asked Elizabeth if she didn't think it time to leave. I offered, for the sake of convenience, I said, to drive her to Whispering Hill Road, but she preferred going with her escort. His blush had faded and he looked at me in triumph as he left with Elizabeth clutching his arm.

Pique prevented me from visiting her until that glorious afternoon when the first crisp wind of autumn tempted me to work in the garden, but duty committed me to the dreary task of correcting sophomore papers, Elizabeth arrived without invitation. Rosy-cheeked and panting, she had run the half-mile to find refuge from a horrid couple who had been advised by the FBI of the presence of the amnesia victim in the Royce's house and had come to identify their missing daughter.

'What did they say when they saw you?'

'They didn't.' There was an impish gleam in her eyes, sly laughter on her lips, triumph in her voice. 'I listened in the hall and when Kate called me, I ran out the back way.'

'Oughtn't you go back and face them even if it's to prove you're not their daughter?'

'I'd die if they were my parents. Don't make me go, Mr Greenleaf, please don't.'

I wavered, thinking of odious virtues such as right and duty, but was diverted by the insidious charms of soft flesh, silken hair, the delicate scent of a young body. She had pressed herself close, flung her arms about my neck. 'Oh, please, please, Chauncey.'

My given name, heard for the first time in that sweet voice, was an aria by Mozart. It shortened the gap between our ages. I kissed the top of her head, her forehead, her cheeks. The sound of a passing car parted us. It went up the road towards the Royce's place. She wrapped her arms about her body and, although the afternoon was warm, shivered.

'Why are you so frightened?' I asked.

She tried with a shrug to thrust off whatever had caused undue distress. Shadows deepened around her eyes. I led her into the house and established her in the library. Here my mother had worked from breakfast to tea-time on her novels. The room was cosy, protected from light and heat by dark green jalousies. 'Elizabeth, my sweet girl, tell me what are you so afraid of?'

She clutched the arm of her chair with such tension that her knuckles rose like snowy peaks on tremulous hands.

'They'll come,' she whispered, 'they'll come here and find me.'

'Who?'

'Why do you ask me? You know I can't remember.' Her eyes softened with reproach, the tone was of a rueful child.

I took her hands, drew her from the rocker and led her to the couch so that we might sit close together. I kept her hand in mine to give her the assurance of male strength. Without words I attempted to communicate courage, to let her know that for better or for worse I would defend her. When at last I spoke it was without caution; my heart spoke.

'You'll be safe, my darling, if you marry me. No one can take you away if you're my wife.'

There was no response. No muscle moved, no nerve twitched. Her silence unnerved me. I considered the statement and wondered at the impulse that had led me to speak the rash words. Having suffered the experience of marriage, I had no desire for a repetition of grievance and irritability. Since the divorce I had been intimate with more than one interesting woman, but had never been tempted towards matrimony.

After a few heavy moments a question interrupted my musing. 'Was that a proposal? Were you serious?'

Now it became my turn to tremble. Impulse or, perhaps, the urge to gallantry forced my answer. 'I love you, Elizabeth.'

She shifted her position, turned, looked at me with gratitude so tender, so moving, that I became ravenous for her love, seized her, pressed my lips upon hers, forced her body close to mine. She neither responded nor resisted, but lay limp in my arms so that I was free to do as I willed with her.

My temperature rose, my heart beat with such fury that I ached with desire.

It was not the pounding of my heart that thundered in my ears but the clamour of the knocker on my front door. I wiped perspiration from my face and straightened my tie. The knocking continued as the impatient caller demanded entrance. Elizabeth retreated to the couch, curled among the cushions, tense, her face a white mask of terror.

'You've got nothing to fear, I'll handle the situation.' I closed the library door as I left.

Through the screened door a question was hurled at me. 'Is Elizabeth here?' asked Richard Shannon.

'No,' I said.

'Has she been here?'

'No.' Brazenly I compounded the lie. 'I haven't seen her today.'

'Mrs Royce thought she might be. Sorry to have disturbed you, sir.'

I returned to the library to find Elizabeth still crouched among the cushions. I took her in my arms. 'Sweet Elizabeth, you have nothing to fear while I'm here to protect you.'

My reward was a wan smile. 'Was it someone for me?'

'It was a Fuller Brush man.'

'Oh!' She pressed closer to me.

My love for her had not diminished although ardour had waned on my journey to the front door. The short absence of her physical presence had cooled my body and brought my mind to the temperature of reason. Before my marriage and after the divorce, as I have remarked, I have enjoyed relations with a number of charming women, but have never bedded a virgin. Such forbearance may seem odd to a generation given to heedless intercourse, but to those of us who have inherited our fathers' prejudices, to 'ruin' a maiden would be considered more a lapse of gallantry than an immoral act. For the protection of both, I suggested that I drive Elizabeth back to the Royce's. In the car I kissed her and enjoyed the light touch of her lips on my cheek. No more was said about marriage, but it was to be mentioned again soon in startling circumstances.

# Chapter Two

# Leaves from a Notebook

## by Elizabeth

She told me to write down everything . . . everything . . . random thoughts, dreams, etc. Not possible. If I tried to write down *all* my thoughts there wouldn't be enough paper. My thoughts come too fast—too many at a time, like I can be wondering if I should cut my hair at the same time I'm asking what life is about and wishing I had a lemon squash. She said to concentrate on one thing . . . bits of memory might rise out of my unconscious and maybe one tiny little thing would open up all the rest. I hope so.

Funny that I remember books and games . . . I say poems to myself and conjugate French verbs. I found a Scrabble set and played solitaire for hours just to prove I could remember words. But I do not know my own name or where I live or my friends or parents and where I went to school. Where? I must have gone to school somewhere because I can spell and write and punctuate. Right?

Doctor Tish. Tich? Tisch? Can you trust an elderly lady who wears a dirndl? A psychoanalyst too. Why does that bother me? She is a very kind lady.

She said to keep a pencil and pad on the table next to my bed and write down everything I dream, but I can't remember dreams, only horror. I get so frightened I wake up sweating. Sometimes I scream. I hate to wake up Kate . . .

she's so good to me. She bought me blue jeans and a bikini. I try not to scream, but how can you control yourself asleep? It's like wetting the bed.

Flashes of things come to my mind. Subliminal is the word. Below consciousness. Subliminal images go too fast for me to name or recognise them.

I remember a blue dress. Crêpe-de-chine with tucks and the tiniest little buttons I have ever seen. Why do I remember that dress?

Another dream—six people at the table. All speaking different languages. I am one of them. Was it a dream? It seems more like something I remember.

Dr Tisch (spelling correct . . . I asked Kate) told me to concentrate on my mother and father. I must have had a mother. *Most little boys have mothers* . . . Lord Dunsany . . . *Six Who Pass While the Lentils Boil?* Why do I remember Lord Dunsany when I can't remember my own father. If I had a father.

Whited sepulchre. Why do I keep thinking that? Remembrance of things past? Dr T. told me to read Proust before going to sleep. He's full of associations. I might associate in reveries, she said.

A dead man is lying on the floor. I see the pattern of streaks in a marble floor, but not the man's face. Maybe he is not dead.

Rick. Rick Shannon. Could I care for a detective?

We walked in a park. I was happy. Lilacs were in bloom. Some are shreds of dreams . . . some are flashes of thoughts. They come and go too fast for me to catch them.

Elizabeth X. X is the unknown quantity. Will I be X the unknown forever?

The room is filled with roses. White roses, red, pink, maroon, tea roses. The odour is heavenly but it keeps getting stronger. Too strong. Chauncey goes out to make tea. The fragrance is too strong. I try to open a window but none of the windows will open. And the door is locked from the outside. I fainted. Then I woke up in Elizabeth's room. I am Elizabeth again.

Richard Shannon.

I wish I knew who *they* are. My enemies.

Mr Greenleaf asked me to marry him. Not exactly asked. He said if we were married no one could take me away. I cannot imagine being married to an old man. He must be forty at least. Maybe more.

Kate keeps getting mysterious phone calls. About me? I am allowed to hear ordinary conversations like when she says she doesn't feel like playing golf or can't come to a committee meeting or doesn't want a new vacuum cleaner. When she gets these mysterious calls she closes the door of the room so I won't hear what she says. I could listen on the extension but when I think how good she is to me I put temptation behind me.

Kate is like a mother to me. Is my mother anything like that? If I love her how can I forget her? Could I ever forget Kate?

*Sic transit Gloria mundi.* What makes that go through my mind all the time?

Dr Greenspan says I'm a virgin. So I must be.

I hate lies . . . loathe and despise liars. Lies have surrounded me all my life . . . I can't remember what they were but know they existed. Worse: lately I've told lies and I know I will lie again and again and again when I have to.

# Chapter Three

# The Private Life of an
# Amnesia Victim

## by Kate Royce

As the story would not be complete without details that I am obviously not able to provide, I asked Kate to flesh out the bare bones with an account of Elizabeth's actions and conversations while residing in the Royce house. Strong protests were overcome only after I had promised to act the ruthless editor. If my influence is over-evident, I ask the reader's forgiveness.

C.J.G.

## 1

I am not a writer. The only writing I've done since my master's thesis has been statistical. Reports like: 'Since 1970 the increase in the Latin-American population in this area has been 37·09%. The annual increase has been 6·27%.' When I first got my job with the Bureau I was very proud. Young. Just out of college. Eleven years later when I had become assistant to the chief, I was bored and uptight. I was sure no one ever bothered to read our reports. My work was sterile just as I was. I had been married eleven years and had never conceived. My husband and I both wanted children. Allan

41

had designed our beautiful house for a family. At last after special exercises and mammoth doses of thyroid I found myself pregnant. No woman had ever been happier. No one had ever given up her job so eagerly. No one ever shopped so joyfully for a layette.

There had never been a more beautiful baby than my Elizabeth. At birth she had hair curling around her face in gold ringlets like a cherub. Her eyes were a deep violet blue. I cannot describe her death. It is still too painful. At first I could not believe her to be gone. She had seemed quite normal at the 3 am feeding. It was what the medical profession calls a cot death. There are thousands per annum and the cause is not known to the most eminent paediatricians.

But why my baby? Was I to blame for her death? Had I done something wrong? I tore myself apart trying to answer these questions. I could accept no solace. Even my good thoughtful loving husband could not comfort me. For Allan's sake I regretted my beastly disposition but could not climb out of the deep depression. My obstetrician said I could have other babies. I did not believe him. I was spiritless and lazy, could do nothing but menial tasks in the house and garden. People suggested that I go back to my old job. The thought made me physically sick. My social life was meaningless. I could not live through a day thinking of a concert or play or barbecue supper. On the first Saturday in September I agreed for Allan's sake to go to a party given by a client of his in Redding. I was soon bored and offended by the dull jokes and loud voices, and around half-past ten begged Allan to take me home. It was whilst driving on a back road that wound through a wood that we found the lost girl.

I have read what Chauncey has written and there is no need for me to repeat any of it, but there are many things he could not know. Like Elizabeth's nightmares and her terrified reaction to blood and killing on television. Although my husband is the most intelligent person I've ever met and with excellent taste in everything else, he has a peculiar weakness for those ridiculous plays about murder and mayhem on TV. He loves to stretch on the couch with the television on at full blast and me sitting quietly in the room, ready to leap up and switch stations or fetch another bottle of beer. 'Stay with me, hon, don't run away,' he says if I try to escape. The only way I can take it is by keeping my hands busy and my eyes on my knitting.

'Why don't you come and watch with us?' Allan asked the third or fourth night Elizabeth was with us. She was very shy at first and would slip off to her room as soon as she'd made the gesture of helping me stack the dishes.

On this one particular evening the show was noisier and more brutal than usual. I looked up from the socks I was knitting and saw a big ugly monster seize a slender young man by the shoulders, slam him down on the sidewalk and smash his head against the concrete until the victim became unconscious. I turned from the horror to see Elizabeth curled in the armchair, shrunken and as white as a ghost against the black leather upholstery. The look on her face is unforgettable. I still see it misshapen by terror, lips drawn back, teeth clenched, projected bones seeming to thrust through her taut flesh. Her whole body was shaking.

'What is it, Elizabeth? What's the matter?'

She gave no sign of having heard me and did not seem aware that I had come to stand beside her. I let my hand fall upon her shoulder. She twisted around and stared up at me as if she'd never seen me before, then jerked away and ran to her room. Allan, unaware of her panic, gave full attention to the beer and the carnage. I was glad he hadn't noticed as he probably would have called the girl unstable and said again that it was not safe to keep her in the house.

Towards morning she had another of her nightmares. Allan always slept through the moaning and sobbing, but I was sensitive to her anguish and hurried to the guest room to put my arms around her and hold her until she was fully awake. She stared at me and the room as if it was all new and strange to her, then smiled in that lovable way and said, 'Oh, Kate, I'm so glad you're here with me.'

She could never remember the nightmares. Dr Tisch, when she came to observe Elizabeth, was particularly anxious to hear about them, but the poor kid could not remember what she had dreamed about. At first she had been afraid to talk to the psychoanalyst and had asked me to stay with her during the ordeal. As it turned out this was not necessary as Dr Tisch soon won Elizabeth's confidence. I found Tisch nothing like my first impression of her, no Gorgon but a friendly fattish woman. Not more than twenty minutes after she arrived, Elizabeth went into Allan's study with her and did not suggest that I come along. When the session was over Elizabeth was as relaxed as when she was alone with me, and certainly not as shaken as after a questioning by the detectives and FBI men who came to identify her as a criminal fugitive.

Allan had gone out to play golf, so that while they were in the closed study I was alone and dying to hear what they were saying. As I had been brought up on a code that made eavesdropping a mortal sin, I went into the kitchen where I could not hear the tempting hum of their voices. Then Chauncey Greenleaf arrived with an offering of his precious Golden Champion pears. He tried to cover his curiosity with a show of neighbourly generosity which did not fool me a bit. We discussed garden pests. I invited him to dinner but got no response.

When Elizabeth came out of the study and Chauncey saw her he practically jumped out of his pants. He and I drank whisky while Phoebe Tisch had her *Punt e Mes* and Elizabeth meekly obeyed the doctor's order to take her medicine.

Walking to the car with Dr Tisch, I asked her if Elizabeth had said anything about the 'enemies' pursuing her.

'She's told *you* about them?' Dr Tisch's surprise made it sound like I was unworthy of private information.

'She talks to me a lot.'

'Confiding in you?' Scepticism was not concealed.

'There's not much to confide. She remembers impersonal facts but absolutely nothing about herself or her home or people. Only *them*, the ones who are after her.'

'Paranoia is part of the syndrome.'

'You think she's—' I tapped my forehead, hesitating over the ugly word—'sick?'

'Sick!' Dr Tisch snorted. 'How the layman cherishes that euphemism. Afraid of plain words. No, I don't think the girl's insane. She's both quick-witted and clear about the present. The area of paranoia is the past. Clearly she's run away from the physical presence of someone or something too painful to contemplate. Or guilt. Amnesia could be her escape from unbearable guilt.'

'Guilt? What could she be guilty of, that sweet kid? She's so well-mannered and considerate, anxious to be helpful, and very grateful.'

'She should be. I wonder if she realises how much you've done for her. Harbouring a criminal fugitive can be a serious crime, you know.'

The argument was not new to me. Detectives had warned me. Friends had called on the phone to caution me against the risk. Allan had mentioned the danger several times, but had promised that Elizabeth could stay as long as I wished. He believed that my interest in the lost girl was helping me out of the depression which I'd endured since my baby died.

'Look, Allan, if there should ever be anything criminal in having her here, it's my crime and mine alone. I cannot believe that Elizabeth has ever done anything criminal.'

I had willed myself to dismiss the thought that she could possibly be one of the fugitives sought by the FBI, girls who had committed incredible crimes. While an FBI agent had read a list of six names—Alice McIntyre, Lorraine Riordan, Jane Gold, Marilyn Schmidt, Barbara Fortescue, Lillian Brush—his partner had studied Elizabeth's facial expressions. There had been no sign of recognition, no twitch of a nerve, no flick of an eyelid. They had left these names with me, suggesting that I drop them casually, one at a time, and watch the reactions.

Dr Tisch did not think much of their methods. While I talked to her on the driveway, Elizabeth made a conquest. When I came back to the living room Chauncey announced that he would gladly accept my invitation to dinner. He stayed until Allan, worn out after a day of exercise in the open air, had excused himself, and Elizabeth and I were yawning. So I had to wait until 3 am to hear her version of the Tisch encounter. I had been aroused by cries from Elizabeth's room. Another nightmare had awakened her. When I soothed her we went into the kitchen where I warmed some milk for her and made myself a cup of tea. She told me that Dr Tisch had asked no questions. To begin with the lady doctor had told the girl that the amnesia would probably not last more than a few more days, and that the most effective cure was free association. Something irrelevant—a name, a tune, a picture, a voice—might bring to mind the memory of a time, a place, a person that would bring it all back. Meanwhile it might help to concentrate on something she could recall, our meeting with her in the woods, for instance.

'I can remember a forest,' Elizabeth said. 'But is it that one? I can't remember anything before I woke up in that room with the light on and the yellow walls and the bathroom door open. I had to go and when I came back I was hungry and then I saw the glass of milk and sweet biscuits on the table. Like in a fairy tale. It didn't bother me that I didn't know where I was, I was too tired to care. Have you any Proust in the house?'

'Proust? What's Proust?' I said like an idiot. 'A new detergent?' The way she asked the question and the irrelevance caught me off balance so that the single syllable sounded like the name of one of those miracle soaps they shout about on television.

Elizabeth laughed gleefully. 'Proust, the French writer. Dr Tisch thinks that if I read him I might associate with things, you know—' she waved her hands in circles to illustrate her point—'the way Proust does, things in my early life. I might associate with just one thing and it would remind me of other things, you know.'

I leaned across the table and kissed her. She was as soft and sweet and fragrant as a baby after its bath.

## 2

On Monday, the day after poor Chauncey fell in love, Elizabeth met Rick Shannon. Picked him up at Compo Beach. The weather had become outrageously hot, I had a yen for cool salt water and Elizabeth was eager to wear the bikini I had bought for her at a sale.

A strong warm wind was blowing and the sea was rough. A cautious and mediocre swimmer, I keep close to shore. She plunged into the breakers before I'd waded knee-high. 'Be careful,' I shouted, but I doubt that she heard me through the roar of the waves. Her speed and confidence inspired me so that I swam more than my usual few sissy strokes. Back on shore I looked for her. She was nowhere to be seen. I became alarmed. 'Now, Kate, don't act like a nervous mother,' I said in fear of becoming like my own mother who had always irritated us with her futile worries. I fumbled in my beach bag for dark glasses so that the glare of sunlight and its reflection on the water should not totally blind me. When I was not worrying or scolding myself, I heard Dr Tisch's voice. 'Part of the syndrome.' Would a death wish be part of a mind that rejected memory? My heart was behaving as wildly as on that morning when I stood paralysed beside the crib of my dead baby.

The lifeguard passed, talking to a girl who skipped beside him. I started towards him with the intention of telling him that my companion was missing when I looked towards the sea and saw a head far out in the water. I recovered my breath and looked again. Two heads. Fear returned. Swimming side by side, they might have been a couple of friends or lovers who had come to the beach together. When they came close to shore I saw Elizabeth's black hair shining like sealskin and a red head beside hers. Treading the foam near shore, they laughed together. On dry land they separated. I recognised the man as the suspicious character who had peered in at us from the garden.

As she stood on the sand beside the mat where I lay stretched under a beach parasol, Elizabeth twisted her head from side to side to shake the water out of her hair. 'You oughtn't to go out so far. The waves can be dangerous,' I said, and bit my tongue in anger at the echo of my mother's querulous voice. 'You scared me half to death.'

'You needn't worry, I'm a good swimmer.'

'So you remembered that?'

'It was instinctive. When I was putting on my bathing costume I wasn't sure if I could swim but the minute we got here and I smelled the salt water . . .' She laughed merrily. 'Would Dr Tisch call that an association?'

'Bathing costume. Isn't that what the English call a bathing suit?'

'Is it?' She threw herself down upon the mat next to mine, lay back with only the brief bits of her *bathing costume* to protect her from the sunshine. I suggested that she move the mat closer to the parasol, but she declared emphatically that she wanted to tan her body. 'I'm so pale this year. Usually in summer—' She paused, became thoughtful and said, 'That's another association. But with what? With what?' Her face tightened so that she seemed to be wearing a protective mask. Her expression changed as a shadow fell across the outstretched body. Beside her stood the red-head. He was wearing a jockey cap and had a shirt tied across his shoulder.

'Hi,' he said.

'Hi,' she answered. Both laughed as though they shared some precious secret. She started to introduce him but was stopped by ignorance of his name.

'Rick Shannon,' he said. 'How do you do, Mrs Royce?'

'You know who I am?'

'Doesn't everyone around here recognise Mrs Royce who took this lovely wood nymph into her home?'

Elizabeth loved to laugh, but I had never heard such joyous tones as those that rang out then. Any female eye would recognise the reason. He was so positively masculine and so colourful with his coppery hair not entirely hidden by the jockey cap, by the impudent grin and the strong freckled body. There were flecks of red in his brown eyes. He squatted beside Elizabeth on the sand, glared up at the sky for an instant, adjusted the shirt so that no ray of sun touched his body. I invited him to sit under the parasol. He thanked me. 'That's better. This damned skin, one sunbeam and I'm burned to a crisp.'

Elizabeth moved her mat and invited him to sit with her in the shade. He spoke to her through me. 'You know you're harbouring a mermaid in your home, Mrs Royce.'

Elizabeth laughed as at deathless wit. 'A wood nymph and a mermaid. You're very literary.'

'God forbid.'

'Are you anti-literature?' I asked.

'I'm anti-starvation. Whatever literature I turn out is a hundred percent realistic.'

'What sort of realism?' I said.

'In many areas, mostly investigative.'

'You're a detective!' I exclaimed.

He thought about it before he confessed.

'You certainly don't talk like a detective,' I said.

'I happen to have an M.A. from Columbia.'

'Lots of detectives are college graduates,' Elizabeth said, addressing me but slanting her eyes toward Rick. 'Those FBI agents who've been coming to the house are well educated and refined.'

'Are you with the police or a government agency?' I asked him.

'I'm independent. What might be called a private eye.'

I asked a direct question. 'Is that why you've been snooping around our house?'

'A private eye doesn't discuss his work,' he said.

'You're trying to find out who Elizabeth is,' I said. He tried to shrug off the question. 'Why didn't you come to the door and tell us who you are and what you wanted?'

'I was checking on the possibilities before declaring my purpose.' He smiled and tilted a bit of a wink at Elizabeth.

'I wish you could tell me,' she said and smiled at him archly.

'I suppose it was Chief Potts who told you Elizabeth was staying with us.'

'Pop did mention you to me.'

'What did he say about me?' Elizabeth asked.

'That you are mysterious and beautiful. That you are the loveliest creature who has ever graced this town or its environs.'

Elizabeth accepted the exaggeration with girlish laughter. I doubted that Pop had said any such thing. From Rick's use of the nickname I came to the conclusion that he was a native. I asked if he lived in the neighbourhood.

'Part of the time. I have a pad in New York but my grandmother lives in Norwalk. She's sick and my mother's with her, so I usually come up on weekends.'

'Long weekends?' Most commuters were not able to spend their Mondays on the beach.

'I've got some special work around here,' he said.

I started gathering up the beach bags and towels. He offered his hands to Elizabeth, pulled her to her feet and kept hold of her wrists for longer than necessary. 'You'll see me soon,' he told her, and to me with mocking formality said, 'Have I your permission to call, Mrs Royce?'

'Come to the front door and ring the bell,' I said.

On the drive home Elizabeth was silent. Her eyes were soft with dreams. I felt it my duty to warn her, 'Be careful with that fellow, darling. He's a detective.'

'Is that bad?'

'It looks to me as if he were after you for some reason or other.'

Apparently she did not think he was working for her nameless enemies. 'Do you think he knows who I am? Maybe my memory will come back when he tells me my name.'

'Like the prince whose kiss wakes the sleeping beauty.' I spoke ironically but she accepted the idea with delight.

'Then I'll know who I am.'

And leave us, I thought, and saw my house empty, the rooms bare of life. I could not say this and make a show of my selfishness.

Traffic lights changed to red. On our left brakes screeched as a foreign convertible came to a sudden stop. Elizabeth didn't notice. She was wrapped in dreams of the prince's kiss. I saw Rick staring into our car as if he too were in a trance, but whether it was in admiration of Elizabeth or anticipation of a detective's fee, I couldn't tell.

# 3

After dinner Elizabeth would insist that I let her clear the table and stack the dishes in the machine. She took a childish pleasure in simple household tasks at which she was incredibly inept. She couldn't cook, she couldn't iron, she was helpless when she tried to mop the kitchen tiles after she'd spilled a pot of beef stock. It was as if she'd never seen a mop before, much less handled one. On this evening she was relentlessly trying to ruin a frying pan.

'Good heavens, Elizabeth, don't you know you shouldn't scour Teflon?'

'What's Teflon?'

'Have you forgotten that too?' I pulled the pan out of her hand. 'Was Teflon so important to you that you had to forget it?'

'I don't know.' She was so humble that I embraced her as I begged her pardon for my bad temper.

'I shouldn't fly off the handle about trivial things. But it was my good omelette pan.'

'I'm sorry.' She pressed her soft baby lips against my cheek. 'I hope I didn't ruin it.'

'Oh, it's nothing to fuss about.' I turned my head away so that she shouldn't see the tears in my eyes. She was so eager for love, given and received, that her humility softened me to the texture of a sponge.

'Kate,' she said and rubbed her eyes with her fists like a rueful child, 'may I ask you a question. Did Dr Greenspan definitely say I'm a virgin?'

'Does it bother you?'

'I want to know. Am I?'

'Dr Greenspan wouldn't have said it if it weren't a fact.'

'It's funny, isn't it, not to know a thing like that about yourself?'

'You'll find out as soon as you—'

The doorbell interrupted. I started towards the hall but Elizabeth caught hold of my arm.

'As soon as I what?' She held on until I answered.

'Fall in love.'

Allan went to the door. 'Elizabeth,' he called, 'someone here to see you.'

'Hey, Elizabeth, sea nymph!'

She ran into her room so that Allan had to talk to Rick Shannon until she came into the living room, walking sedately and wearing the white linen Cardin dress which I had washed and ironed several times since she'd come to our house in the stained and dirty garment.

'Oh, hello.' Her voice was tuned to a note of casual acceptance. 'So nice to see you again.' I wondered where she had acquired that cocktail party manner.

At dinner we had told Allan of our meeting with the 'snooper' and Elizabeth's eagerness and rosy cheeks had given him the message. After a few minutes of polite conversation he winked at me and said, 'Hey, Katie, would you mind looking over some stuff I've brought from the office?' A wink and a nod let me know that he was offering an excuse for leaving the kids to themselves.

Presently Elizabeth came into the study to ask if I'd mind her going out for a short drive with Rick. I forgot to give her a key so that she had to ring the doorbell when she came back. She was so distressed at having awakened me and I so sleepy that I didn't ask until the next morning if she had enjoyed the date. She bubbled with excited glee. I've never heard cokes and hamburgers described so ecstatically.

'You seem to like him,' I said.

'He's terrific. But terribly nosey. I wish he wouldn't ask so many questions.'

'What sort of questions?'

'About me. Things I can't answer. I feel so foolish. It's embarrassing not to know your name. You know what else he asked?' She smiled as if she were about to divulge a treasured secret. 'Whether I'd ever been in love.'

'Have you?' A stupid question from me who was so well aware of her condition. Dr Tisch had warned me against probing.

'I felt like an idiot saying I didn't know but,' she said, shaking her head, 'what can you do when your head's filled with a vacuum and you can't think of the most important things in your life?'

We were still at the kitchen table lingering over coffee when Rick phoned to ask if he could take her to a seafood restaurant that evening. Elizabeth was all a-twitter, washed her hair, painted her nails and would have spent the whole afternoon primping if Pop hadn't called to ask if I'd drive down to headquarters with Elizabeth. There was a lady in his office who thought Elizabeth might be her daughter.

Mrs Fortescue definitely looked out of place in the Chief's dusty office. Her clothes were costly and conservative, her face bare of make-up. On the table beside her chair lay an elegant suede bag, a pair of white gloves neatly folded beside it. She gave no sign of emotion at the sight of the girl who might have been her missing daughter.

'I am sorry I caused you the trouble of coming here,' she said in an upper-class voice. 'Of course you understand that I hoped desperately—'

'I'm very sorry to disappoint you,' Elizabeth said.

'How dear of you to say that. Naturally I'm disappointed. My daughter's a very naughty girl but I love her and want her back.' She touched a fine handkerchief to dry nostrils. 'I'm sure your mother feels the same way about you.'

'If she does, she hasn't come to find me.' For the first time I heard Elizabeth speak aggressively.

With the excuse that she had caused us to make this futile journey, Mrs Fortescue begged to be allowed to take us to tea. Her reason, I found out later, was to talk to us without Pop's listening. Elizabeth, sensitive to the lady's distress, turned to me with an appealing glance. Since the tea room is almost as extinct as the dinosaur in this country, I drove them over to the White Lion Inn where we were served by a sulky waitress in a huge empty dining-room.

Elizabeth's sweet smile and melting eyes offered Mrs Fortescue the sympathy she craved. For a full hour she talked about her daughter's naughtiness which was nothing less than arson. 'Of course it was our own property that was burned, a row of tenement buildings belonging to Barbara's grandmother. I'm sure she'd never have destroyed anyone else's property. She was to have inherited it.'

'Why did she do it?' asked Elizabeth.

Mrs Fortescue set her fork down upon her plate and wiped her mouth clean of crumbs. 'She was an idealistic girl, too idealistic, I'm sure, for the world of today. She was fine before she got modern ideas—'

'What kind of ideas?' Elizabeth asked eagerly.

'Not the nicest kind, I'm afraid, certainly not the kind she'd been brought up to. She was a Bramley girl.' The gentle monotonous cultivated voice somehow achieved dramatic effects. 'Bramley was my school, but we had different, oh, very different ideas in my day. Even at Bramley nowadays the girls have become rebellious. Somehow Barbara got it into her head that our society is corrupt. If I happened to disagree with her or question these new attitudes, she would flare up and ask if I condoned injustice and corruption. Corruption, corruption, corruption. If I ever hear that word again I shall go stark raving mad.'

Elizabeth had become tense. It was unlike her to push away an unfinished banana split, to rest clenched fists on the table and to speak harshly. 'But there is a lot of corruption nowadays, an awful lot, and lying and hypocrisy.'

This reaction startled me. Until this afternoon she had shown nothing but indifference to the state of our society. Was Barbara Fortescue's rebellion an association that aroused some latent emotion? Did the intensity of her response give evidence of buried recollections? She demanded every detail of the actions of a girl who had been so affected by her disgust of corruption that when she learned that her grandmother owned some of the filthiest, most run-down, vermin-ridden tenements in New York for which the poorest tenants paid exorbitant rents, she had, with two of her friends, placed cans of kerosene in the basements and set them afire.

I remembered reading about the incident in the *Times*. No one had died but several tenants were badly burned. Apparently one of Barbara's companions had phoned the superintendent and instructed him to have the flat evacuated before the fire started. 'That was surely Barbara's doing,' said her mother. 'She was always considerate, not at all the type who'd kill people in a bank robbery.'

Although it was not at all necessary to whisper in that empty cave of a room, Mrs Fortescue leaned across the table and in a hushed voice said, 'I'd rather not have the police or FBI find Barbara. You know what that would mean, a trial, and if we lost, a conviction and jail, probably a long term, her life utterly ruined.'

Elizabeth nodded to show understanding.

'Of course I have to use the police and FBI men for leads but I'm carrying on myself. I've become quite a detective,' she said with a small harsh artificial laugh. 'If I find her myself the police will never know. We'll fly to Canada and from there to Europe. I've got her a new passport under a false name and one for myself so that we can travel together without anyone suspecting.'

'Can you get a passport under a false name?' asked Elizabeth.

'Dear child, you can get anything in this world if you're willing to pay for it.'

My sympathy was with Mrs Fortescue, Elizabeth's with the fugitive daughter. On the drive home I remarked on the tragedy for the mother of a nice girl turned criminal. 'I think Mrs Fortescue sort of enjoys it. It's probably the first time she's ever had a purpose in life,' Elizabeth said. I thought this very astute, and afterwards, telling Allan about Mrs Fortescue, said that in her forgotten life Elizabeth had probably been familiar with women of that sort. 'If she was my mother I'd have rebelled. That kind of complacence drives me up the wall,' I said.

Allan wondered if Elizabeth was trying to escape the memory of a past similar to Barbara's.

The thought sent chills down my spine. 'Oh, darling, you can't believe she's done anything criminal.'

'If her reaction was as violent as you say, there must be some guilt buried in that torpid mind.'

'I didn't say violent. I said she was upset and very sympathetic.'

'There must be some association. I wonder, Katie, if we ought to keep her here.'

'Oh, Allan, please don't send her away. Just when she's beginning to come to life.' To me the lost memory seemed a kind of death. 'She's happy with us and I'm so fond of her.'

'Okay, if she means that much to you,' Allan said in the indulgent voice he had used during the worst of my depression.


# 4


Elizabeth had been on pins and needles until Rick came to fetch her. She skipped out to meet him before he'd parked his car. I ran out after her with one of my sweaters as I was afraid she'd be cold riding in the convertible when the evening grew chilly. 'Oh, Kate, you're so good to me. Like a mother.'

There was a warm glow in me, a kind of happiness that threatened to explode. Allan said I was getting to be my old self again and took me to the new show at the Playhouse. Afterwards we drank beer and ate hot dogs in a joint full of high school kids. It was like old times when we were first in love.

We got home after midnight. Allan went to bed and fell asleep immediately, but I kept thinking about Elizabeth and couldn't keep my mind on the book I was trying to read. It was after two when I turned out my light. I heard the clock strike every half-hour.

Again I had to remind myself that I was becoming like my mother. 'It's none of your business what time she gets in,' I told myself. 'There's no reason why she shouldn't stay out as late as she pleases.' But I kept thinking of her childishness and vulnerability and could not control my fear. When I heard his car in the driveway I listened for the sound of the key and the door opening. Time passed. The clock struck the half-hour. I thought of the times I'd sat with boys in cars and of kisses and clumsy love-making. I fell asleep before she finally came in.

The next morning she was dreamy and silent, walking in the garden or lying on the chaise, smiling at the sky. At lunch, while she spread mustard on a ham sandwich, she said, 'Tell me, Kate, what's it like, I mean how does it feel to be in love?'

'Different probably for different people. And at different times you feel differently too.'

'How did you feel when you fell in love with Allan?'

I scraped at shards of memory. 'How did I feel? At first I guess I just liked him a lot and then suddenly—' suddenly I remembered the acid smell of the cleaning fluid used in the vestibule of my sorority house—'he was the most important person in the world, the only important person. I felt dead, positively dead, when he wasn't with me. Hey, the mustard!' She had spread it as thick as frosting on the ham.

'Oh, sorry, I wasn't thinking.'

I was sure she had been thinking of that hour in the parked car. 'Take it easy, dear. You've only known him a few days.'

She retreated into her dream. Only Elizabeth could look so beatific while chewing a ham sandwich. I doubt that she noticed when I gathered the dishes on a tray and carried them into the house. This was unlike her for she was always eager to help me and often more of an obstacle than an aid.

One thing she knew was how to make a bed. Since it's a nuisance to walk around our king-sized monster when I tuck in sheets, I welcomed her assistance. She folded in the corners with practised precision. 'You make a bed beautifully. Wherever did you learn?'

There was no immediate answer and I expected her to remind me that she could remember nothing. 'I suppose at summer camp. Where I went our councillors were terribly strict about hospital corners.

'Pricey taught me.'

This was her first affirmative reference to the past. I decided not to make any remark about it, but simply to let her go on with the revelations. 'Pricey did?'

Her smile faded and her face took on the blankness assumed whenever she struggled to remember. 'Pricey?'

'Someone who taught you to make beds.'

She shook her head in bewilderment. I thought it best not to probe farther and kept quiet so that she'd be free to concentrate on a name that might open some door of memory. When we had finished the bed she went out to the garden and walked about aimlessly, her head lowered, her arms crossed over her chest. She came obediently when I called her in for lunch.

At once she began to chatter. 'That was an association, wasn't it? I've been trying to concentrate on it, but it didn't bring back anything at all. Nothing. And then I forgot the name. What was it?'

'Pricey.'

'Oh, Pricey. I'll write it down and keep looking at it just

before I go to sleep. That's when you associate best. Sometimes I see things, places I might have been, I guess . . . unless . . . no, I don't think I made it up. A house. I saw it while I was swimming, a different seashore, rocky, huge rocks and on top of one this house. It was pink, a pink house.' She was solemn and a bit sad. 'I only saw it for a second and it was gone. Pricey?'

'Have you been reading Proust?'

'I haven't got very far. It's not easy reading.'

'No other associations?'

She hung her head like a rueful child.

# 5

Soon the story of our amnesia victim was spread on the town grapevine. When Mrs Maple came to clean the house her first question was about our mysterious guest. 'It's a sad thing, Mrs Royce, when a person don't know their own name,' she whispered. Elizabeth was eating breakfast in the kitchen when Mrs Maple came in. She stood still and stared as if the girl was a sideshow freak. I introduced them. 'It's a real pleasure meeting you, Miss, I've heard so much about you.' Elizabeth replied courteously, but then jumped up and ran out of the room, leaving the coffee I'd just poured. She beckoned me to follow.

'How come she's heard so much about me? Mr Potter promised it wouldn't get into the paper, and the doctor said he'd keep it a secret.'

'You can't keep anything secret in a town like this,' I said.

Pop had dutifully informed the FBI, and circulars with descriptions of Elizabeth had been sent to police departments all over the country. Telegrams had been sent to bureaux of missing persons in towns and cities which had reported runaways and female fugitives.

'Am I a female fugitive?' Elizabeth had asked. 'I wish I knew what I'm fugiting from.' We both giggled.

I asked why she was so afraid of having the story appear in newspapers.

'My enemies would find out where I am.'

'Who are your enemies, Elizabeth?'

She gave me a reproachful look and came out with the answer I had heard so often. 'I don't know. I can't remember.'

'Then how do you know they exist?'

'I must be running away from something. Or somebody.'

I considered this a symptom of paranoia and wondered if it was the cause or effect of paranoia. I meant to ask Dr Tisch but never got around to it.

Soon after that, only a couple of days, I think, (probably the day she went to lunch at Chauncey's as she was not in the house) I had the first phone call from Fort Worth. The voice did not sound like Western voices in the movies, but more like the lower East Side of New York where I practised social work as a college project. 'Am I speaking to Mrs Allan Royce?' the voice asked.

'Yes.'

'Are you the lady that took in a young girl with amnesia?'

'Yes.'

'Just a minute, please. Mr Gordon Hildebrandt would like to speak to you.' He paused as if he expected a reaction from me. As none came he added, 'The second.' Then a different voice came on the line. 'Hello, Mrs Royce, I'm Gordon Hilde-brandt.'

'What is it you want of me, Mr Hildebrandt?'

'I'd like to speak to the young lady.'

'She isn't home now, Mr Hildebrandt.'

'She isn't?'

'No, she isn't.'

'She's still staying with you, Mrs Royce?'

'Yes.'

'Then she'll be back sometime today.'

'Yes, she will.'

'Tell her I . . . no, don't . . .' he stopped, breathing heavily. 'I'll call again and speak to her myself.' He seemed definite about this but changed his mind again. 'I'll be there in a day or two, maybe three. I've got to wait here until my lawyers finalise some contracts that have got to be ready when my associates arrive. From Japan and Switzerland. On a deal like this you can't take chances. International business is most demanding.'

'I'm sure it must be,' I said.

'You'll surely keep her with you until I get there.'

'I'll do my best.'

'Don't let her out of your sight. It's very important in the condition she's in. Promise me.'

'I'll try.'

'And tell me, is there an airport near you? A small one where a private plane can land. Never mind, Mrs Royce, I'll have one of my secretaries check it out. Thank you, Mrs Royce, for your . . . no, wait . . . did I tell you not to mention my name to Claire?'

'Claire?'

'The young lady who's with you. My fiancée. Don't let her know I've been in touch with you. Let me surprise her.'

Was this man, Gordon Hildebrandt, the enemy she was

afraid of? 'I wonder if that's wise. In her condition, psycho-
logically.'

'You may be right. On the other hand it—the confrontation, that is—the shock of suddenly seeing me may restore
her memory. Let me talk to my analyst. I'll phone you again.
In the meantime don't mention my name. Thank you again,
Mrs Royce.'

What a strange person, I thought. Changes his mind every
second second. How would his unannounced appearance
affect Elizabeth? Would there be a happy reunion before
he carried her off in his private plane? Between snatches
of sleep that night I thought about Elizabeth's fiancé with
his international business deals and his uncertain plans. The
next morning I bumped into Chauncey in the supermarket
and told him about Gordon Hildebrandt the Second. News
about Elizabeth's fiancé did not please the professor.

I must confess that my attitude towards Elizabeth was
affected. Not that I am mad about money nor that I dream
of wealth for myself, but the fact that she was (probably)
engaged to a multi-millionaire changed our waif into a romantic heroine. Like Cinderella sitting in the ashes while
Prince Charming roamed the town looking for a foot that
fitted the glass slipper. Gordon Hildebrandt phoned again
and again. I saw this as a sign of the prince's passion and
awaited his arrival as anxiously as if he were coming for me.

His big international deal took more time than he had
expected, and the meeting with the Swiss and Japanese
associates was postponed for several days. On the telephone
he kept assuring me that he trusted me not to let Claire out
of my sight. All I could promise was that I would do my best
as I did not think it wise to tell him that she was spending
her evenings with one of her two admirers.

I guess Allan understands me as well as any male can understand a woman. He laughed at my romantic fantasies but went so far as to concede that her engagement to Gordon Hildebrandt the Second confirmed his opinion of Elizabeth's background. 'It explains her tennis,' he said.

'Just how?' I asked him.

'She was obviously coached by a top pro and has had plenty of time for practice.'

Allan is a born athlete, plays both golf and tennis. When he planned this house, he insisted on a tennis court instead of the usual swimming pool. There is nothing he likes more than two sets of tennis and a shower before he sits down to dinner. What a disappointment I was to him, an absolute dud in spite of the expensive lessons I had from the club pro. A couple of nights after she came to us he asked if she played tennis. She answered with the inevitable, 'I don't know,' and added that she'd like to try. I think this aroused a glimmer of memory in her unconscious, for the moment she had a racket in her hand old habits reasserted themselves. She played like a demon, beat poor Allan to a pulp. Every night, except in bad weather or when he worked late, he was no sooner in the door than he yelled, 'Hi, kid, are you ready?'

Then he told me to buy her a proper outfit—not at Sears or a Penney store. On the day we went to buy it I also bought her a good dress—not an import like her old white Cardin which had to be washed every time she wore it—but a charming, rather old-fashioned summer frock of dotted Swiss with tiny puffed sleeves and a velvet sash. She fussed at first, saying I should not spend so much on a charity case, but looked so like a doll in it that I made her take it.

Meanwhile I dreamed. My consciousness-raising group

would certainly not have approved the reveries of those days. Instead of concentrating on my growth into the power of mature womanhood and my rights as equal to any male of my IQ and education, I retreated into childish fantasy. My mind was filled with visions of the princess, Elizabeth, in the great restaurants of Paris and Rome; I dressed her in creations by fashionable couturiers, built or bought for her mansions and palaces and a remarkable modern house—designed by Allan, of course—and furnished it with priceless antiques and custom-made modern pieces, also designed by Allan. No doting mother ever had more luxurious hopes for a beautiful daughter than I for the waif we had picked up in the woods.

I am not certain about the sequence of the incidents I am writing about. A lot of time has passed so that I cannot remember which evenings she spent with Rick or those, when he went to New York in relation to his work, when she saw Chauncey. I do remember a night when Rick brought her home early, before twelve, and did not stop for the usual smooching in the car but drove away at once. Elizabeth opened the front door stealthily and went on tiptoe to her bedroom. The next morning when I asked if she'd enjoyed the evening, she answered brusquely that Rick Shannon was a liar and hypocrite and she never wanted to see him again as long as she lived.

His name was not mentioned that day. Whenever the phone rang she quivered, and if she heard a car, usually a delivery truck, turn into the driveway she would peep out from behind the curtains. After supper she and I were in the living room reading while Allan, in the study, watched a television detective solve a bloody murder. When the doorbell rang she popped up like a Jack-in-the-box and ran to her room, but kept the door open to hear the visitor's voice.

Chauncey had come with the usual tribute. Elizabeth hurried out to welcome him effusively. The little minx had been reading a magazine, but she now had *Swann's Way* in her hand with a finger marking a page. She knew he would ask what she was reading and she would impress him with her intelligence and taste. This delighted him so that he gave us a long lecture on the significance of Proust's work and its influence on Western literature. Elizabeth's sorry mood had evaporated so that she smiled sweetly, laughed at the professor's jokes and openly enjoyed his flattery. I thought her a bit too enthusiastic in accepting his invitation to lunch the next day. He did not invite me.

She left the house at noon. At five o'clock I drove down the road to fetch her. Chauncey was rather rude. He seemed to resent my intrusion.

There was another afternoon she spent at his house. I'm not sure whether it was after or before she said Rick Shannon was a hypocrite and a liar and she never wanted to see him again. Not that it matters much. I do remember it as the day I became a liar. Pop Potts had telephoned to say that he had a couple named Riordan at the station house. 'They want a look at the little lady you've got with you,' he said. 'If you don't want to drive down, Mrs Royce, they'll gladly drive up to your place.'

They came in a white Cadillac. I led them into the living room and called Elizabeth. No response. I called again and heard a door close and a lock click. Elizabeth had barricaded herself in her bathroom. Mr and Mrs Riordan said they'd wait when I told them that Elizabeth was in the tub. I had to look at photographs of an overweight kid on the beach and a studio portrait of an older girl in cap and gown. She was nothing like Elizabeth.

'She was heavier then. She dieted and lost nineteen pounds,' Mrs Riordan said. 'Weighed only ninety-nine the last time we saw her. And her hair's short in the picture. She's been wearing it long.'

'She's got a scar on her body. Appendicitis,' said Mr Riordan digging his finger into his bulky left side.

'Two years ago Easter.' Tears flooded the mother's eyes as she started a long detailed account of the operation. 'We almost lost her.'

They were not willing to believe they had lost her again for they wanted to think that when they found her and brought her home, she would be the same loving child as before she went to California to work for her Master's degree. Although the State claimed to have definite proof of her guilt, her parents could not understand how their darling Lorraine, brought up in their beautiful home with strict morals and her own car at sixteen, could possibly have placed and set off a bomb in the Ladies' Room of the State Capitol.

'She got in with the wrong crowd at college,' her father said.

'Grubby girls and boys with long hair. And dirty finger-nails regardless of sex,' added his wife.

Mr Riordan was the perfect type of self-made man with a house in the suburbs and a car for every member of the family. His wife wore refinement like a transparent garment. Both were smug and without imagination. I felt sorry for them but wished they had not settled themselves so comfortably in my living room. I called Elizabeth several times, then went into her room to demand that she come out and face these improbable parents. Her bathroom door stood open. Elizabeth was gone. I looked in every room, but the only clue was a paper handkerchief behind the door of the study. From this I concluded that she had posted herself there and listened to the Riordans' descriptions of their daughter. Fear held me paralysed. If she was not their child, why had she left the house? When I had regained composure I returned to tell them that she was neither in the house nor garden. One of them asked if I knew where she had gone.

'I haven't the slightest idea.'

This was the first lie. A moment later, shaken by the sin I had committed, I told another. Mr Riordan asked if she had any friends in the neighbourhood to whose home she might have gone. I answered that Elizabeth had not one single acquaintance nearby.

'Then she'll probably come back soon,' said Mrs Riordan settling back on the couch.

'Not if she sees my car outside,' her husband said, but plonked himself down in an armchair and asked my permission to smoke a cigar.

They sat like a pair of stone pillars, but were not as silent as stone. Finally I escaped further descriptions of life in the Riordan manor by offering to make tea. Water had never taken so long to boil, toast never browned so slowly. Their gratitude for my hospitality embarrassed an ungracious hostess. I perched on the edge of a chair, nervous, listening for footsteps outside, hoping Elizabeth would not return while they were there. I barely heard Mr Riordan's cautious explanation of the reasons he wanted to find Lorraine before she fell into the hands of the police. When at last they decided to leave, I gave them my promise that I would call them when Elizabeth returned. Mr Riordan left me his home and office telephone numbers in Bronxville and New York. I was not sure that I would keep my promise although I am usually punctilious about such things.

'Don't forget the appendicitis scar,' said Mrs Riordan.

Just before we reached the door the bell rang. Hope sprang to life in the Riordans' chests. But it was Rick Shannon who stood outside. I had to introduce him to the Riordans who showed him the pictures of Lorraine. His verdict was negative. This restored my courage.

When they had gone I asked if he honestly thought the photographs could possibly be of Elizabeth. He stared at me in amazement. 'Are you crazy? How could you possibly have thought that klutz was Elizabeth?'

'I didn't at first, but you know when you're nervous . . .'

'Where is she?'

'Not here now.'

'Christ! She hasn't gone away, has she? I brought her this.' He was carrying a large box tied up with ribbons. 'Peace offering.'

'You'll probably find her at Chauncey Greenleaf's. Next house down the road.' I told him this as eagerly as I'd said the opposite to the Riordans. 'Will you do me the favour of driving her back here?'

'You've got a deal,' he said.

To my surprise it was not Rick but Chauncey who brought Elizabeth back. He apologised for not coming in, saying he was late in starting for an appointment in Ridgefield. Elizabeth asked to be forgiven for running off without telling me, but she had not been able to face those awful people.

'Why, if they weren't your parents?'

'I wouldn't want them to be.'

'Have you forgotten your parents' faces?'

Her face became the rigid mask that concealed her struggle to overcome the obstinacy of a crippled memory. To relieve her I asked if she had told Rick that she never wanted to see him again.

'How could I tell him anything? I haven't seen him for days.'

'Didn't he stop for you at Chauncey's?'

'When?'

'Twenty minutes, half an hour ago.'

'Oh! Oh!' She slapped her forehead. 'So that's who it was.' She smacked her forehead again and stamped on the floor. 'Someone came to the door and Chauncey answered. I was in the library at the back of the house. Chauncey said it was the Fuller Brush man. What a foul trick. I'll never speak to that liar as long as I live.'

I went into the kitchen to start dinner. She followed. 'May I make the salad dressing, please?' Elizabeth was herself again, the child learning grown-up ways, the pupil proud of success in the domestic tricks I'd taught her. She was measuring olive oil when I asked if she'd ever been operated on for appendicitis.

She laughed. 'For heaven's sake, whatever gave you that crazy idea?'

Was she stalling? I insisted that she tell me. She asked if I'd forgotten that she could remember nothing of her past life.

'You ought to know if you've got a scar on your belly.'

'You ought to know, Kate. You've seen me naked.'

The mockery could have been a way of teasing, but it could also have been an evasion. I mentioned none of this to Allan.

# 6

It was on a Friday evening that Rick was turned down at Chauncey's front door and on Saturday morning that he arrived without phoning and surprised Elizabeth in the garden. Apparently she was willing to speak to him again for they talked for almost two hours and she agreed to have dinner with him that night. In the box tied up with ribbons was a beautiful handbag he had bought for her in New York.

'He noticed I didn't have anything but that little clutch you gave me—not that I don't appreciate it, Kate, I was very glad to have it—but wasn't it thoughtful of him?' In preparation for the dinner date she filled the bag with a few trifles I had given her: a comb, lipstick, mirror, paper handkerchiefs and whatever was left of the five dollars Allan had put into the little old clutch. She wore the new dotted Swiss dress, piled her hair on top of her head and bound it with a coral ribbon she had found in my sewing box.

She was in such high spirits when Rick came to call for her that I was tempted to warn her against staying out too late. And again recalling my mother's most deplorable habits I controlled the urge. Not that it made any difference. She came home before eleven, hurried into her room and closed the door with a slam that said Do Not Disturb. I supposed that there had been another quarrel, but decided not to ask unless she mentioned it first.

That Sunday began in misery and ended in terror. Dark clouds gave morning the look of midnight. By noon the sky was clear, the sunshine as bright as if no such thing as a cloud had ever existed. Allan, whose scowl had been as dark as the atmosphere, whistled gaily and out of tune, and went out with his golf clubs.

Elizabeth and I carried our lunch out to the garden. There was no mention of Rick. She had been quiet and subdued all morning, and would begin to say something and then stop as if she were afraid of her thoughts. Quite abruptly she said she felt sick and went to her room. I took her temperature, but she had no fever so I thought the sudden sickness was psychosomatic. While I was in the garden clearing the lunch table she must have made a phone call for she was talking when I came into the house and the phone had not rung. She told me she was going out to tea, but did not say with whom. Her sickness seemed miraculously cured. She washed her hair and had the dryer going when the doorbell rang.

Chief Potts was there with a dapper man he introduced as Dr Hyde. I took an immediate dislike to him because his black hair touched with grey and his neat Van Dyke beard reminded me of the doctor who used to come when I had a sore throat and gag me with tongue depressors. Like our old family G.P. his manner was formal and his voice pitched low to soothe the frightened child. As he shook hands he thanked me for my kindness to the lost girl. 'Very generous of you, Mrs Royce, and very courageous. I'm sure your kindness has been a good influence.'

'We've become fond of her. She's like a member of the family.'

'I understand. She can be charming when she isn't,' he paused to find a tactful word, 'rebellious.'

'She hasn't been rebellious since she came here,' I said.

'No?' The word had a sceptical sound.

'How do you know she's the girl you're looking for?' I had become belligerent.

'I showed him her picture,' Pop said.

The doctor nodded. 'She's clearly the patient I'm looking for. If you'll ask her to come out and meet me, you'll have no further doubts, Mrs Royce.'

Elizabeth skipped in lightly, stopped dead at the sight of Dr Hyde and hugged herself as if she'd been assaulted by a cold wind.

Dr Hyde said, 'Aren't you going to say hello to me, Grace?'

She drew a deep breath before she spoke. 'Do I know you?'

'Why, Grace dear, you haven't forgotten me, have you?'

'My name's not Grace and I don't know you.'

'Now, Gracie, you haven't forgotten all our long talks.'

'I've never seen you before in my life.'

The doctor nodded, sighed and looked towards me with raised eyebrows.

'Come on, Elizabeth, tell the truth. You know him,' urged Pop.

Elizabeth turned to me. 'Hasn't Dr Tisch come yet?'

'Oh, so that's who you're having tea with,' I said.

'Dr Phoebe Tisch? You're expecting her?' Dr Hyde sounded less than enthusiastic.

'She's a very famous psychoanalyst,' said Pop as if we didn't know.

I heard a door slam and saw that Elizabeth had left. Through the window I saw her running towards the road. At this very moment Dr Tisch's car turned in at our driveway. Elizabeth clambered in and Dr Tisch turned the car. Pop jumped up.

'Come along, Doctor, we'll go after them.'

'Never mind,' said the doctor. 'Let her have her tea. Dr Tisch will bring her back. As long as we know where she's staying, we have nothing to worry about. I'd like a few words with Mrs Royce.' He came to sit beside me on the couch. 'Tell me, is Dr Tisch treating Grace?'

'She's interested in amnesia,' I said.

'What does she say about the patient?'

'Dr Tisch doesn't confide in me.' My tone was anything but pleasant. I disliked Grace as a name for Elizabeth. Pure prejudice. In school I'd loathed a girl named Grace Waterbury. 'Are you quite sure Elizabeth's the girl you're looking for?'

'I know my patients.'

'She didn't recognise you and she said her name wasn't Grace,' I argued.

'Symptomatic of the condition,' he said. 'All the time she's been at the sanitarium she's denied her name. This isn't as unusual as you may think.'

'What kind of sanitarium?' I asked.

'Mrs Royce, I think you'd be more co-operative if you knew the truth about the girl you've so generously sheltered.'

'What kind of sanitarium?'

I believe he delayed the answer in order to heighten the dramatic effect. Pop squirmed in the big chair. He looked extremely uncomfortable.

'I notice that she's put on some weight since she's been here. Wasn't she awfully thin when you found her? Not that we don't feed our patients well. One of the things Shady Oaks is known for is its excellent table.'

Remembering how starved she had seemed when she first came to the house and how she had attacked her first meals, I wondered if the doctor's sanitarium was one of those freak food resorts where they serve the straw bread and nut cutlets known as health food. I wouldn't blame anyone for escaping from a place of that sort. 'What kind of sanitarium is it, Doctor?'

'A home for disturbed adults.'

'An insane asylum?' I cried.

'It's a private hospital, very exclusive,' Pop said.

'Elizabeth isn't crazy!' I had risen and come to confront him at close range.

'Calm yourself, Mrs Royce. Grace has probably seemed a charming young woman. Many patients are able to disarm people ignorant of their condition. As I said before Grace can be charming when it's to her advantage.'

'I've been in social work, doctor. I've seen many disturbed adults. Elizabeth has shown no symptoms of any psychological disorder.'

'Don't you consider amnesia a psychological disorder?' he asked with the smooth condescension of a councillor speaking to a difficult child.

'That's not exactly insanity. In every other way she's completely rational.'

'Quite so. But have you ever considered the idea that the amnesia is not real? Patients are often able to simulate symptoms of other than their own disorders. In fact they are sometimes better at imitating rational behaviour than so-called normal people.'

'May I ask you a question, Doctor?'

'I'll answer to the best of my knowledge.'

'Who put her into your sanitarium?'

'I am not at liberty to say. Mr Dearborn's a prominent member of the political community and prefers not to have it known that his daughter is not quite . . . shall we say mentally stable?'

'Dearborn,' I said, and asked Pop if he knew of any

important politician named Dearborn. 'Never heard of him, but how can a busy man know every name in Washington?' Pop said. I asked where Mr Dearborn lived.

The doctor fitted a cigarette into a long ivory holder, settled back in his chair and blew out smoke rings. I asked again where the prominent Mr Dearborn lived. The doctor preferred not to say. We sat in silence as if each of us were alone. Finally Dr Hyde asked if I thought Dr Tisch would keep Grace out much longer.

'I haven't the vaguest idea,' I said.

Pop was visibly embarrassed. After clearing his throat several times he suggested that they leave. 'We've imposed on Mrs Royce long enough.'

The doctor sat firm. 'I'll wait.'

'How about a drink at the White Lion? They've got a great bar. Mrs Royce can phone us when Eliz . . . when Grace comes in. I'll tell Sheila, the switchboard operator, to ring you in the bar.'

The doctor agreed reluctantly. 'Thank you for your gracious hospitality, Mrs Royce.' I had never been less hospitable in my life but could not refuse to shake hands. 'Now that you know the truth about Grace, Mrs Royce, you'll turn her over to me, of course. For her own safety as well as your own. You'll surely notify me at the White Lion.'

I said I would. What else could I say?

# 7

I drank two big whiskies and walked a hundred miles between the front and back doors. I rearranged furniture, I looked out of the window a dozen times. The wind scattered dry leaves and rain had begun to fall. I moved the furniture back to where it had stood before. Trying not to think about Elizabeth I could think of nothing else. I wondered how to tell Allan. What would he say? That he'd guessed all along? That I'd been a sucker? That he'd coddled me, indulged my whims so I'd stop mourning my baby? I stood quite still, remembering how in the weeks after my baby died I'd walked the floor, rearranged furniture, polished the silver and tried to drown myself in Canadian whisky. The symptoms of neurosis had come back. I was hopeless as ever.

Thunder boomed like cannons in a siege. A streak of lightning came through the window and for an instant turned the room green. I considered not telling Allan, keeping the hideous information from him lest he insist that we turn her over to that odious doctor. Mammoth raindrops hammered down on the room. Why hadn't Allan come home? I grew angry with him for lingering to drink with his cronies at the club while I sat alone in the dark house. I was not worried about Elizabeth. There could have been no safer companion than Phoebe Tisch. I went to the phone to call her home but hung up before I dialled the number. What would the famous analyst have thought of such a neurotic fool? When she brought Elizabeth back I'd take her aside and ask her opinion of Dr Hyde's diagnosis. I'd ask her to stay to dinner. The thought sent me flying to the kitchen. I had completely forgotten to put my roast into the oven. There was spinach to wash and a salad to make. These simple tasks should have calmed me down but I could not stop thinking and every thought unstrung me.

There was a cliché for that sodden Sunday: it never rains but it pours. Besides the sudden violent storm there was the coincidence of two sets of visitors, both in search of a lost girl. Not much more than half an hour after Dr Hyde left, the second couple arrived. I was chopping an onion when I heard wheels on the driveway. I thought Allan had come home or that Dr Tisch was bringing Elizabeth back and wondered whether I should keep my promise to phone Dr Hyde at the Inn. From the kitchen window I saw a car that made my heart beat faster, as no one less than Prince Charming would be driving that costly custom-built Mercedes, a car that made Allan, otherwise rather modest in his tastes, absolutely wistful. Certainly I was disappointed at the sight of the short rotund man who jumped out of the car and stood staring as if he had never seen a really handsome modern house. Before the bell rang I rushed to my room to comb my hair and rouge my lips.

'Is this the Royce residence?' he asked.

'Yes, it is,' I said.

Apparently he thought I was the maid for he asked if Mrs Royce was at home. I had forgotten to take off my kitchen apron. With as much dignity as I could summon up I said that I was Mrs Royce. He turned around and nodded towards the car. When the passenger got out and started towards the house I hurried to untie my apron. Prince Charming! As tall, slender and beautiful as the heroic princes in the old fairy books illustrated by Edmund Dulac. He was fair with light hair brushed back from a high forehead, sculptured features, elegant in grey flannels, a navy blazer and a turtle-neck sweater—the correct outfit for a Sunday in the country. How stupid I had been not to realise that the smaller man was the assistant or secretary whose lower New York accent I had heard on the telephone.

'I'm Gordon Hildebrandt and this is Mr Abel, my lawyer.

It's kind of you to receive us.' His manner was formal and seemed to me princely. I hoped he would not kiss my hand which probably smelled of onions.

I invited them into the house.

'We won't be long, Mrs Royce,' said the lawyer. 'We'd like to see the young lady.'

Mr Hildebrandt nodded. When I said she was not here he looked as if I'd hit him. I said that if he had let me know he was coming, I'd have kept her at home.

'We were uncertain of our plans, Mrs Royce. We only just arrived in New York at midnight and this morning had an important meeting,' said Mr Abel.

'You allowed her out alone.' Mr Hildebrandt's tone was reproachful. He reminded me that he had asked for a promise that I would not allow her out of my sight.

'You asked but I didn't promise,' I told him. 'She's a grown woman, I can't keep her a prisoner. But there's no reason to be alarmed. She's gone for a drive with a most reliable woman.'

'A drive in this weather!'

One would think I had cast a fragile child out into the storm. Still I found it necessary to offer an excuse. 'It was nice and sunny when she left. That's Connecticut weather for you. Changes from arctic to tropical in minutes and vice versa.'

Mr Abel spoke up, 'Do you remember, Mrs Royce, what Mark Twain said? New England had fourteen different climates in a day. Or was it forty?'

'One hundred and thirty-six in twenty-four hours,' I said.

Gordon Hildebrandt said he could not understand people wanting to live in this climate, and wondered why the responsible lady hadn't brought the girl home immediately the rain started. 'Would it disturb you if we waited in this delightful room?'

I assured them that they were welcome and asked if they would like something to drink, alcoholic or tea or coffee. Mr Hildebrandt praised my generosity as if I had offered the nectar of the gods. Somewhat miffed by his remark about people who chose to live where the climate was so uncertain, I said that it would bore me to death staying in a place where there were no exciting changes of season. I had visited a cousin in Santa Barbara and had driven through much of the South-west which, I felt, had none of New England's beauty.

One cannot go on forever talking about climate and scenery. Mr Abel then went into a long explanation of their movements since they had left home. They had gone first to San Francisco, then to Washington, and on to New York, travelling in Mr Hildebrandt's plane which he liked to pilot. They had dined the previous night and spent the evening in conference with the chairman of the board of one of the companies Mr Hildebrandt controlled, and this morning had breakfast and a conference with his New York attorneys. The next morning they were to meet with Swiss and Japanese executives who were to join with Hildebrandt in that international conglomerate.

I paid little attention as Gordon—he had suggested that we call each other by our first names—had given me a leather case filled with photographs of the lost fiancée. Nearly all the pictures were in action, playing tennis and golf, dancing at a costume party, preparing for a dive from a high platform. As I had never thought of Elizabeth in these activities, except her tennis with Allan, she seemed something of a stranger. In three portrait photos she was made up like a model, her fair skin covered with a matte paste, her eyes shadowed in green, her hair done in an elaborate arrangement of curls. But there was a very definite resemblance.

Gordon had grown restless. He travelled around the room and from time to time stopped to pick up an ornament or ashtray, turn it over and examine the hallmark. At the shelves holding our pre-Columbian pieces he stopped for a longer time to study a small but lovely jadeite god from Peru. 'Nice pieces you've got here. Someone in this family has excellent taste.'

When we were still living in the city I had taken a course in pre-Columbian art so could not keep from showing off. I told him the piece in his hand was my favourite god, gave its probable date and said we had bought it on a trip to Peru. I did not mention that I had an awful row with Allan who had said we could not afford it.

'How much will you take for it?'

I was startled. Guests do not ordinarily offer to buy one's possessions. 'It's not for sale,' I said loftily.

'Name your price, my dear.' His smile was indulgent, almost whimsical.

I stood firm. 'It's not for sale.'

'I also collect, but have nothing in this category in my collection.'

'We don't want to sell it,' I insisted.

'We'll pay any reasonable price. Ask what you like, Mrs Royce.'

The way Mr Abel included my name in every remark reminded me of those old radio shows where they name every character in every speech so that people who tune in late know who is talking.

'You gentlemen don't seem to understand. I said it's not for sale.'

Mr Abel turned his back to signal some kind of question. Mr Hildebrandt nodded. 'Five thousand, Mrs Royce?'

I was tempted less by the profit than by the thought of triumph over Allan who had said the piece was not worth the 675 dollars we paid for it. 'I wouldn't sell for double that,' I told them.

'I'm afraid I must accept your decision although I am very sorry to lose this lovely thing.' He set the god back on the shelf and smiled at me ruefully. He looked so like an unhappy boy that I was tempted to let him have the god. He must have been a beautiful child, to his doting mother, a golden-haired blessing. Although he was easily thirty, perhaps more, his face still had something boyishly winsome about it. He had taken off his gold-rimmed sunglasses to reveal very bright, very blue eyes. 'I bow to your will, dear lady. We'll say no more about your Peruvian god.' Everything about him, his stature, the grace with which he accepted rejection, the very blue eyes, the excellent manners added to the princely role. All this and millions too. I wondered how a girl lucky enough to have captured him could forget the prince.

He came to sit beside me on the couch. 'Let's get down to the business of the day. You know I'm here to fetch Claire—'

'Claire? Is that her name?'

'She hasn't told you? Has she ever mentioned me?'

'Amnesia,' I said, 'wipes out all memory of the past. She hasn't told me anything because she can't remember who she is or where she's from or how she got here.'

'Do you believe that, Mrs Royce?' Mr Abel was sitting uncomfortably on a chair whose seat was too long for his short thighs.

I became indignant. 'What do you mean? Do I think she's shamming? Why should she?'

'Don't be angry, Mrs Royce. It was just a thought that occurred to us.' He glanced towards Gordon who gave no sign of having heard. 'We've considered every possibility.'

'Elizabeth—your Claire—so far as I've known her, hasn't that sort of character. She's utterly sincere.'

'You haven't known her very long,' Mr Abel said.

I exploded. 'Do you feel that way, Mr Hildebrandt? If you do, why are you so anxious to have her back?'

'I love her.' The tone was so plaintive that I hoped Elizabeth would turn out to be Claire not only for Cinderella's sake but for the comfort of Prince Charming.

'You misunderstand us, Mrs Royce. We were merely considering possibilities. Don't think we're criticising Miss Foster, it's . . .'

'Foster, is that her name, Foster?' My mother had some distant cousins named Foster. They were horrible.

'Claire Margaret Ravage Foster, Mrs Royce. Her mother was a Ravage of San Francisco, one of the finest families of California.'

My mother's Fosters never got west of the Ohio River. I tried to think of Elizabeth as Claire Margaret Ravage Foster, daughter of a first family. To Gordon Hildebrandt I said, 'But I thought you were from Texas.'

'He has homes in Fort Worth and Los Angeles, Mrs Royce, a place in Palm Springs and apartments in New York and London. Miss Foster's folks live in Pasadena, California, where she was to have married Mr Hildebrandt just three days after she was kidnapped.'

'Kidnapped!' I had never thought of that possibility.

'Indeed.' Gordon had taken a handkerchief out of his pocket, unfolded it carefully and blown his nose. 'Just three days before she was to have become my wife.'

'All the preparations for the wedding had been made, guests invited, Mrs Royce. Two hundred and seventy-nine phone calls had to be made. For some guests it was too late, they'd already left London, Paris, Zurich and Tangiers. We had four girls at the switchboards. At daytime rates, Mrs Royce.'

'I don't think Mrs Royce is interested in petty details, Abe.'

Mr Abel smiled like an indulgent parent. 'He's modest about his expenditures, Mrs Royce. Doesn't want people reminded of his money. Never let newspaper men know he'd paid 250,000 dollars ransom.'

I was awed by the amount. 'Then why is she missing? I thought that when a ransom was paid the victim was returned. Isn't that what happens?'

'That was the understanding, Mrs Royce. But when we went to pick her up at the place designated by them in their final phone call—'

'The gate of Forest Lawn Cemetery,' Gordon blew his nose again, 'but she wasn't there.'

'No sign of her, Mrs Royce, no indication that she'd ever been there. We haven't seen her since.'

'How long ago was it?'

'June ninth. Our wedding was to have been on the twelfth. The last time I had contact with her was on the morning of the ninth. I always phoned her at nine-thirty to say good morning. She told me she was going out to buy something blue.'

'Nothing has been seen of her since, Mrs Royce. The police believe she's been—'

Gordon interrupted. 'Don't mention it, Abe.' To me he said, 'I refuse to believe she's dead. Claire is alive and on her way to us now.'

'Sorry, Gordon. I'm surprised you haven't read about it, Mrs Royce. The kidnapping was reported in papers all over the country.'

The only newspapers I read are *The Westport* which provides local news and *The New York Times* where crimes are usually reported in the second section. Mr Abel was indignant. Texas and California papers reported the kidnapping of and search for a multi-millionaire's bride in bold type on front pages. As the kidnapping occurred weeks before we found Elizabeth there was no reason to think she was the missing bride.

'Now my faith has been rewarded.' Gordon took off the sunglasses again and wiped the misty lenses. 'When our Chief of Police in Fort Worth phoned me personally with the information that they had a report of a girl with amnesia in Connecticut who fitted the description of Claire, I knew I'd been right in believing her alive. The pictures sent by telephoto confirmed it. How soon do you think she'll be here?' He went to the window. The storm had ended but a steady rain was falling. Turning back, pacing the room, Gordon said that it made him nervous to sit idle and wait. He proposed that he and Mr Abel drive around a bit and see the famous Connecticut countryside. 'With all you hear about New England I'd like to judge for myself. I've been around the world five—'

'Six times,' said Mr Abel.

'Seven, Abel. You forgot the trip to Iran when we came back by way of Asia. I think nothing of flying to Hong Kong or Johannesburg, but I've never been north of New York. Come along, Abe.'

After shaking—not kissing—my hand Gordon started off, but paused at the door to ask a favour. Would I pack

Claire's bag so that there'd be no delay in leaving. 'You mean you want to take her away now?' It had not occurred to me that I was to lose Elizabeth so suddenly.

'We must get back to New York tonight, Mrs Royce. We have a very important meeting tomorrow morning. International business.' Mr Abel went on to tell me again that their Swiss colleagues were already in New York and the Japanese would arrive that evening. 'So if you'll be kind enough to have Miss Foster's bags ready we'll be grateful.'

'She has no bags. When we found her wandering in the woods she had nothing but the dress she was wearing and her shoes, nothing else—not even panties.' I hoped to shock them as I resented the high-handed assumption that they could just snatch Elizabeth away from us. 'She has a few trifles and those I'll have ready so that you won't miss a moment of your important meetings.'

'Thank you so much,' said Gordon. 'You're a kind and generous woman. How can I show my gratitude.'

A deliciously wicked thought came to mind. If he had paid a quarter of a million dollars to the rogues who kidnapped his bride why shouldn't he give as much to those who had rescued her? Or even half a million? I'd be grateful for a mere hundred thousand. Not that I am greedy or overfond of money. Allan earns enough to keep us in comfort of the kind that many people would call luxury. It was the glamour of sudden wealth that aroused dreams; I would buy that costly Mercedes for Allan, throw away all the carpets we had admired when we furnished the house, subscribe to the Metropolitan opera and contribute to all the worthy causes that stuffed our letter-box.

From the wardrobe in 'Elizabeth's room' I sadly took from the hangers her two dresses, an old shirt of Allan's which she sometimes wore with her blue jeans, the bikini, and one of the two cheap blouses I had bought for her (she was wearing the other with the jeans). When I started to fold them I was overcome with the sense of loss I had felt when I cleared my father's wardrobe after he died. At the same time I thought that if she was Claire and married Gordon Hildebrandt, I would give them the Peruvian god as a wedding present. This was only slight consolation, and before I let depression get hold of me I hurried to the kitchen for therapy.

Allan found me stirring up an unnecessary pudding. I tried to welcome him with a smile, but within two seconds he sensed trouble. Dear Allan, so sensitive to my moods and so compassionate. During the dreary months when I'd been so impossible there had never been a word of complaint. It would have been unfair to keep anything from him so I spilled out my news quickly. Without much coherence, I'm afraid. I began with Dr Hyde's visit, keeping the pleasanter news about Gordon Hildebrandt for the end. My description of Dr Hyde and his diagnosis of Grace Dearborn's condition must have been horrendous, for I could tell by the look on his face that Allan thought I was exaggerating.

He said, 'You're the one who sounds insane, hon. Are you sure this really happened?'

I was in no mood to be teased. 'Oh, please, darling. This is serious. Do you believe she's crazy?'

'Sh-sh, not so loud. She'll hear you.'

'Don't worry. She's not in the house.'

'Where is she? Don't tell me you let that phoney doctor take her away.'

'She went out for a drive with Phoebe Tisch.'

'In this weather.'

'For heaven's sake, Allan, Dr Tisch knows enough to come

in out of the rain. They've probably gone to her house.' Allan's concern delighted me. It showed that he had grown fond of Elizabeth. He called Dr Tisch's house. There was no answer. I began to worry, less about Elizabeth than about the roast which would be overdone if she was not here by seven o'clock. Allan called Tisch's house again and again and with each call took a stiff drink. He grumbled about some people's lack of consideration, blaming Dr Tisch and Dr Freud and all who practised psychoanalysis.

'They can't think of anything but complexes and psychoses, the lot of them. Elizabeth would have called to say she'd be late if she weren't afraid of that witch.'

'If Elizabeth had wanted to phone I doubt that Dr Tisch would have prevented it.' I was proud of my cool. But his next question threw me into a panic.

'What are we going to do about her now?'

'Oh, Allan. We can't let her go back to that . . . that asylum.' The word tasted like poison.

'If she's been committed we'd be sheltering a fugitive.'

'She was committed unjustly . . . if she was committed,' I spoke passionately. 'Elizabeth is not insane.'

'According to that learned authority, Dr Kate Royce.'

The sarcasm distressed me. Allan had swung around to the wrong side of the argument. 'You want to get rid of her, is that it?' I snapped.

'If it were up to me I'd keep her here—'

'For afternoon tennis?'

'It'll soon be too cold for that. I'd keep her because it makes you happy. But it isn't up to me and, besides, I wonder if it's safe for you. With me gone all day and you alone here with no one within hearing distance.'

'For heaven's sake! You don't think she'd ever hurt me.

That's the dopiest thing I've heard in a long time. She's the gentlest person I've ever known, she wouldn't hurt a fly.'

'Yeah? What about those bank robbers and bombers and killers, such sweet girls?'

It was time to change the subject. Smiling, I said, 'There's no need to worry, darling. She may be leaving us this evening.'

Our argument was hardly logical. Allan switched around to the other side again. 'You're not going to let that phoney doctor take her away? Without proof!'

'It's not that phoney doctor. It's Gordon Hildebrandt. He swears she's somebody called Claire Foster.'

'He phoned again?'

'He was here.'

'Hildebrandt?'

'He left just a little while ago, but is coming back. Ought to be here any minute now. He wants to take her back to New York this evening because he's got a big meeting tomorrow morning. Colossal. You'd think it was the Geneva conference. Or Potsdam. Or Versailles. He'll tell you he's madly in love with Claire but it seems to me business comes first. If he's so wildly wealthy why does he have to rush around making deals?'

'It's a peculiarity of the rich that they want to be richer,' Allan said, stopped and shouted, 'Hey, where's your Peruvian idol?' He was standing before the shelves that held our pre-Columbian collection.

'Isn't it there?' I rushed over to point it out to him. 'That's funny. It was there just a little while ago. Gordon Hildebrandt was crazy about it. He offered to buy it for—'

'He did?'

'No, he didn't. I refused to sell even for—'

'Look at this!' Allan waved a cheque at me. It was for 5,000 dollars.

'The dirty thief,' I said. 'I told him it wasn't for sale. I'm going to make him give it back.'

'Not at this price. Katie, do you realise we've made over a hundred percent profit?' He laughed like a lunatic. 'Now there's a guy who gets what he wants by fair means or foul.'

Foul, I wanted to say when the doorbell interrupted. We both sprinted. Outside stood Dr Tisch in a hooded raincoat like the one I wore to kindergarten.

'Is Elizabeth here?'

'Isn't she with you?'

'I've been looking all over—' She had to pause for breath. 'May I come in?' She jerked off the raincoat and yanked off her wellingtons. 'For almost two hours. Have you any idea of where she could have gone?'

'Why did she leave you? What happened?' Allan and I asked at the same time.

'I wish I knew. I meant to take her to the Inn at Southbury, they serve a real English tea with crumpets, but the weather,' Dr Tisch sighed, either with disapproval of the weather or with disappointment at being cheated out of the English tea with crumpets, 'so we stopped at the White Lion. Elizabeth had something which she wanted to tell me, but first I excused myself to ring a patient I'd promised to get in touch with this afternoon. He kept me for quite a while, and when I got back Elizabeth wasn't at the table. The waitress said the young lady had left shortly after I'd gone to phone. I thought she'd got tired of waiting and gone out to the car. She wasn't there, she wasn't anywhere around. I walked about the grounds but no sign of her. Then I drove down the road, stopping at intervals to call her name. Then I went the opposite way, and drove about three miles in the other direction. She couldn't have walked much further. Where could she be?'

I thought of the night we found her shivering in the woods. The weather had turned colder so that I shivered to think of her outside with only a thin sweater over her dress. 'Somebody might have picked her up,' Allan said.

'Do you suppose Dr Jekyll found her and took her back to his sanitarium?' I asked.

'Who's Dr Jekyll? What sanitarium?' demanded Phoebe Tisch.

I told her about the doctor's visit, his identifying Elizabeth as a girl named Grace Dearborn who had escaped from his asylum before we found her.

'How did she react to that?'

'She said she'd never seen him before and then ran off to meet you.'

Dr Tisch was upset. Allan asked if she'd like a drink. She said she certainly could use one but when I explained that we still had the bottle of *Punt e Mes*, she asked if she might have a straight Scotch. 'Ran away from a sanitarium? I see her actions as a pattern, a pattern repeated three times. From the sanitarium, from the doctor, but from me! Why, she'd phoned and asked if she could talk to me this afternoon.'

'I can understand why she ran away from Dr Jekyll. He looked like a phoney to me.'

'My wife's impressionable,' Allan said. 'She doesn't know anything about him but she's sure he's a quack.'

'But why should Elizabeth run away from *me*?' Dr Tisch repeated like a dumb layman who had not been trained to study the human mind. 'She appeared to trust me implicitly.'

'You don't think she's crazy, do you?'

Phoebe Tisch looked at me scornfully. She disliked the word. 'It is used,' she said, 'too widely, too carelessly—used to describe every condition from slight eccentricity to severe dementia. Elizabeth appeared rational until this escapade today but, as I said, her pattern may indicate a tendency towards sporadic and spontaneous derangement due to delusion, hallucination . . . does she take drugs?'

'Of course not,' I said.

'What makes you so sure?'

'Certainly not since she's been here. How could she get them? She's had no money except five dollars she won from Allan on a bet, and most of it she spent on cosmetics at the discount drug store. Besides she's hardly been out of my sight for more than two minutes.'

'Except when she's out till two or three in the morning with her boy friend,' Allan said.

'Rick brought her home early last night. They must have had a quarrel. She hasn't mentioned him once today, and usually she chatters. There was something different about her this morning, a sort of withdrawal.'

Allan had another theory. 'You may be right about that doctor. He may run one of those fake sanitariums where they "cure" addicts by giving them daily doses, thus keeping them in captivity at high prices.'

'I would like to meet this Dr Jackal. Then I will tell you whether he is a fake or not,' Dr Tisch said.

While I went to phone the White Lion Inn Allan had to listen to a lecture on probable causes of Elizabeth's loss of memory; the result of shock or a retreat from the accumulated experiences of her entire life or even guilt due to sin or omission. Now that she had heard that Elizabeth may have escaped from an asylum, the doctor's theories would be altered. 'Will this doctor . . . what's his name . . . Jackal . . . come here or shall I go back to the Inn to see him?' she asked when I returned to the living room.

'He's not there. Never has been. Funny, isn't it, that he didn't leave his name at the desk when he expected me to call him the moment she got back.' The clock struck seven and I ran to the kitchen to turn out the light under my roast. When I came back I interrupted Dr Tisch's second lecture, 'I wonder why Gordon Hildebrandt hasn't returned. He was so sure she was Claire and so keen on taking her back to New York this evening.'

'Who are you talking about? Someone else beside this phoney doctor from the sanitarium?' asked Dr Tisch.

So I had to repeat the story of Hildebrandt's visit to which Allan added the incident of the Peruvian god and showed off the 5000 dollar cheque.

'An aggressive personality with an inflated ego,' was the analyst's analysis of the man we described. 'I do not think he is at all the sort of man Elizabeth should marry.'

I disagreed with her, not because I am familiar with the tools of her trade but because I had met the man. 'No, that's not a fair description. I guess I skipped some of his positive assets. He's very handsome and courteous and rather fascinating except that he's a bit spoiled like someone who's always had his own way. An aristocratic type. I wonder if Cinderella lived happily ever after with the prince.'

'Prince? Or do I misunderstand?' Dr Tisch used her bedside voice as if I were a patient in her office. 'Do be more coherent, dear. You go off at tangents that are indeed puzzling. Now who is this person you are talking about?'

'Don't you know about Cinderella, Doctor? With the pumpkin coach and the glass slipper.'

'Oh! Oh!' She fairly bounced off the couch. 'You refer to Aschenbrödl. How stupid of me. Oh, my dear, I wrote my dissertation on the influence of that myth on the mores of modern marriage. So this is Elizabeth's prince. Is he coming here?' She danced over to the window and looked out upon the dripping trees. Had she been young and lovely with a foot that would fit into the glass slipper, she could not have been more eager.

'Good God,' said Allan pouring whisky for all of us, 'we've been dumb. It's obvious that she's with Chauncey.'

'Obvious?' I said happily.

'Isn't that where she always goes when she runs away?'

'Always runs away?' said Tisch, happy to have her theory confirmed. While I went to phone Chauncey, Allan was fed another dose of psychoanalytical theory.

Chauncey gave me no chance to ask a question as he rattled away about the inconstancy of the weather, and his journey to Oxford to see an old college chum bedridden after a stroke. He even offered details of his chum's condition as well as a mile-by-mile description of the horrors of driving fifty miles in a storm. At last, 'How's Elizabeth?'

'Isn't she with you?'

An irritable voice asked, 'Haven't I just told you I came in five minutes ago? How could she be here? The house has been locked since ten this morning. Don't you know where she is? Probably with that Shannon fellow.'

This was a possibility. Rick might have arrived at the White Lion by coincidence. 'She may be,' I said, not wanting Chauncey to panic at the idea that she was missing.

'Don't you know?' Chauncey asked accusingly.

'I don't. Perhaps she met him outside.' I proceeded

cautiously. 'If she has another fight with him and lands at your house, call us right away, please.'

'Fights with him, does she?' His voice rang with happiness. He would have liked to go on asking questions about the quarrels. I asked him to excuse me as I had something on the stove that needed immediate attention.

I was getting to be quite an accomplished liar.

Frustration was my lot that abominable evening. In the Norwalk phone book I found three Shannons. None had a Richard in the family, but the last person I disturbed told me that the newspaper reporter came from Rowayton. I found the number in the phone book but got the engaged signal twice. At last I heard from Rick's mother that her son had gone to New York early that morning. There was nothing more that we could do so I decided to serve dinner without Elizabeth. Dr Tisch agreed to stay. We were all edgy and bad-tempered. Allan was cross with me because I couldn't eat. This had been one of the symptoms of my depression. He and Tisch ate heartily of the overcooked roast.

Tension was increased when Allan asked if Dr Tisch thought it possible that Elizabeth was shamming the symptoms of amnesia.

'Oh, Allan, for God's sake . . .'

'Don't get sore, hon. I like Elizabeth, she's a lovely kid but I can't help wondering if she isn't using us for her own purposes.'

'What purposes?'

'To keep her, take care of her. Obviously she doesn't want her folks to find her, doesn't want that doctor to find her, doesn't want to be sent—'

Dr Tisch cut in sharply. 'Mr Royce, I can't agree with you that Elizabeth is shamming amnesia. From my short meeting with her this afternoon I find that she's making a serious effort to find in every stimulus some association which might relate to her past. Just this afternoon she looked at a woman in the tea-room and remarked that her mother had once dyed her hair the same colour. I did not wish to disturb the stream of consciousness and said nothing, but Elizabeth laughed in her charming way and said, "Yes, Dr Tisch, I remember that I had a mother." I do wish she'd told me what she felt it so urgent for me to hear.'

Allan tapped his forefinger on the arm of his chair. The rhythm was erratic. I had become so nervous that a moment of silence distressed me. I thought of the empty bed in the guest room and the emptiness of the house after Allan's departure in the mornings. Elizabeth had become too important to me, a crutch for my loneliness. I almost shed tears at the thought of going back to a job of collecting dead statistics to be interred in filing cabinets. 'I wish you'd stop that tapping.' I glared at Allan's hand.

'Don't be so nervous, hon. She'll be all right.'

The phone rang. Allan got to it first. While we waited for him to bring news we were as still and silent as mourners. Before Allan was halfway back to the dining-room I shouted, 'Was it Mr Hildebrandt?'

'Will he come soon?' asked Dr Tisch.

Allan gave me a peculiar look. 'It was Dr Hyde.'

'Hyde!' I sank back in my chair.

Allan laughed in the way of a husband exercising machismo. 'No wonder they told you he'd never been at the Inn. Dr Jekyll indeed! Hyde's going back to Newbury. If she returns we should phone him and he'll either come for her or send someone.'

At that moment I decided never to let Dr Jekyll-Hyde or

any of his minions take her back to the asylum. To my mind she was as sane as any of us and probably more normal than that quack. I said nothing of my resolution knowing that Allan, in spite of his promise to humour me, would be on the side of law and duty. What have duty and the law to do with love and compassion?

Every half-hour Chauncey called to ask if Elizabeth had come back. He was perturbed when I said we had no idea what had happened to her or where she might be. He wanted her absence reported to the local police. I argued that Pop had been involved with Dr Hyde and was also a slave of duty. At this time Chauncey knew nothing of the Grace Dearborn angle, Dr Hyde's establishment nor the accusation of insanity. He became indignant and promised he would do nothing that could endanger Elizabeth's freedom.

Until she left Dr Tisch kept running to the window, looking out at the driveway, hoping, I suspect, that the prince would arrive. When finally we heard from him it was almost ten o'clock. His Mr Abel called to ask if Claire had returned and to say that 'we' had been obliged to hurry back to New York.

'On important business,' I said, 'a deal with Nidji Novgorod.'

He laughed dutifully, said he would continue to call me but left no number where I could reach Gordon Hildebrandt. He called early on Monday morning, and again in the evening. On Tuesday he said they were putting a private detective on the case. Did I object? I was no less anxious for news of Elizabeth and gave my permission with the stipulation that I was to be informed as soon as she was found. So far as I know the private detective never came to Westport, for none of us saw hide nor hair of him.

\*

On Monday morning I changed my mind and reported Elizabeth's absence to Chief Potts. He called the State Police, then rang me back to say they had no trace of her. I was convinced then that Dr Hyde had discovered her at the White Lion and taken her back to his sanitarium. As soon as Allan had dashed off to catch the early train I started on the long drive to Newbury. When I reached the town and stopped at a gas station to ask the attendant if he knew of a place called Shady Oaks he stared as if I belonged in that institution. Not to know Shady Oaks was, in that community, to be not quite right in the upper storey.

The mansion built in the age of railroad tycoons and copper kings stood on the highest hill in the area. Fifty acres of park and forest were protected by high iron railings. At the main gate I was stopped and asked for identification and my purpose in demanding admission. I said I had come to ask Dr Jekyll about a patient.

'Dr who?' said the guard.

I realised that in my confusion I had repeated yesterday's error. 'Dr Hyde,' I hastened to say.

'Name of the patient?'

About to say Elizabeth, I avoided further suspicion by naming Grace Dearborn. Scornfully the guard made me wait while he telephoned the house saying some dame who didn't seem to know what she was after wanted to see the Doc about Dearborn. Wasn't that the kid who'd escaped a couple of weeks ago?

On well-kept lawns patients played croquet and badminton or wandered about aimlessly, supervised by male and female attendants in starched white uniforms. I experienced the terror common to visitors of such institutions and tried to avoid the eyes of inmates whose curiosity was aroused by my presence. A simian creature, with crouched shoulders and overlong arms hanging to his knees, blocked my path, gazing into my face with lustful yet appealing eyes. A male nurse hurried to jerk him away. 'Don't worry, Miss. He's harmless.' My heart was still pounding when I entered the reception hall. A refined lady informed me that I would have a long wait before the doctor could see me.

'He is with a patient. We are not allowed to interrupt his encounters. Would you care to read a magazine while you wait?'

I was impatient. 'Maybe you can tell me. Is Grace Dearborn here? Did the doctor bring her back last night?'

'You will have to speak to Doctor personally,' the lady said, and departed.

It was almost an hour before she returned to say that Dr Hyde would see Mrs Royce. At the door of his office he greeted me like a long-lost love. 'I'm sorry to have kept you waiting but it's our strictest rule that I am not to be interrupted during an encounter. Have you brought Grace with you?'

'Isn't she here?' I asked.

'I wish she were,' sighed the doctor. 'You're sure you don't know where she is, Mrs Royce?'

'Are you sure you don't know?' I retorted.

'Do you doubt my veracity, Mrs Royce?'

'You seem to doubt mine. If I knew where she was, do you suppose I'd have driven ninety miles to accuse you of hiding her?'

This logic was acknowledged with a nod and a sigh so woeful that I could not, in spite of my distrust, dismiss as insincere. 'I can't imagine where she can be,' I said. 'In this weather. It's gotten so much colder. With only that little sweater, she'll catch her death.'

The doctor sighed again. 'I'll have to notify her father. If we don't find her at once there'll be hell to pay.'

Before he permitted me to leave, Dr Hyde insisted that I see the room Grace had occupied so that I would know that the girl had suffered no hardships. The building was not as elegant as in the days of the tycoons, but it still retained the carvings and gold leaf of its grandiose past, and the patients' rooms (several were shown to me) were spacious and pleasantly decorated. If it had not been for barred windows and locked doors that isolated various parts of the upper floors, residence there would have been not unlike a stay in a large country house. Shady Oaks is (according to Dr Tisch who spoke to several colleagues about it) an institution where the rich could save themselves embarrassment by stowing away mad, drunk, addicted and retarded family members. The besotted were kept content with a daily pint of the favourite beverages, addicts shot with drugs, the mad and the morons allowed their sex games and toys, all under supervision. A wealthy transvestite was provided each month with a new female wardrobe, a sodomite given a pet goat. The meals were said to be excellent, the cost exorbitant.

On the long drive home I kept my spirits up by hoping and half-believing that Elizabeth had come back and let herself in with the key. When finally I got there I rushed from room to room looking for her or some sign that she had been there and gone out again. Like in the months that followed my baby's death the house seemed an empty box, all angles and dark corners. I gave Allan a potluck supper and while we were eating confessed to my useless journey. Allan said I was a nut but a nut with a heart.

'Can you believe she's Grace Dearborn?'

'Why not?'

'I just feel she can't be. Like I felt that she wasn't the Riordan girl or Mrs Fortescue's daughter.'

'Do you feel that she's Hildebrandt's lost bride?'

'More than the others.'

'A romantic nut,' Allan said.

Exhausted, I went to bed early but couldn't sleep, and whenever I heard a sound that might be a door opening or closing I'd creep to Elizabeth's room to see if she had come home. Early the next morning Allan found me perched on Elizabeth's bed shivering in a chiffon nightgown.

'What the hell are you doing here?'

'Sinning.'

'Wouldn't it be just as easy to sin with something warm on?' He stared down at the loose-leaf notebook in my hands. 'What's that?'

'Elizabeth's private life. I found this the other day when I was turning the mattress. I was too honourable to read it then.'

'Does it tell who she is?'

'I haven't finished it yet. But there's one thing I'm sure of now.'

'What's that?'

'She's not shamming. There's no doubt of the amnesia. The poor kid's heartbroken at not knowing who she is. Here, read this.'

I tried to thrust the notebook into his hands. He rejected it, saying he hadn't time if he was to catch his train and telling me he'd like something to eat before he left. I put the notebook back under the mattress in case Elizabeth should return and look for it while I was making Allan's breakfast.

# Chapter Four

## More Leaves from a Notebook

### by Elizabeth

The dead man keeps coming back. He opens his eyes and I scream. I do so hate disturbing Kate. She's my good angel.

Day dreams are better than night dreams. I dream about Rick sometimes. I am afraid he respects me.

I woke up in the middle of the dream. I still felt that I was falling. Somebody came to the edge of some rock or ledge to catch me. Hughie. He fell past me.

*Sic transit Gloria mundi.* This keeps going on and on in my head like a disc on a stereo machine somebody forgot to turn off.

A sweet biscuit, a madeleine in a cup of tea brought Marcel Proust memories of his youth. With me it was a blanket, the feel of wool and the colours of the cover Kate put on my bed last night. I was just about to drop off when she came in with the extra blanket. She tucked it around my shoulders and rested her hand on my cheek and suddenly it was another hand soft and loving on my cheek. Then I was in a different room, a different bed. Big bed, mahogany, Victorian, with carved roses and pineapples and blue curtains at the long windows. Then I fell asleep.

Something else I remembered. It went through my head a minute ago. I saw a place and things happening but now they are gone. While I was getting out my notebook the vision went away. Please, God, help me to be someone. I remember you, God.

Tonight I can't sleep so I might as well write out my thoughts. Not that there are any helpful associations. What I have been thinking is that I ought to be grateful if Rick is a detective working on my case. How can he be working on it if he doesn't know who I am? Maybe he does? Then why doesn't he tell me? It is really painful not to know who you are and what you have done and if you're a good person or bad. Am I wicked? What is evil? Evil is telling lies and cheating and hurting people and hypocrisy and betraying someone who trusts you and adultery. Dr Greenspan says I'm a virgin so I must be. That means I never committed adultery or unchastity. What about those terrible sex things? I get flashing pictures of Certain Things that make me feel sick all over. I get cold shivers when I think of things I might have done and forgotten about.

Rick is falling in love with me. I may be in love with him but am not sure.

Kate and I have been talking about love. She and Allan had an affair when she was nineteen and he was twenty-three. They were in college, she was a sophomore, he was doing post-graduate work in architecture. She was not a virgin. She had an affair when she was sixteen. Allan did not mind. Their affair lasted three years and then they got married and are never mean to each other.

I wish I had an affair when I was sixteen. I wouldn't feel so dumb now.

Rick kisses passionately but I think he is afraid to ask me to go to bed with him. I am not brave enough to say I would like to. I do not think that is the worst thing a girl can do.

I like playing tennis with Allan. It helps. There was a

different court. Where? Who did I play with? I have a sense of a man hitting balls with violence. Was he my enemy?

I keep dreaming that I am about to go somewhere on a ship or a plane. And just as I hear the ship's whistle or the announcement that the plane is to leave, I cannot find my passport. What does that mean, Dr Tich . . . or Tish . . . or Tisch?

*Sic transit Gloria mundi. Gloria mundi* sounds like a girl's name. I don't think I'd like her.

Tomorrow Rick and I are going to the beach in the afternoon and then he is going to take me to his country club for the Saturday night dinner dance. I am going to wear the dress Kate bought for me. It feels like being awake after a long long sleep.

I will arise and go to my father and say unto him, Daddy, I have sinned against heaven and . . . why did I write that? Dr T said I should write everything that comes into my head. Why did that come when I picked up the pen? I have no father except who art in Heaven . . .

It did not come back all at once. No miracles for me. Bits and pieces, faces, voices, happenings. I get a flash and then it goes and I am in the dark again. Last night when I saw him on TV I got so scared I didn't know where I was. And tried to find my way. Things went on and off like different coloured lights in my head. After I got in bed and the darkness was real I got scared and turned on the light again and looked hard at the blanket. It was like the blanket Pricey put on my bed on cold nights. Pricey!!! I KNOW NOW.

Was it only yesterday or last week I felt sorry for myself as an anonymous girl named after a dead baby. All along I tortured myself because I thought I wanted my memory back so I could be myself. Maybe what I really wanted was to be Elizabeth, Kate's petted child. I want it now. I don't like remembering. I don't want to go back.

What a fool I was to believe in people. In him.

I remember THINGS. Like the quilt and the white suède Bible and a string of pearls with tiny little diamonds set beside each pearl. Yes, and a white dog with sad eyes and an old writing desk with secret drawers. Most of all I remember the ring. My finger feels empty without it. Was it an important ring like an engagement ring? Was I engaged? But it is the fourth finger of my *right* hand that feels empty.

I ought to tell them. Right now. It is unfair to let them bother about me, buy me things, etc. I did try to tell Kate just now while we were having lunch in the garden. I could not talk. Or eat. Kate asked if I felt ill. She said I usually had such a wonderful appetite. I said I felt sick to my stomach, and she asked if I had a lot to drink last night with Rick. I could not bear to sit with K and look her in the face and pretend. So I ran to my room and locked the door. She came and knocked at the door and I let her in. She took my temperature. It was normal so I knew I couldn't go on pretending much longer. I must tell them tonight. It is important because they may be in danger. *He* will find out soon and come after me. *He* is afraid I will talk about him and tell what I know. *He* will stop at nothing. After what *he* did to me he could do anything.

If I tell them will they believe me? They will think I made up this weird story. It is too weird. Suppose they think I am really crazy.

I called Dr Tich . . . Tish . . . Tisch and asked if I could talk to her today. She was very nice and said she would pick me up and take me to tea at some inn. I'll tell her everything and ask her to help me tell K and A.

This is it. What I hoped and prayed for. Waking up. Remembering. Real, not a nightmare. But I think nightmares are real and real life is a nightmare. I am here. In this room, a yellow room in Kate's house. Elizabeth's room, they call it. Please God let me stay Elizabeth.

# Chapter Five
# The Waldorf Letters
## by Abraham Abel

One of the persons I asked to contribute to this account of the 'Elizabeth period' was Gordon Hildebrandt II. His refusal, although courteous, was so positive that I had not the heart to try again. Instead I asked Abraham Abel who, at our single meeting had showed greater sympathy for Elizabeth, to provide information relevant to the Hildebrandt affair. Mr Abel regretted that in his position as counsellor and confidant to Mr Hildebrandt he could not comply with my request. How I came into possession of his letters and was granted permission to use them will be told at the end of this narrative.

C. J. G.

WALDORF ASTORIA HOTEL
Park Avenue
New York, New York

Sunday night,
September 27th

Beloved Ruth:
In our phone conversation last night you complained that I have become secretive about our activities here. I agree but

will give you three reasons: a) details of business negotiations and transactions would bore you; b) despite his spendthrift generosity G.H. can be miserly in many ways, most notably with regard to long distance calls so that while he can talk to Tokyo on business for three hours he will hover around the telephone if anyone uses it for more than three minutes on a personal call; c) every instrument in these seven rooms is bugged so that every conversation is on record. Therefore if any associate or employee should deny an assertion or lie about an agreement, G.H. will have indisputable evidence. If what I am about to disclose came to his attention the result would be fatal.

I hope you told Debbie that her old Dad was unhappy about not being home for her birthday but that he was kept here by important business. I hope the presents will console her. I bought her the Polaroid she's been hinting about, and G.H. when he heard it was her birthday went immediately to Cartier's and bought her a solid gold wristwatch. Idiotic for a ten-year-old girl who will break or lose it in a week.

We begin the last stages of our negotiations tomorrow morning. Our Japanese associates will arrive at midnight and the Swiss are already here. A curious thing about G.H. is that because he was panting to find his 'lost Lenore' we didn't go up to Connecticut until this afternoon. We drove the new Mercedes to Westport where Claire was said to be staying at the home of Mr and Mrs Allan Royce, which by the way is fantastic modern architecture (Mr Royce designed it). He was out but we found Mrs R a pleasant lady with the accent and manners of your WASP friends from Vassar. Claire was not in when we got there, but as Mrs R expected her soon, we waited there. As usual G.H. got restless and wandered about the room, turning over antique ornaments to look at the marking and determine the value. He got excited over some god or idol from Peru and offered to buy it. Mrs R refused to sell. After an argument G.H. who will stop at nothing when he wants something simply put the idol in his pocket, but as he is no thief he left a cheque for 5,000 dollars on the shelf. When he told me about it subsequently I was horrified. 5,000 dollars for an ugly clay figure about eight inches high.

Not wishing to have his trickery discovered while present he suggested that we drive around the environs of Westport and return in half an hour or so to find Claire. During this drive in the rain I thought about us, you and I, my darling, when we were young and poor and came for a day in the country to this beautiful area.

What happened on that drive is hard to believe. We were heading back to the Royces when . . .

Later

I had to quit writing because he barged into my room, saying it was imperative that we discuss the deal before tomorrow's meeting. It was not at all necessary as we had gone over all the possibilities of disagreement, had all of our arguments typed in triplicate and rehearsed our answers to certain questions.

Well, I was telling you what happened on that drive. But before I give you that part of the story, let me brief you on the background. You know what you read in the papers and heard on TV about the kidnapping. I must confess that when you asked me about it, I was not completely honest. The true story is top secret. I had to swear on G.H.'s mother's Bible that I would not reveal the truth to anyone, including my wife. Something that happened as the result of that drive has caused me to change my mind. So I am writing this to you now to let you know the true facts, also to have a record of these complex events. Do not let anyone else read this letter and *do not destroy it*.

Claire Foster was not kidnapped.

To give you the complete facts I must go back to the beginning of the so-called romance. In some special tournament at one of his clubs he was paired with a woman player who beat the hell out of him. He was furious. To be beaten by a female was a challenge, and if there is anything G.H. responds to it is a challenge. He was compelled to beat her in the same way that he forced certain mergers because the deals were difficult. So he started working on his tennis with a pro and also dating the young lady. She was beautiful and intelligent and a constant challenge because she would not kowtow to him like most of the women he knew. There is no reason to add that he fell madly in love as you undoubtedly remember the night I brought him home to dinner and you achieved the ultimate in potato pancakes. You will recall that he spent the evening raving about the wonderful girl he was going to marry.

Did I tell you about her folks? They consider themselves the *old rich* and look down their aristocratic snoots at anyone whose forebears came to California after 1900. Except Gordon Hildebrandt the Second. They could sympathise with a poor fellow handicapped by millions. They could also overlook the fact that his grandfather, a poor immigrant Dane, had the bad taste to settle in Texas and become the *new rich*. In the meantime they had become the *new poor* but made a great effort to hide the disgraceful fact. Nothing is as expensive as pretensions. God knows how they paid their bills if they ever did. Claire's mother is like those snotty society dames you see in old movies. G.H. was not fooled, but could not have cared less about their financial status.

Claire fought with him about the wedding. She wanted to spare her father the expense of a big fancy affair. G.H. backed up the mother. The Fosters were Society and he fancied his picture on the Society pages. He had his Publicity Relations Department send Mrs Foster a check for 50,000 dollars, then discussed with me the legitimate deduction he could get as a publicity expense.

Claire went along with the elaborate plans until about ten days before the wedding. She wanted it called off, she wanted to break the engagement. They were not compatible, she said, they disagreed on fundamentals. G.H. said this was just a whim, reminded her that she had a history of changing her mind. There were few details of her life he had not investigated; he knew how impermanent her affections had been, how transitory her interests, how she had gone from débutante parties to transcendental meditation, from marijuana to maharaja, from yachts to yoga. For once in her life she would have to stay firm. He promised her a life of love and luxury.

Three days before the wedding she had an appointment for the final fitting of the wedding dress. She did not keep it. That same afternoon a letter was brought to G.H.'s Los Angeles office. Ten minutes later he called me in. With the door locked and the blinds closed he told me that Claire had run away. She hoped he would not try to find her. She would be using an assumed name. Still fond of him she knew that she could not be his wife. This way was better than divorce. To G.H. this was failure. He swore he would find her and bring her back if it took the rest of his life and his entire fortune. She was his and he would never let her go. Never, never, never.

This was the origin of the kidnapping story. It was concocted to save the face of a man who did not know how to cope with defeat. Pride would not let him face the world as a jilted bridegroom. I tried to dissuade him by naming the hazards. Nevertheless he was determined to go on with the deception. He planned the details with the precision and cunning of Napoleon on the eve of battle. Through me a meeting between G.H. and the Chief of Police was arranged. This took place in a secret apartment G.H. kept for another sort of rendezvous. He explained that his fiancée had been missing since early afternoon and that at 8 pm he had received a phone call from an unknown person who said that Miss Foster would be returned to him on payment of 250,000 dollars. Furthermore, his informant had warned him against instigating any action by the police or private detectives as such interference would result in the girl's death. The time, place and manner in which the cash was to be left would be provided in a phone call the following day. He had reported this to the police as a citizen's duty but asked that they refrain from immediate action lest Miss Foster be murdered.

He proceeded as if the kidnappers' instructions were not his own invention, obtained 250,000 dollars in cash from a bank partially owned by one of his corporations, and at the hour said to have been named drove to the appointed place and deposited a brown paper shopping bag filled with old newspapers in a dustbin behind an antique shop on Los Feliz Boulevard. I was then sent to pick up the alleged ransom. At the same time he drove to the place where he was to find

Claire. Of course she was not there. He then reported to the police, urged them to act, also hired a private . . .

2.35 am
Monday, Sept. 28th

I had to quit again as G.H. heard the sound of my typewriter and came in to ask why I was working so late. I had to sit practically on the machine so that he would not see what I had written. God help me if he had! Darling, I can't write any more tonight. I am exhausted. The rest of the story will be 'continued in our next issue'. Goodnight, my love. Sleep well and keep well and God bless you and our beautiful children. Kiss them for me.

Your loving Abe.

WALDORF ASTORIA HOTEL
Park Avenue
New York, New York

Monday, Sept. 28th
8.40 pm

Dearest Love:

I hope you weren't hurt or upset by the brevity of my call this evening. When you get the letter I wrote yesterday you will understand why I'm so cautious on the phone. I have to hear your sweet voice every day and know that all is well on the home front. I have caught a slight cold, nothing to worry about, but it gave me a good excuse for not going to the theatre and a night club with the Swiss bankers whom G.H. is entertaining. So I have the evening free to continue the serial story I began yesterday.

We were at the point where he hired private detectives to search for the missing sweetheart. He was still in love with her in his fashion. The 250,000 dollars alleged ransom money has been invested in various stocks so that his bankers and accountants will not discover that he is re-investing money supposed to have been given to the kidnappers.

Well, the search went on. There were reports that a young woman of similar appearance and proportions had been discovered. Every disappointment made him more determined to find and bring her back. Last Wednesday the Chief of Police of Los Angeles reported that a young lady in Westport, Conn. was suffering from amnesia and had no recollection of her name or home. A teletyped photo showed a definite resemblance. He was sure this young lady was the missing bride. I, knowing how deep his dejection was after previous disappointments, cautioned him against optimism. Without avail. He was prevented from leaving at once for Connecticut by the obligation to attend a meeting with the directors of his AQC Company. It was imperative that we attend this meeting before we begin negotiations with our new Swiss and Japanese partners. As you know we did not leave L.A. until Friday night and spent Saturday in Washington where we had engagements with two representatives. On Sunday we breakfasted with a deputy Cabinet member, then flew to N.Y. where we picked up the new Mercedes and left our luggage here in the hotel. Throughout all of this G.H. was nervous and impatient, not at all like his usual poised self. I must tell you that he was unduly anxious about his appearance, he had changed from a turtle-neck sweater and Paisley ascot to a white shirt and Countess Mara tie, then back to the turtle-neck and ascot which he declared more appropriate for Sunday in the country.

As I wrote yesterday Claire was not at the Royce home

when we got there and after half an hour we left to drive around in the rain. Now comes the astounding part of the story. We were on our way back to the Royce house when we passed a dark-haired girl running along the road. G.H. looked back and braked so hard that we went into a slight skid. He said nothing but I could see from the set of his jaw how tense he was. He stopped the car, leaped out and stood in the girl's path.

'Claire,' he shouted and held out his arms. The girl backed away. 'I've found you at last, love,' he said.

'Do I know you?'

These were her exact words. I may not report other conversations precisely but these I remember distinctly.

The girl said, 'I don't think I've ever seen you.'

I got out of the car and stood behind him, a witness of all that took place. To me the girl in jeans and sweater darkened by rain, with her hair in strings, bore little resemblance to the elegant young lady I had seen twice in my life. Her face was pinched with cold and she was bent against the wind. Gordon whispered to me that a person with amnesia has a total lack of memory. He kept a tight hold on her wrist.

She was very tired and very wet. G.H. offered to drive her to wherever she was going. She thanked him and said the Royces lived only about a mile away. At the mention of the Royces he looked over his shoulder at me and nodded. He asked me to sit in the back so that he could have Claire with him on the front seat. Then he pulled off his blazer and tucked it around her shoulders.

'How gallant you are. Like Sir Walter Raleigh,' she said.

'How is it you remember him when you've forgotten me?' he asked her.

She told him that she had amnesia and could not remember anything about herself, but had not forgotten impersonal facts like books and music and history. In the rear seat I could not hear what they were saying but from the way the girl laughed it was apparent that she was enjoying the company. We should have been at the Royce's in a couple of minutes, but I thought he was driving around in order to have more time with the girl. Suddenly she cried out that we were on the wrong road.

'I know,' G.H. said.

'Where are you going?'

We had left Westport and were on the Connecticut Turnpike. Signs pointed to New York. The girl insisted that he take her back to the Royce's. He turned around to speak to me. 'Now she can honestly say she's been kidnapped,' he said and laughed heartily. The girl turned sulky. I heard no more laughter.

So here we are in the suite he keeps in the company's name. The moment we got into the hotel he started giving orders: the phone taken out of her bedroom, maids only allowed in for cleaning and bedmaking when G.H. or I are in the suite. When the rest of the rooms are being cleaned she is locked in her bedroom, ditto when he and I are out. 'I'm not going to lose her again,' he says when I protest against him keeping her a prisoner. He has hired a security guard to keep watch in the corridor outside. If she wants anything she knocks on her door, from the inside of course, and he unlocks the door. All her meals are ordered by him, and when Room Service sends up the trays the guard takes them in to her. Except for the arrangements that prevent escape, she is treated like an invalid queen. He has had books and magazines sent up, made sure the TV in her room is in order, has ordered flowers for her and imported chocolates at nine dollars a pound. And asks tenderly if there is anything else she wants.

Her freedom, she tells him. She is a spirited girl full of fire and zest. A great fuss was made because he would not let her telephone Mrs Royce. 'After we finish with these meetings I'll give out the news that I've found you and you can phone anyone you want,' he told her. Until he is ready to make that announcement no one is to know where she is.

I cannot quite make her out. When she is not sulking or brooding, she is as gay and charming as our little girls. At times she is angry at G.H. for keeping her a prisoner and at other times she admires and flirts with him. Does this all sound insane? You have often remarked when I told you about his *mishegas* that G.H. must be crazy. Darling, I haven't told you the half of . . .

11.09 pm

It seems I can never write a letter to you all in one piece. This time the interruption was by Claire who came into my room and asked if she could talk to me. As I did not care to entertain a young lady in my bedroom I suggested that we adjourn to the sitting room. She began by flattering me, telling me I had a kind face and sympathetic eyes. I cannot honestly say I did not enjoy these pleasant words from a pretty girl. She began by asking why Gordon kept her a prisoner. I told her it was because he loved her and did not want to live another day without her.

She said, 'Yes, he told me that last night, but I want to know. How did he lose me?'

'You honestly don't know?' I said.

She said, 'Please forgive me. With amnesia you can't remember.'

'Excuse me, I should have thought of that.'

She said, 'It's crazy, not remembering who you are and what you were like. Like one of those dreams that seem so real when you're sleeping but you wake up and it's gone and all you know is that you dreamed.'

I asked her if there was anything about her past she could remember. 'Sometimes. Things come and go. Fast, much too fast for me to recognise them,' she said with a sigh. 'The other night, when was it? Saturday, Saturday night on television—that's slipping my mind already—Saturday night on television,' she kept repeating these words, 'on television I saw something, someone, and I was shocked—it was shocking.'

'Someone you knew?' I asked.

'I thought—he was, yes, someone—please, Mr Abel, I can't talk about it.' She beat her forehead with tight fists. 'I was so sure the other day—when was it? Sunday, that was yesterday, yesterday before he, Gordon, came along. Now I'm not sure of anything.' The poor kid was shaking.

I went to the bar and poured a Scotch for her. She refused it saying, 'I am sure of one thing, Mr Abel. I do not like Scotch.' So I drank it myself and brought her a glass of sherry. She smiled. When that little lady smiles it is like the sun coming out. She does not look like the stray cat we found in the rain. She washed her blouse and her hair and made up with some of the cosmetics G.H. had sent up for her. She laughed when she saw the variety of powders and rouges and perfumes and eye stuff and said, 'That drugstore must think Gordon's harbouring a tart.' She has a lively sense of humour and can be so sweet that a man would have to be unconscious not to fall for her. Don't worry about that, Ruthie darling, I can admire a girl but never love her as I love the girl I fell for twenty-one years ago.

She then asked if I had known her before she disappeared and I said I had seen Claire twice and had been the recipient of many confidences concerning her. 'Was I a nice person?' she asked.

'According to him you were a goddess and an angel.'

'He must have been very much in love with me,' she said.

'Can't you see that he still is?'

'Was I in love with him?' she asked me.

'He thought you were.'

'He told me last night when you were in your room typing that I should say I was kidnapped. Was I? Do you know about it?' She seemed troubled.

I was tempted to tell her the truth but did not want to betray G.H. (as I am betraying him in these letters) while he pays me so well. So I said, 'Don't you remember anything about it?'

'Nothing at all. I just don't get any vibrations. It's funny because I thought I was getting better after I saw that TV show on Saturday night. I seemed to remember a lot of things but maybe it was only imagination. The associations don't seem to add up.'

'Don't you get any vibrations from him?'

'Gordon? Yes, in a way,' she nodded enthusiastically, then all of a sudden, became still. 'If I weren't so angry with him I might, you know. But he had no right to bring me here and keep me locked up. That's no way to make a girl love you. Don't you agree, Mr Abel?'

I was in total agreement, but again in loyalty to G.H. I could not tell her so. I said that his love for her was so great, his need for her so pressing that he had resorted to unfortunate tactics, and that as soon as he had completed this complex and difficult deal he would give her complete freedom as well as everything her heart desired.

'He *is* attractive.' There was no doubt that she meant it. 'And good-looking. And in some ways kind. But so bossy. He has to have his own way about everything, doesn't he? I suppose it's because he's so rich.'

'Richer than you can imagine,' I said. 'So rich that he has only to snap his fingers and he can get anything he wants.'

'Except me.' She grinned, and those beautiful eyes lit up with the same elfish look as our Sally puts on when she's up to some new mischief. The next minute she became serious and asked if I would help her.

I inquired as to the sort of help she needed and she said she wanted to get back to Westport. I answered sternly that I could do nothing that was not in the interests of G.H.

'So you approve of his unfortunate tactics,' said the clever girl.

'My approval or disapproval has nothing to do with it. While I work for Gordon Hildebrandt I owe him my loyalty,' I said in answer.

She took from the pocket of her jeans the leather folder G.H. always carries. 'He said these might help me remember. Would you say these are me?'

I had seen the photographs many times. G.H. admires his photography almost as much as he admires the subject. He had snapped her wielding a tennis racket, posing in a big hat under a tree, preparing to dive into a swimming pool,

and in a head shot flirting with the camera. 'Don't you recognise yourself?' I asked.

'The tennis pictures and the pool and the riding seem sort
of familiar. But I don't recognise the horse.' She laughed,
throwing her head back and screwing up her eyes. Her
face became quite different. Faces have a way of changing
the characters of those who possess them. There are times,
sweetheart, when you look like a stranger to one who has
observed you for twenty-one years.

'I remember doing all those things, tennis and swimming
and riding but I don't remember doing them with Gordon.
If amnesia is an unconscious desire not to remember, what
would there be about him that I'd want to forget?' Then with
another switch of mood and facial expression she said that
if Gordon came in, I should say she was asleep. 'Goodnight
and thank you for being so kind to a nut.'

She was on her way out when I stopped her with a question. 'You don't like being bossed, do you?'

She answered quickly. 'God, no. I've been bossed too
much in my life,' and ran to her room.

The speed and vehemence of her answer made me
wonder. Why, when she can't remember the man she was
to marry, can she so easily recall this emotion? There must
be scenes or incidents related to such intensity. Is she playing a game, knowing that G.H. wants most what is hard to
get? She cannot have planned a strategy since she did not
know she was going to be kidnapped. I am puzzled. This
girl is a mystery to me. Yet I am fond of her and angry with
him for keeping her locked up. It is no way to make her
love . . .

Tuesday, Sept. 29th

2.10 am

G.H. came in while I was writing and kept me up with a lengthy report on everything the Swiss said during the evening. Thus, having greater knowledge of the man's character, G.H. had developed a new tactic to be used at our meeting tomorrow morning. Will I ever get enough sleep? This letter is going down the post right now so that I don't worry about it in bed and get up and tear it up because I feel that I'm disloyal in telling you all this. I know you will never breathe a word to anyone, my loyal love, so I can safely say, 'Goodnight, sweetheart,' and God bless you and the kids. I miss you so much that it hurts. And once more, I love you.

Your Abe.

P.S. We may be home by the weekend. Hopefully.

WALDORF ASTORIA HOTEL
Park Avenue
New York, New York

Tuesday, Sept. 29th

Dearest:

I have other secrets to tell. It has gotten to a point where I can no longer keep everything to myself. Today I committed an act of disloyalty. I did something I never dreamed I could do in all the years I have been trusted with G.H.'s confidences. This morning we had a lengthy and fruitless meeting with our Swiss and Japanese colleagues. Long arguments over nitpicking details in the contracts. Between them they had seven lawyers while G.H. had only Yours Truly and Sandy Whitelaw of Stone, Sloan & Cohn. As the laws of our countries differ in many ways, there were strongly diverging differences of opinion. It was almost 3 o'clock when we adjourned for lunch. It was decided that while the lawyers retreated to their offices to study ways and means of adjusting the disputed clauses, a cooling-off period would be to the advantage of the principals. We will not meet until tomorrow morning. I fear that my return home will be delayed again.

Instead of going with Whitelaw to work on Clause 21.C, I returned to the Waldorf with G.H. who wanted me to discuss the points of difference with him. He was in a great hurry to get back to Claire. She had eaten her lunch but was not averse to a huge portion of ice cream while we ate sandwiches in the sitting room. G.H. insisted that she sit close to him on the couch. She was subdued and very sweet like our kids when there are guests at the table. G.H. asked if she could guess how he intended to spend the afternoon. 'I can't have my girl looking like a hippie,' he said. 'We're going to Fifth Avenue and I'm going to buy you a complete wardrobe from the bottom up.'

She was ecstatic. The prospect of new clothes always sends a woman into raptures. Even you, my darling. Claire rushed to her bedroom to comb her hair and put on lipstick. 'Adorable,' said G.H., 'just the way she used to be. It's obvious that she's getting over that mental block. Haven't you noticed a terrific improvement in the last couple of days?'

I felt that he was too optimistic. This phase of his character should not have surprised me. It is his habit to believe what he wants to believe and everything that he desires will be just as he wants it to be. This is the rich boy syndrome that we have discussed during arguments about not spoiling the kids just because we have a big income and live in a neighbourhood where their playmates have their wishes granted too easily.

As they were about to start out on their shopping spree, Whitelaw phoned with the good news that the lawyers of our Swiss colleagues had informed him that the Zurich gnomes had been persuaded to give in on Clause 21.C and would initial the paragraphs as soon as the others did. The Japs had been notified and were on their way over to the lawyers' offices, and Whitelaw urged G.H. to come at once to add his initials before the gnomes changed their minds.

Claire pouted. Her heart had been set on having those new clothes right away. She was tired of having to wear old jeans all the time and that one shirt. Couldn't Gordon sign those silly papers tomorrow? The more he insisted on the importance of getting Clause 21.C initialled immediately, the more she fussed at him for neglecting her. 'Just like old times,' he said happily, and reminded her that she had promised last year not to fuss when important business forced him to break dates.

'You know I can't remember things,' she said.

'Please don't be angry, sweet. I'll take you shopping to-morrow.' He tried to pet her. She jerked away.

'I want to get out of here,' she said.

'Aren't you happy to be with me again?' he asked.

'You think I can be happy locked up in this over-stuffed jail?'

'You won't be alone, dear. Abe will stay here and keep you company, won't you, Abe?'

I had expected to accompany him as he never signs anything that I have not examined and approved, but in this instance we were getting our way on the clause and he had only to write his initials beside a paragraph which embodied the terms as I had written them. 'It will be pleasanter for you to spend an hour with this lovely young lady than with my unlovely colleagues,' he said.

Claire drooped like a fading flower. 'You won't take me tomorrow. I'll never have anything decent to wear. You never have time for anything but business.'

'What about you taking her, Abe? Buy her anything she likes. He leaned over to kiss her. 'Now do you love me?'

'You're not as bad as I thought.'

'Be a good girl,' he said, and left.

'Shall we go?' I asked.

'I don't care.' She had planted herself on the couch. All the sparkle had gone out of her. Bent over, hands between her thighs, head drooping, she was a picture of despair.

'But I thought you were so anxious to have those new dresses.'

'All I want is to get back.'

'Back where?' I asked her.

'To Westport, to the Royce's. That's my home now.'

I told her to be patient. Gordon would give her a beautiful home, several homes in glamorous places.

She got up and walked around the room, finally stopping at a window to look down upon the street below. With her back to me she said, 'His dearest possession, am I? Do you call that love, Mr Abel?'

I tried to be loyal to him by telling her how he had grieved when she disappeared, and how much time and money he had spent trying to find her. 'He wants to own me. That's not love,' she said. Nevertheless I went on defending him, telling her how much he talked about her, how he would stop during a business discussion to declare his intention of getting her back. The more I tried to practise loyalty the more hypocritical I felt. She was correct in saying that possessions meant more to him than human affection. He loves his cars, his boats, his houses, his real estate, his dogs, his investments because they belong to him. He feels the same way about a woman. She belongs to him and he would stop at nothing to keep her.

So I asked her if it had been his possessiveness that had caused her to run away from him. The words were hardly out of my mouth when I realised what an unforgivable mistake that was. She drew my attention to it immediately.

'Run away? He told me I was kidnapped. Wasn't I?'

Unable to answer honestly I asked, 'Don't you know?' and received her usual reply. An amnesia victim cannot remember. I was not sure I believed her. But I was sure that she did not want to marry him. This was the basis of my ultimate disloyalty. I did not think of loyalty to G.H. when I acted. Only later when I considered what I had done I thought of G.H.'s faith in me, looked back over the years as his confidant in private affairs, his best—perhaps his only—friend. Where G.H. goes, Abe Abel goes; when he has problems Abe is asked to supply solutions; when he is hurt he expects Abe to soothe the maimed ego. With the exception of social and romantic affairs he must be accompanied by his personal attorney so that he makes no costly errors. His fears are irrational. If we ordinary folk guarded our lives as sedulously as the very rich protect their money we would be a nation of hypochondriacs.

I feel that I am myself no longer. Ruthie darling, do you remember a young attorney who believed so religiously in the law, whose ambition it was to serve justice, who saw himself as the brave defender of the poor and helpless? How then can you stand the sight of this lily-livered stooge? How often have I resolved to end this servility? Yet while despising myself I ask how can a man of small stature serve justice courageously whilst giving his family the *good American life* and accumulating enough money to nourish, clothe, house and educate four beautiful daughters.

Well, all the time that I had been straining to take G.H.'s part, my sympathy for Claire had been mounting. Over the couple of days in the hotel I had become increasingly concerned about her and more indignant with him; I had tried to make him understand that he had committed a crime.

'Stop nagging, Abe. She's my fiancée, she's going to marry me. She's sick up here,' he would say and tap his forehead. 'I've every right to take care of her.'

'But you got her into your car under false pretences and carried her into another state without her knowledge or consent,' I argued. 'Besides you're keeping an unwilling adult under duress.'

'It's more for her safety than my convenience. It would be dangerous for a person with a mental disturbance to go out on the street alone,' he insisted.

When I reminded him that kidnapping was a capital offence he reminded me that I would be considered his accomplice. I knew and did not relish the idea.

All of this was eating me when I proposed that we start on our shopping tour. 'You'll feel a lot better getting out of these rooms. You need air. Besides it's getting late, the shops will close soon.'

She came reluctantly. To save her the embarrassment of walking through the lobby in jeans I took her out by way of Lexington Avenue exit. As you know this is not the way to the Fifth Avenue shops. I had a different idea, I hailed a taxi and told him to take us to Grand Central. Even with traffic the drive took no more than two minutes. I bought a one-way ticket to Westport, then gave her a ten-dollar bill. 'Take a cab to the Royce's.'

Tears shone in her eyes. 'How can I ever thank you?'

'Forget it. And forget that this ever happened. Amnesia will be a convenient excuse.'

I left her weeping happily and a prickle in my own eyes. Not that I'm such a benevolent guy but her gratitude weakened me. Walking back to the hotel I invented my excuse. As expected G.H. had a fit when he returned and found her gone. I did not say we had gone out on our shopping tour but told him that she had slipped out of the suite while I was in the bathroom. Thus he was to blame for having dismissed the security guard when he went out. He always let them go when either he or I was in the suite with her. Another of his petty economies as the guard service is paid by the hour. As always when he loses anything G.H. has a tantrum like the spoiled child that he is. He cursed me as a bastard, an idiot, a lazy slob. I asked if he wished to get rid of me. If he had given a hint of assent I would have resigned on the spot. Since he gave no answer I pursued the question no further thinking of the tuition fees for four girls at good colleges.

'Do you have any idea of where she'd have gone?' he asked me.

'She didn't say.' This was no lie.

'Westport probably. She kept nagging me about letting her phone that Royce woman. God damn it, man, why did I invite those Japs for dinner tonight? I'd like to drive up there right now. Do you suppose I could squirm out of it with the Japs?'

'They'd consider it an insult,' I said, and advised him not to endanger negotiations at this delicate moment. He agreed sadly. 'How long do you think we'll be tied up with the creeps?'

Later when he'd had a few drinks and cooled down I asked why he continued the pursuit of the reluctant bride. 'Do you think you'd be happy married to an unwilling woman?'

'Happy,' he said in a tone that made happiness sound obscene. 'That's not the chief reason I've got to get her back. It's what she knows. Too much, Abe. What would it do to me, to my image, if people found out Claire was never kidnapped? What would they say about me. I'd look like a bloody fool.'

'She was kidnapped. Only it was after you reported it.' I had to laugh. G.H. did not think it funny. But the irony pleased me and I went on, 'And you were the kidnapper and she ran out on you the second time.'

'God damn it, I've got to keep control of the bitch. She's dangerous to me. The next time I'll make her stay with me.'

'Suppose she doesn't?'

'I'll kill her,' he said.

This remark is too common to be taken seriously, but I could not help thinking of the time he got into a tantrum and shot his favourite hound.

I hope these long letters have not bored you, but you'll forgive me for spilling out my guts to the one person in the world who I can trust. Please keep this and yesterday's letter in the wall safe as I may want them in the future.

I love you, I love you, I love you and can't wait until I hold you in my arms. Kisses to my little girls and a big you-know-what for yourself.

Your devoted Abe

Note:

While working on this ms. I received the following letter which greatly facilitated the task of giving the narrative a coherent structure.

C. J. G.

Malibu, California
February 29th

Dear Mr Greenleaf:

In going over my husband's papers I found your letter requesting detailed information about the period of Claire Foster's imprisonment at the Waldorf Astoria, and a carbon copy of his reply refusing your request on the grounds that while he served as Mr Hildebrandt's confidential attorney he could not give out information about Mr Hildebrandt's personal affairs.

I regret to tell you of my husband's death as the result of an accident caused by his car having been hit and edged off the cliff of the Coast Highway by a speeding car whose hit and run driver has not been identified.

As my husband's death occurred shortly after he had resigned his position with Mr Hildebrandt (after a rather nasty quarrel about his client's personal and business ethics, or lack of ethics) I believe that Mr Hildebrandt no longer deserves the protection my husband believed his client's due. The wish to 'expose the bastard' was expressed so often and so ardently (and directly to Mr Hildebrandt during the quarrel, I believe) that I feel Abe would approve of my giving you permission to publish the letters written to me at the time you need to know about. I have had photographic copies made and am sending them to you by registered mail.

Incidentally I think you'd like to know that Abe was favourably impressed the one time he met you and wished he had known you under happier circumstances.

With good wishes for your work in progress,

Yours sincerely,

Ruth Abel.

# Chapter Six

# Passion and Investigation

## by Richard Shannon

Unhappily I confess that it was at my suggestion and with my encouragement that Richard Shannon wrote this account of his search and discovery. Believing the story would be incomplete without his contribution, I urged the strictest honesty and the inclusion of any detail that might be relevant. Although I fear that he took my advice too literally, I have not changed, deleted nor added so much as a comma, and do not take responsibility for what follows.

C. J. G.

1

When Dr Greenspan told me of his mystery patient I had visions of a siren in a clinging black gown that revealed every curve of an irresistible body. I saw her greeting me, a scarlet tipped hand extended, head tilted back, eyes narrowed, a Mona Lisa smile on lips whose startling crimson gave violent contrast to powdered flesh. The vision collapsed when the doctor added that his examination had shown her to be a virgin.

'She must be very young, probably another runaway.'

The prevalence of teenage runaways had become a bore. No freelance writer would speculate on such a story.

'I take her to be over twenty although you can't tell nowadays. They mature so early.' The doctor yawned.

'Twenty and a virgin. Must be a freak.'

'Wait till you see her.'

I was not sure I cared to. What kind of story can you write about a virgin of twenty? I tried to let Old Doc down easily. He'd conducted me on the long journey from womb to moustache, had dosed me through measles and whooping cough, deprived me of my tonsils. Although he no longer made house calls he came regularly to see my grandmother and lingered to chat with my mother over coffee and doughnuts. Up in Grandma's room he said I should wait for him downstairs as he had something important to tell me. He spoke as if he were bestowing a rare gift. Why are non-writers so anxious to provide us with material? They're always sure they've discovered a remarkable tale that will bring the writer Fame and Fortune. Some even expect to share the take. What would the doctor say if I told him I'd discovered a terrific brain tumour and expected to be cut in on the fee?

'She may not be a virgin except technically. There are cases where a woman's had intercourse without the hymen having been penetrated. It's not common but it sometimes happens.'

'Some fun,' said I.

'She might have had vaginal orgasms, or intercourse with a man who practised *coitus interruptus*.'

I enjoyed an instant reverie of the passionate gratitude of a beautiful gal whose only previous experience had been with a jerk-off. Driving on the highway that evening, I passed the road that led to Whispering Hill and it occurred to me that I had nothing to lose by looking into the story. If the chick was photogenic there might be a chance to sell a short piece to one of those magazines whose publishers believe that a picture tells more than ten thousand words. I visualised the lay-out: double-spread, photograph of girl in bikini, and story of *The Girl Without A Past* by Richard Shannon. Who was she? Where had she come from the night the Royces found her wandering in the woods? According to the doctor there was no indication of physical trauma. So what had caused amnesia? What had horrified her so that she had lost her identity?

A piece like that might not pay a lot, but money wasn't all I was after. I was tired of being a stringer, I wanted a job with a future. My sights were fixed on *The Weekly*. It was a new rag, sort of a combination of *The New York Magazine* and *The National Enquirer*. A year-old entry in the publication sweepstakes it had already achieved the threshold of competition with leaders in the field. Out of three ideas I'd presented I'd been given two assignments. When I told Dinsmore, the editor, that I wanted a place on his staff he'd said, 'Bring me something sensational, something we can feature on the cover. Show us that we need you.'

'I'll do that,' said I.

There was nothing very sensational about the story Dr Greenspan had told me but I thought I might find an angle. If not, there'd be little harm in looking over the situation. And the girl. I knew the Royce place, having done a story for a Bridgeport paper on the unique home a Connecticut architect had built for himself in the woods. I parked the car a few yards down the road and walked through the garden.

Nothing is easier than spying on a glass house. Concealing myself behind a group of shrubs I had a first-class view of the kitchen and the two females inside. Kate Royce had the correct Connecticut commuter's wife appearance; tweed skirt, matching sweaters; short string of pearls, pony-tail. She was stirring something in a pot. At the other end of the table a girl was arranging flowers. She wore jeans rolled up to the knees and a man's shirt that was too big for her. Long black hair hung over her shoulders. Her back was to the window.

She finished the flowers and carried them to the dining room. The lights were switched on and I got a quick glimpse of her face. At that moment I was surrounded by the glow of headlights. I was on the garage side of the bushes and could easily be seen by the driver of a car. Before he could jump out, I ran like the devil through the garden and down the road.

No one pursued me.

All that night and the next day I thought of the mystery girl. I couldn't be sure that the hasty first impression was accurate. The idea of beauty might have come from an eager imagination. I thought of a story about a lovely lost girl and saw myself directing the photographs to get shots of her as I had first seen her, arranging flowers. At the end of the day I spied on the Royce house again. Instead of the levis and white sweater I'd worn before, I dressed in dark clothes, and was careful to see that Allan Royce's car was in the garage before I approached the house.

They were at the dinner table, Royce's back towards me, his wife facing the window, the girl in profile. I moved stealthily to a place where I could view her full-face. Mrs Royce must have caught sight of me for she jumped up and pointed towards the garden. Royce made for the back door. An experienced interloper would have hurried away but I stood like a fool hypnotised by a sensational face.

The kitchen door swung open. Allan Royce dashed towards me. 'What are you doing here?'

I was off like an Olympic sprinter. He followed me to the road. I leaped into my car which I had parked on the road facing downhill. There was no real danger in the situation. I could have said I was a private detective on the trail of a missing girl and that I wanted to establish her identity before announcing myself. To tell the truth would have defeated my purpose. After Dr Greenspan had told me about his mystery patient I talked to the Police Chief and learned that Elizabeth X would never talk to a reporter. Although she could remember nothing of her past, she had a fixed idea that enemies were after her and had consented to be photographed only after he had promised to keep her story from reporters. So there had to be another way of approaching her.

A lucky coincidence brought about our meeting. Not such an unusual coincidence. It was a scorching day and everyone who could went to the beach. What better place for a pick-up? I kept myself in the background while Elizabeth plunged into the water and Kate Royce hesitated at the edge. A couple of minutes later I dived in and swam like the devil to catch up with her. She swam lazily, turning over on her back to float, letting the waves carry her a few yards, turning again to do a neat crawl. I took a parallel course a few yards behind, and dreamed like a teenager that she might get a cramp and valiant Richard Shannon, for five summers a life-guard, would rescue her. At last she turned towards shore. I had waited long enough. The tide had to be taken at the flood. I swam towards her.

'Hi,' said I.

'Hi,' said she, and turned her head to show me the prettiest smile I'd ever seen.

'You've come out awfully far. Aren't you afraid?' said I.

'Of what? Water?' At which she dived in and swam under water.

I kept close by. We came to the shore at the same time, walked side by side without speaking until she went off to join Kate under a striped parasol. I went in the opposite direction to fetch my cap and shirt as I cannot expose my damned skin to sunlight without raising a crop of blisters. With the shirt tied around my shoulders and the cap angled to protect my face, I strolled jauntily towards the parasol. For some seconds I stood looking down at her. She affected not to see me. Her eyes were the colour of huckleberries. If the long lashes had been blackened artificially, black rivers would have run down her wet cheeks. Her flesh was as lustrous as the inside of a seashell. At the sight of her body any of the Old Masters' mistresses would have hastened to the nearest reducing parlour.

'Hi,' said I.

'Hi,' said she.

These were not like the 'hi's' of our meeting in the water. They were more like the greetings of old friends. She laughed deliriously, started to introduce me to Mrs Royce but had to acknowledge that she did not know my name. I introduced myself, and we soon got into the question and answer game of new acquaintances. I did not state directly that I was a detective but hinted at it in such a way that Mrs Royce guessed it immediately. She asked if I was working on any special case. I answered that a private eye could not talk about his work. When we were getting ready to leave I asked if I might come to their house that evening.

'Oh, do!' exclaimed Elizabeth.

Kate said, 'Come to the front door and ring the bell.' So I knew she recognised the spy who had sneaked into her garden. Nothing more was said of it. Did she think that a private detective was on the trail of the runaway daughter of some celebrity whose image would suffer if it became known that there was discord in his family? Or that I had been hired to find a kidnap victim whose captors had threatened her life if word of the snatch got out, and had kept secret her escape in order to collect the ransom? This was all pretty far out but typical of the way my mind works.

Not wanting to appear a too eager beaver I waited until quarter to nine before I rang the Royces' doorbell. After a bit of polite conversation Kate and Allan retreated like the parents of an eligible girl. I am not usually self-conscious, but being alone with Elizabeth made me feel like a kid on his first date. I had plenty of questions to ask but did not want to sound like an interviewer. We sat silent for a while, looking at each other, looking away, then letting our eyes meet again.

Elizabeth broke the ice. 'Tell me, what did Mr Potts tell you about me?'

'I wasn't kidding when I said he told me you were a beautiful girl without a memory.'

'Sounds like a deformity. It is, I suppose, a mental deformity. Silly, isn't it, not to know who you are or where you came from or how you got here?'

'The human condition,' said I.

'Not exactly. Because even if you wonder who you are and what life's all about, you know your name and where you live and who your parents are. But when you can't remember *anything* it's like—' she paused to find words—'like being born blind and not knowing what anything looks like, or deaf, never hearing sounds.'

'I never thought of it that way.'

'I wouldn't have either if it hadn't happened to me.'

Laughter seemed irrelevant but, turned against herself, rather touching. I liked the way she tried to smile off self-pity. How pleasant it would be, after the string of heels I'd glorified (in a former job as a press agent), to write about someone I could honestly admire. It would not be a tough yarn to write. I saw it set up, the title in bold type—*The Girl Without A Past*.

Ideas erupted. I became restless, paced the floor. The Royces' big living room was too limited for my impatience, the air-conditioned atmosphere too lifeless. I suggested a drive. Like a child Elizabeth ran to ask permission. Like a child she was delighted with everything. We stopped in a joint for cokes and hamburgers. You'd have thought she'd never tasted a hamburger, never heard the clamour of a juke-box, never taken a night drive in a convertible. Her pleasure made me feel like a rajah distributing gems, like a Rockefeller sharing the wealth, like a sugar daddy with mink.

If she'd been a normal date, the kind of girl you take out for obvious reasons, I'd have made love to her before the evening was over. Not that I wasn't tempted. But Elizabeth meant more to me than fun and games. She was a story, she was opportunity. This worried me. Deep in the gut I was irritated by scruples not usually suffered in my profession, the sense of being a heel in taking advantage of her innocence.

I had still to find substance in the story, something more sensational than amnesia. Saying I was a detective had not been a mere gag. To find an angle I had to investigate her background, discover the facts she had forgotten—if I was lucky enough to find a clue. From her manners, her movements and carriage and the peculiar inflections of a voice that was either English or finishing school, I could tell that she was no daughter of the proletariat nor *petit bourgeois*. Driving home that night after an hour of indecision with the car parked in the Royces' driveway and a chaste kiss on the cheek, I played with improbable fantasies, seeing her as the child of a tycoon, an ambassador, a movie star. Brushing my teeth I made her the fugitive daughter—educated in English schools—of a ruthless dictator. Before I drifted off she became a princess rescued from rebels by a daring reporter.

Early the next morning I phoned and asked her for dinner that night. She said she hadn't anything to wear which is the kind of thing a girl will say when she has thirty dresses hanging in her closet. I told her she looked better in that plain white thing than most girls in their fifty-dollar best—not knowing at the time that the little white thing was an import from Paris and had probably cost more than twice fifty. It was not so much the dress that made men turn and look at her when we walked in the restaurant but her style and the way she carried herself. She had class.

After a shore dinner at The Claw we went to a bar that called itself a discotheque, danced until we were dizzy, then drove to the beach to cool off. Although exciting the evening was not profitable. Questions about her past, her home, parents, school and lovers were answered, 'I don't know.' I tried the exercise of projecting myself into a mind gone so blank that I could not remember our house or my mother's and grandmother's faces. Even my father who had died when I was five remained a living memory. I tried to surprise Elizabeth with sudden, unexpected questions. And once, irritated by frustration I snapped, 'You must be kidding.'

'Do you really think so?' She looked as if she were about to burst into tears.

'I'm sorry, I didn't mean it. It was just one of those things that pop out when you're not thinking.'

'A thought has to be there before it pops out,' she said. 'You don't trust me, Rick. I guess I do sound sort of unbelievable.'

'You're too sensitive,' I said.

'I guess I am, but it's really embarrassing not to know who you are. Like being some kind of freak.'

It was after 2 o'clock when we said goodnight. I kissed her on the mouth. She pressed herself close to me, responding with such fervour that it was all I could do to keep from trying to make out in the open car. Elizabeth X was no child. She might not have remembered other kisses but she had not lost lust.

She asked naïvely if I was in love with her. I answered with more kisses. Words were dangerous. I had to remind myself that it would not do for me to become involved with the subject of a potentially profitable story. Yet while I considered the profit motive I deplored the practical side of my nature which cheated me out of what I desired most at that time.

# 2

I tried the next day to reconstruct the evening, to analyse every remark and to find some clue that would lead to a single substantial fact about her identity. Like every other newspaper reader I knew about the six girl fugitives sought by the FBI. What a yarn I'd have if Elizabeth turned out to be a débutante bank robber, a Junior League bomber, a drug smuggler with a Ph.D. It would have been an extraordinary experience, something of a thrill to have had intercourse—in any sense—with an adventuress of stature, yet I shuddered at the prospect for I had become fond of the girl. Ambivalence was the name for my feeling about Elizabeth. The air of innocence may have been no more than ignorance of her past, the result of her failed memory. A virgin? She kissed like an experienced tramp. Dr Greenspan had qualified the diagnosis by adding that virginity might be technical, a rare case of a membrane that resisted penetration.

The day was a total waste. I had to decide which was more important to me, the girl or the story. A story about a living person demands objectivity. Is it possible to write objectively about your partner in bed? Keep cool, I told myself; smooching in the car was okay if it led to nothing more. If she was a virginal virgin and not merely the creature of an indestructible maidenhead she could be as dangerous as clap. That could be cured in a few weeks, but emotional involvement could go on forever. In the Army I had a pal who was endlessly pursued by a village belle whose little white flower he had plucked. That had been six years earlier. Now girls were taking defloration more tolerantly.

Swearing that I had no need for them I stopped in a drug-store to buy a box of condoms. A virgin would not be on The Pill. When she came running out to meet me I was glad I'd taken this precaution. Midnight was too far away. The preliminaries of dinner and the movies would have to be endured. At the restaurant we flirted. During the movie we held hands.

The picture was about a couple who fell in love and did not get married. The girl was a singer crazy with ambition. When she became pregnant she resisted marriage. The guy said he'd leave her if she had an abortion. She had the abortion. He left her. She hit the big time, became a star, made a fortune with her records but was never happy. One night when she was singing in Dallas she saw him in the audience. Their reunion was terrific, porno to the limit of what could be shown in the cinema. He still wanted to marry her. After a lot of dialogue she agreed to give up her career and settle down with him on his ranch. The marriage would take place as soon as she had made a farewell appearance at a prestigious New York night club. He promised to fly to New York for her final show and the next day go with her for a marriage licence. The show was a terrific success. She was applauded, kissed, showered with gifts and flowers. Her man was not in the audience. She broke away from the throng of admirers and went to her dressing-room where she heard on the radio that a plane from Texas had crashed in Ohio. All the passengers had been killed. He was on that plane. She resumed her career and became the biggest name in show business.

Elizabeth sobbed. She sniffled and groped in her pockets for a Kleenex. In the lobby I wiped her face with my handkerchief. The pleasant task was interrupted by a voice behind me.

'Touching nonsense, wasn't it? I don't wonder at your grief, Elizabeth. Here, my dear. That handkerchief is quite sodden.' Professor Greenleaf held out a clean one.

'Thank you.' She took his handkerchief and gave me back the sodden rag. Smiling at him she asked, 'Do you think I'm a silly cry-baby for getting so upset over a film?'

'I admit to a furtive tear,' said he. 'How about you, young man? Were you as affected by Hollywood's message?'

'Message? In that cheesy flick?' I chose the adjective as a challenge to the professor. From a talk I'd heard him give to writers in the neighbourhood I knew him to be a prig about language. What he 'especially deplored' was journalese which he called 'an assault on the English language by the present generation of reporters'.

He affected not to notice the deplorable word. 'One might conclude that the message or moral of the picture is that love leads inevitably to sorrow. It seemed quite obvious to me. Didn't it strike you that way, dear?'

Tears welled up in her eyes again. 'It's terrible when someone you love dies.'

I wondered if this experience was part of her forgotten past and made a mental note.

'But it's better to have him killed in a plane crash,' she said, and nodded in confirmation of some unspoken thought.

'Better than what?' I made the mistake of asking and was reprimanded with a sharp, 'You know I can't remember things. I'm terribly thirsty. Will someone offer me a drink?'

Crossing the street she took Chauncey's arm. At the café he sat beside her on the banquette while I faced them across the table. He ordered Scotch, I drank beer and Elizabeth had a toasted cheese sandwich and a glass of milk. Conversation was not easy. We were all a little stiff. I told the professor that I had enjoyed his lecture and that friends of mine who had been his students had spoken highly of him. He returned the compliment by saying he had 'been enlightened' by my two pieces in *The Weekly*.

'I didn't know you wrote for magazines,' Elizabeth said. 'Why didn't you tell me?'

'Didn't he? How odd,' said the professor and went on with some inane remark about how most young writers tried to impress girls with talk of their work. 'Why didn't you?'

'Why?' asked Elizabeth. 'He told us he was a detective.'

'Detective!' Greenleaf roared with laughter. 'Were you pulling her leg? For what reason?'

I was growing hot, my skin flushing, but my voice remained cool. 'I happen to be working on a case.'

'Have you joined an agency? Or are you doing an investigative job connected with a story?' continued the nosey professor. He raised his glass. 'Here's to your story, Shannon. Is it by any chance connected with Elizabeth?'

'No! No! Of course not,' she snapped, and in a gentler tone demanded, 'Tell him, Rick, that it isn't.'

'It is not.' I felt no qualms about lying to Chauncey Greenleaf. My work was none of his business. My hand lay upon Elizabeth's thigh. She squirmed away. 'Cool it,' I whispered, 'I'll explain when we're alone.'

'Will you please take me home, Chauncey?' She offered him a little-girl smile.

He beamed like the August sun.

I said, 'You're my date, I'm taking you home.'

He stood up, edged his way between tables, bowed formally and said, 'I shan't intrude any more. Goodnight.' On his way out he paid the bill.

We left the restaurant without speaking. We crossed the street silently. Nothing was said until we were on our way. I kept my eyes on the road and pretended not to hear until she asked for the third time why I had lied to her.

'What makes you think I lied?'

'Chauncey didn't believe you and I don't either. And why did you say you were a detective?'

'What's the use of explaining anything to you in the mood you're in? You won't believe me.'

'Why didn't you want me to know you're a writer?'

I was confused, incoherent, dumb because I was not sure of the way to explain away the stupid lie. 'It was because . . . because . . . I wanted you to be . . . that is . . . not self-conscious the way people get when they're being interviewed.'

'So you are writing about me.'

'I wanted to . . . that is—'

'Well, I don't want you to write about me.' She was very emphatic. Stamped both feet on the floor of the car.

'Why not? Why are you so uptight about it?'

'I don't want you to. That's why.'

'What are you so scared of, Elizabeth?'

She answered with a shrug that had become a customary way of saying she couldn't remember the past. At the same time she asked defiantly, 'What makes you think I'm scared?'

'I don't know but it may be . . . amnesia often is . . . escape from guilt of some sort.'

'Do you think I've got something to be guilty of?' Her voice was hoarse with fury.

'That's what I'm trying to find out. And so are you, I imagine.'

Haughty silence. We were driving up Whispering Hill Road which is not lighted. All I could see of her face was the profile, head high, chin aggressive. She caught me staring. 'Please keep your eyes on the road,' she said.

I begged her not to be angry. 'If you think I've been dating you just to get a story, you're wrong. I fell for you the first time I saw you. Now I may even be falling in love.'

'Oh, Rick.' Tension had relaxed. There was the hint of a sob in her voice.

'You're a very lovable girl.'

'I wish you hadn't lied to me.'

'Don't let it bother you. It wasn't a big lie. Or important.'

'Every lie's important.' She was choked up again. 'People lie too much . . . everyone . . . lies and filth and hypocrisy and lies. The whole world, everywhere, whited sepulchres . . . and now you too, Rick.'

'Elizabeth, you've remembered something. What is it?'

A sigh, a moan, the whimper of a hurt child. Some memory buried deep within had caused this sorrow, this rage, this passionate reaction to the idea of falsehood. 'Somebody's told you a terrible lie lately. Can't you remember?'

'Only little bits and pieces. They go too fast. Like flashes. They don't attach.'

'Try to make them attach. Think hard, concentrate on just—'

'Stop it. Stop pestering me.'

'Look, I'm trying to help you—it's for your own—'

We had reached the Royces' driveway. I had barely stopped the car when she jumped out. I followed and caught hold of her wrist so that she couldn't put the key in the lock.

'Let me go, Rick. And don't come around tomorrow. Or phone me. I don't want to see you again.'

'Look, Elizabeth. Be reasonable. I don't want to pester you. I'm trying to help—'

She freed her hand and put the key in the lock.

'Listen, girl—'

The key turned, the lock clicked. 'Thank you so much for the lovely evening.'

Lovely evening! Wasn't that a lie? Perhaps all courtesy is falsehood. I had no chance to argue the point. She slipped into the house and closed the door. It was too late to ring the bell and disturb the Royces.

## 3

I called three times the next day and was three times informed that Elizabeth refused to come to the phone. The first time I was sore, the second understanding and the third penitent. I had opened a wound. She was acutely sensitive to a condition she likened to a deformity. That she had liked me, responded eagerly to my kisses, made my sins all the blacker. By mid-afternoon I was ready to lie down on the Royces' lawn and bid her walk over my recumbent body. I couldn't see her that night as I had promised to go with my mother to a cousin's engagement party in Port Chester. I was too impatient to wait until the next day to do penance, to kneel before her and swear that henceforth I would seek her company solely for its own sake and that no story about Elizabeth X would be written.

When I arrived at the Royce house I saw a white Cadillac parked in the drive. I had only just touched the bell when the door opened and Kate ushered out a solid couple. They could have walked right out of a comic book. Jiggs and

Maggie. A diamond flashed on his pinkie. She had a face like my father's shanty Irish cousins. If this sounds exaggerated it is because I have inherited prejudices from my maternal grandmother who is lace curtain Irish. Kate introduced the Riordans. Before they departed in their white Caddy they told me all about their darling daughter who had been missing since she set off a bomb in the Ladies' Room of the Capitol Building in Albany.

'Elizabeth couldn't possibly belong to them,' said Kate authoritatively.

'How can you be so sure?'

'You just have to look at Mrs Riordan's ankles to know.'

'Did Elizabeth see them? What was her reaction?'

'She heard their voices and ran out. A deaf mute in Westchester could have heard them.'

'Do you know where she is?'

'Probably at Chauncey Greenleaf's. The next house down the road. I'd be grateful if you'd pick her up there and bring her back,' Kate said.

'With the greatest of pleasure, Madam.' I hurried off, having but a short time to make peace with Elizabeth before I went home and dressed for the family festivities. While on my way I planned speeches of contrition, but never got to use them as the professor told me she was not in his house and that he had not seen her that day.

The party in Portchester kept me from her that night. By the time we escaped the clutches of relations and I'd driven Mom back to the house it was too late to storm the bastion. Early the next morning I called my New York answering service and learned that the editor of *The Weekly* wanted to see me pronto. I lost no time in getting to the city and Dinsmore's office. He had a story he thought I could handle, a rush job that had to be finished in three days. I had to stay in New York to gather material by day and write at night. I barely took time to eat, but I got the copy in by Thursday afternoon.

'Good boy, you've passed the test,' Dinsmore said after he read it. 'Now what about that big story you were going to dig out?'

I was tempted to mention the girl without a past but recalled contrition and a promise I was to make on bended knees. 'I'll have it for you in a week,' I said rashly. I had no idea of where I was to find another story.

Too tired for a confrontation that night I flopped into bed as soon as I reached the house, only going out to eat—the first decent meal I'd had in days. In the morning, without phoning and taking the chance of a rejection, I drove to Whispering Hill Road.

I caught her in the garden. She was on her knees weeding Kate's herbaceous border. When she saw me she jumped up and started to run off. I grabbed hold of the tail of the man's shirt she was wearing, an old one of Allan's, no doubt. Grabbing her shoulders I whirled her around so that she had to face me. There was a streak of dried dirt across one cheek. She had never looked lovelier.

'Hi,' said I.

'You know I don't want to see you,' said she.

'I know that's what you said but you might have changed your mind,' said I.

'I have nothing but contempt for a liar.' She tried to look contemptuous.

'Was it such a bad lie? Did it hurt anybody?'

'There was no reason for it. Why couldn't you tell me the truth?'

'Look, Elizabeth, I'm sorry and ashamed and I swear that I'll never, never lie to you again.'

'And you'll swear not to write a story about me?'

'I'll swear on bended knee if you'll forgive me.'

'Cross your heart and hope to die?'

She was so sweet, so earnest, her eyes were so appealing that I lay my right hand on my chest and swore the childish oath. She became radiant. Colour rose in her cheeks. She stood on tiptoe and kissed me.

In the afternoon I took her to the beach and then to the country club for dinner. The band played rock, jazz and corn. The corn was best because in the old-fashioned foxtrot a man can press his partner tight against his body. Back at the table we pushed our chairs close together. We were drinking whisky sours. Her hand fell with careless care upon my thigh. I kissed the tip of each of her fingers. Club members stared at us and wondered who Rick Shannon's lovely date was. I introduced her to no one. It would have been embarrassing if anyone had asked her last name. Several men cut in while we danced. I gave them no more than two minutes before I cut in on them.

It was early when I proposed that we leave. She seemed disappointed. 'I don't mean to go home,' I said, 'I'll take you to a more interesting place. What do you feel like doing?'

'Whatever you want.'

Her answer could have been interpreted in more than one way. There were tremors in the hand that clung to mine. My blood pressure rose. For a time I drove aimlessly, not sure of where I could take her. Presently I turned off the road and into a thickly wooded grove used by high school kids for secret drinking and sex. I kissed and fondled her. The response was fulfilment of a lecher's dream. When we paused to breathe I whispered, 'You're wonderful, love. Is it possible that you're a virgin?'

She drew away the fraction of an inch. 'Dr Greenspan says I am.'

'Only technically. You must know if you've ever been with a man.'

I guessed the answer before she spoke. 'I don't know.'

'It's strange to forget that.'

'I don't know—I only know . . . I . . . I . . .' she seemed hopelessly confused. 'All I know is that I don't know.' She began to cry softly.

I had my arms around her. She shuddered against me. 'Never mind, love. It's not so important. But I hope you won't forget me.'

'Oh, I wouldn't. I couldn't forget you, Hughie.'

Hughie? Who was he? If I asked I'd get the inevitable answer. Better to soothe her with caresses. With patience and time I'd find out. Oh, it was sweet to feel her softness against my body. I think I could have made it with her if she had not suddenly stiffened and pulled away. She stared over my shoulder as if a ghost had appeared among the trees. Only a luminous ghost could have been seen in that dark grove.

'Let's go, let's get out of here.'

'Why? What's wrong?'

'Nothing, nothing, only I . . . I . . .' she stammered, 'I don't like it here.'

'What's got into you, love? You seemed to like me making love to you.'

'Oh, I do. I do. But not here, Rick, please not here.'

Female moods are beyond understanding. There was such an edge of hysteria in her voice that I decided not to ask any more questions. I started the car and in gratitude she kissed me. For the second time that evening I asked where she'd like to go and for the second time she said anywhere I wished. I wondered where to take her, for with hope restored I knew it would not do to bring her back to the Royce house or into my grandmother's house. It was the old logistics problem. In New York I had no such difficulty. In concupiscent moods I tidied my pad. 'The night's still young,' I said. 'Let's have a couple of drinks.'

I had in mind a bar next to a motel which looked attractive. Perhaps I was over-scrupulous, but I felt that to take her directly to the hotel would be crude.

The bar was crowded. Fortunately for us a couple left and we were led to a booth with high walls. All around was the din of Saturday night voices, the rattle of glasses and tin trays and the clamour of a TV turned on full volume. None of this disturbed us. We were so unaware of everything outside of ourselves that we interrupted a kiss in utter amazement when the waiter coughed discreetly to inform us that he'd brought our drinks.

I touched her glass to mine. She smiled happily and was about to drink when she set down her glass and slid to the edge of the booth. I asked three times what had startled her. No answer. Her whole attention was given to the screen.

The face was not unfamiliar. A politician's face under a shock of silvery hair, a voice as mellow as twenty-year-old Bourbon, an air of injured righteousness, a wholesale package of platitudes. I had missed the introduction and his name, and from what the interviewer asked and his responses gathered that he was more sinned against than sinning and that he trusted in God to prove his innocence.

'Know who that is?'

Elizabeth gave no sign of having heard or even of recognising my existence. She perched at the edge of the seat, motionless, hypnotised. 'Hey, I'm here too,' I said, and gave her a good poke in the ribs. She turned for a split second with a look that asked who I was, then turned back to see and hear the politician's farewell.

'Come down to earth,' I said, while on the screen a dimpled brat asked why Mommy always used plain soap on her washing while all the other kids' mommies used Zip or Rev or Beep.

Once more I asked the name of the guy on the TV.

'Who?' she asked.

'The man you listened to so rapturously. Someone you know?'

'I never saw him before in my life.'

'Then why were you so enthralled? Was it his beautiful silver hair? Or his message? You can find that on every penny. *In God we trust.*'

Her only reaction was a look that combined hurt and scorn. I regretted the smart-Alec retort. Something in that television interview had touched a vulnerable spot. Was it the man himself or a painful memory aroused by a colour photograph and amplified voice?

'Elizabeth! You remembered something.'

She seemed dazed. With a jerky movement she picked up her glass and downed her drink.

'That's no way to drink brandy. You could kill yourself.' She nodded humbly. I gave a short lecture on the dangers of gulping down brandy with reference to a story I'd covered when I worked on the Norwalk paper. 'The coroner's office couldn't decide whether the death was suicide or stupidity.'

I thought this a neat climax and expected appreciation. Apparently Elizabeth hadn't heard a word. She was off in some remote place where the din and the smells of the bar could not reach her. Nor the existence of a man in love and heat.

'Elizabeth! Listen to me. You knew that man.'

She covered her face with her hands. 'Don't keep asking me questions. I don't remember *anything*.'

I was not sure I believed her, but did not think it would improve our relations to mention it at that moment. Crouched over the table, her face hidden, she presented a picture of such sadness that I hadn't the heart to add to her grief. 'Okay, love, I'm sorry. Let's forget it. We don't want to spoil this beautiful evening, do we?'

She straightened. Her hands fell away from her tear-stained face. Her eyes were moist and appealing, her smile grateful and so sweet that I had the urge to grab her and make outrageous love right there in the booth.

We left the bar. A cold wind struck at us. In her thin summer dress Elizabeth shivered and pulled Kate's sweater tight around her. The lights of the motel sign blinked red and green, off and on, off and on. My arm curled around Elizabeth's shoulders. I led her towards the motel office whispering that in two minutes she'd be warm and cosy. 'I'm going to make love to you, my love, like you've never known love before, no matter what your past has been.'

She stopped dead. I tried to urge her on, but she refused to go a step farther. 'You're not angry, darling?' I asked, wondering if the move towards the motel had offended her.

The flickering lights tinted her face green, then red, darkened and turned her green again. '*Decked with purple and gold and precious stones*,' she said.

'What the devil are you talking about?'

She paid no attention but went on . . . *'having a golden cup in her hand full of abominations and filthiness of her fornications.'*

At first I thought she was putting me on but in the glow of the alternating lights I saw her serious face. *'And upon her forehead was written, MYSTERY, BABYLON THE GREAT, THE MOTHER OF HARLOTS AND ABOMINATIONS.* I don't want to go back,' she said in the same tone without a change of inflection.

Now it was R. F. Shannon who shivered. I had turned colder than death. Desire had deserted. I shuddered at the thought of intimacy with a girl who quoted the Bible while her face was dyed green and red by the lights of a motel. One of us had gone mad and I knew it was not Shannon.

'All right, I'll take you home.'

'No! No! That's not my home . . . I won't go there any more.'

'Where is your home, Elizabeth?'

'Not Topeka, not any more. I will never go back as long as I live.'

'Topeka, Kansas?' I asked as if there were a Topeka in every state. Was this a clue to the identity of Elizabeth X?

I decided not to ask questions lest she become hysterical again, but suggested that I take her back to the Royce's.

'Yes, please. To the Royce's, that is my home now.' Her laughter was self-conscious.

With its top up the car became a tight little cell holding two people who had retreated into themselves. I was frustrated and nervous as a man is bound to be when cheated of satisfaction. And baffled by my own stubborn memory. As we bumped over a rock in the road I made the association—the face under the silvery mane—Topeka. 'Of course! That was Claude Dixon, Representative from Kansas.'

Elizabeth had gone deaf.

We turned in at the Royce's drive. I grew angry. 'You must know who he is. Anyone who reads the papers or looks at TV would know him.'

Still the mute indifference.

'What's the matter? Can't you listen when I talk to you?'

'I don't read newspapers nor look at TV news.'

I ran around to help her out of the car, but she ignored my hand. 'Good night, Rick, thank you for the lovely evening,' she said with the hauteur of a lady dismissing a servant. There were no kisses.

## 4

A lie became truth. That day at the beach when I told Elizabeth and Kate Royce that I was a detective, I thought it no more than a convenient whim. The lie went deeper, down to the very soles of my secret seven-league boots, down to the black depths of suppressed yearning. Philip Marlowe, Hercule Poirot, Sam Spade and James Bond had been the idols of my adolescence.

And in an oblique way I did become the detective investigating a mystery. The clues were Elizabeth's reaction to the Face, the Voice on TV and the declaration that she would never go back to Topeka. Who was Claude Dixon? I should have known more about the Kansas Representative who was running for the Senate for the third time. Plenty of dough had gone into his current campaign. Where had the money come from? His alleged transgressions and resulting alibis did not interest me. Too many similar accu-sations and denials had polluted the political air in recent years. What was Claude Dixon to Elizabeth? That was the question.

I had little sleep that Saturday night. I was stimulated by the prospect of the story I could write if my conjectures were valid. Not that my promise to Elizabeth was forgotten. I was eager to know the truth, I told myself. Simply that and nothing more. For the sake of the girl I loved, I rea-soned and fancied that amnesia might be cured by definite identification. And while qualms were soothed by these skittish lies I was composing opening paragraphs, strutting into Dinsmore's office with the news that I had a sensational yarn, seeing my by-line in bold type.

I woke the next day at noon and cursed the laws that closed libraries on Sundays. From back copies of *Time*, *Newsweek* and *The New York Times* I hoped to get the dope on Dixon. I was impatient and irritable. 'God damn Sundays. If I were a dictator I'd ban all Sundays.'

'Why, dear?' asked my mother, a tolerant woman who had endured my blasphemies since I was thirteen.

My aunts who had come from church with her admon-ished me. 'God established the Sabbath as a day of rest for toilers,' said Aunt Matilda. She and Aunt Addie were equally shocked at my having breakfast when their midday dinner was served.

My soul craved madder music, stronger wine. Early in the afternoon I drove to New York. The genteel atmosphere of my grandmother's house oppressed me. 'New York on Sunday!' exclaimed Aunt Matilda. In their circle Sunday in the city was little better than a holiday in purgatory. And so it proved. Nothing was accomplished but the loss of eleven bucks in a poker game. The guy who could have got me into the *Times* morgue was off that day. At ten the next morning, in the Reference Room of the Public Library, I was an island surrounded by seas of information about Representative Claude E. Dixon, b. 1925, Old Indian Springs, Kansas. His present home was in Topeka where he had practised law and served as a judge of the Municipal Court until he entered the House of Representatives in 1957.

Until this present, heavily financed campaign his record had been as clean as a sheet laundered in the leading detergent. The lily-white reputation had been severely smudged by charges that Dixon had accepted over-the-limit contributions from the Drug Lobby while serving on a Congressional committee investigating dubious practices by manufacturers of prophylactics, palliatives, sedatives, carminatives and dandruff cures. The white sheet was further besmirched by a rumour that he had accepted between fifty and one hundred thousand for his personal use. The facts had been vehemently denied while he continued his campaign, charging unnamed enemies with criminal libel. In florid speeches before Elks, Kiwanians, Rotarians, Presbyterians, Catholics, Jews, Republicans and ladies in hats, Dixon denied the slanders. Most of his constituents continued to support him. In twenty years he had not missed a Sunday in church.

As an added attraction to the female voter Dixon was single. What could be more romantic than life in Washington as a senator's mate? Maiden, wife, divorcee or spinster, the gals' dream. Dixon was handsome, Dixon was virile, Dixon was mature but not elderly. He had been married to and divorced from the former Evelyn Waterfoot, daughter of old J. C., chief of the beeftrust tribe. Waterfoot's only son had died in World War II. The bulk of the fortune had been left to Evelyn Waterfoot Dixon-Clayborne-di Grassi-Wells, now Lady Harrington-Clark. She had twin sons by her third husband, a daughter Gloria by Dixon.

Gloria Dixon? It was not the right name for Elizabeth.


# 5


At 3.47 that afternoon I came down to earth at Topeka Airport. When I gave the taxi driver the address he said, 'Oh, the old Waterfoot place.' The house and grounds had been settled on Dixon in his divorce from Evelyn. She had given out an interview saying she never wanted to see Topeka again. She never had.

The house stood well back in a formal garden. Red brick, turrets, ivy, mullioned windows. Henry VIII would have slept well in this house built for a beeftrust king. A pair of gardeners watering the lawn and trimming the hedges stared as I got out of the taxi. I nodded and waved my hand in what passed as a regular visitor's nonchalant greeting and they went back to work. 'Good afternoon,' I said when a dignified woman in a dark cotton dress opened the door.

'Good afternoon,' she said, and waited to hear whether I was trying to sell vacuum cleaners or subscriptions to a combination of magazines that no home should be without.

'This is the home of Mr Dixon?'

She jerked a nod. Tightened lips, narrowed eyes marked suspicion. Worse than door-to-door salesmen had invaded the territory. Reporters had probably swarmed after the accusations and denials.

'Mr Dixon's not here.'

'It's Miss Dixon I've come to see. Is Gloria at home?'

'No.'

'I'm very anxious to get in touch with Gloria. Can you give me her address?'

'Are you a friend of hers?'

'Yes indeed. A good friend.'

'And you don't know where she is?' The woman was nervous. She twisted a narrow gold chain from which a Phi Beta Kappa key dangled.

'Gloria said that if I ever happened to be in this city I should look her up.'

'She did?' A hint of scepticism in the tone. 'And did she tell you she'd be here at this time?'

'She wasn't definite. She just said I should drop in if I was ever in the city.'

'How long is it since you've seen her?'

I answered cautiously, 'Not long ago.'

'When? When?' The woman stiffened with the tension of suppressed excitement. 'Since June?'

My nod gave no information beyond a suggestion of assent. The woman came out of the house to look me over in the sunlight. I saw then that she was extraordinarily handsome. Ivory skin, sea-green eyes, swan's neck, Nefertite's profile.

'You've been in Europe? At Cap Ferrat?'

I had to move with assurance, to adjust my thinking to this new concept, to play my role as private eye. How would Humphrey Bogart have done it? What would Sam Spade have answered? I said, 'Is that where she's supposed to be?' I was tough but nonchalant. The trick worked.

'Are you a detective?'

I owned up to the role.

Agitation was no longer suppressed. There was a marked change in her manner. 'Come in, I'd like to ask you a few questions.'

Inside, the house lived up to its exterior pretensions. Panelled walls, dark oak chairs, marble floor, pompous portraits. From the murk of the great hall I was led into a sitting room that overlooked a flower garden. 'Gloria's favourite room. She had it done over, the house was too gloomy, she said. She did the decorating herself. Her taste is impeccable.'

The woman asked me to sit down, established herself on a sofa and took up a piece of needlework. Her hands trembled. 'Would you like tea, Mr . . .'

'Rick Shannon.'

'Or coffee, Mr Shannon? Or a drink?'

'Coffee if it's no bother.'

'No bother at all. Mr Shannon, who hired you to look for Gloria?'

'I'm not at liberty to disclose my client's name.'

'It wasn't Mr Dixon?'

'Doesn't he know where his daughter is?'

'Then it must have been Dearborn. Did Roger Dearborn engage you to find Gloria?'

'I've never heard of any Dearborn.'

'He's Mr Dixon's pilot, pal and general factotum. He takes care of everything for him now.' Her mouth puckered in bitterness.

A young coloured girl in a grey uniform came in. 'You rang, Miss Price?'

'Coffee, please, Emma.'

When the girl had gone Miss Price let her needlework slide to the floor and left the sofa to sit closer to me. She spoke softly. 'There's no use beating about the bush, Mr

Shannon. I'm as anxious as you are to know where Gloria is. So let's be frank.'

'Is there something you want to tell me?'

'I've been told not to worry about Gloria, she's supposed to be with her mother, but since you've come—a detective—looking for her, something must be wrong.'

'What do you think could be wrong, Miss Price?'

'I don't know. It's just ... she usually writes to me every ... two, three weeks at least, sometimes oftener. I haven't had a word since the middle of June.'

'You asked if I'd seen her at Cap Ferrat. Is that where she's supposed to be?'

'I don't know. She usually spends most of the summer there. With her mother.'

'Haven't you tried to get in touch with her? You can phone her, you know.'

The lady seemed offended. She snapped out an answer. 'I was angry with her. She left without a word for me, I was away that week and I fully expected to see her when I got back. It's not like Gloria to treat me discourteously. Her manners are perfect if I say so myself.'

'What does Mr Dixon say about it?'

'He says he's not worried. I don't dare talk about it any more, he gets into such a temper when I say we ought to do something. She's just careless about writing, he says. I can't believe that. Gloria was never careless before.'

'Are you a relation, Miss Price?' I wondered about her position in the household. The maid had called her Miss, but she certainly did not have that hungry old maid look.

'I'm Mr Dixon's housekeeper.'

Again I noticed a touch of bitterness. The maid brought in a tray with cups and coffee in a silver pot. Like Miss Price the girl had a long graceful neck, a proud small head, sculptured bones. Unlike Miss Price who was old ivory the girl was golden brown.

'This is Emma, Mr Shannon. Emma's my niece.'

It was a green-eyed black's way of telling me.

We spent more than an hour over the coffee cups. She had both praise and criticism for Dixon. 'I don't want you to think he's unsympathetic. He adores Gloria but lately . . . lately . . . he's been . . .' she chose the word carefully . . . 'preoccupied. It's these accusations . . . unfair . . .' Head held high, she addressed judge and jury. 'His political rivals . . . unscrupulous . . . have spread these vile canards.' She went on with a string of oratorical phrases probably gleaned from Dixon's speeches. Perhaps he rehearsed them with the housekeeper as audience. 'He's a good man, hasn't missed church for twenty-nine years of Sundays.'

Fondling the Phi Beta Kappa key, Miss Price told me that she had never meant to become a domestic. She had had higher ambitions. 'But fate was not kind to me.' Her language had the stilted dignity of strict self-discipline. Her story was typical, the stereotype of an old-fashioned novel. Poverty, an unemployed father, sick mother, tubercular sister. Lucy Price had been lucky in getting a job that might have been conceived by a Brontë sister or Daphne du Maurier. The gold of the Phi Beta Kappa key was not tarnished by her employment as governess to the five-year-old victim of a failed marriage. The divorce court had given little Gloria to her mother for nine months a year, to her father three. The child had been taken to live in England, returned after the first nine months like the souvenir of a broken engagement. The snob nanny who had brought her refused to remain in a house where the staff were black and there was no one of her class to provide companionship. She left without notice.

Lucy Price had been hired as a three-month substitute, spent eleven years as Gloria's teacher, nurse maid and surrogate mother, had crossed the Atlantic twenty-two times coming and going, had stayed in great town houses and luxurious country mansions, had travelled with her charge, visited the famous museums of England, France, Italy, Germany, Austria, Holland and Spain. The ex-Mrs Dixon, respecting Lucy's character, M.A. and gold key, had kept her on even when Gloria was away at boarding school.

She was careful to inform me of these facts in order that I did not consider her a servant. When Gloria had grown too old to need a governess and travelling companion, Lucy Price had become Mr Dixon's housekeeper. Having lived in formal houses abroad, she knew how to arrange dinner parties when he entertained influential people in both his Washington residence and the house in Topeka. Her intelligence was appreciated, her education valued. She helped with his correspondence and criticised his speeches. Best of all she could be close to her darling Gloria when the girl came home to spend holidays in her father's house.

'Not that she has to obey the custody ruling now that she's of age, but she loves it here, she adores her daddy, and why not, he's a wonderful man. Her hero, her ideal, like God in her eyes. She's always been happy here until . . .' The sentence, accompanied by a sigh, was left unfinished. 'She was different this visit. Secretive, sulky, cold. Came here unexpectedly, only letting us know by a phone call the day before. The Congressman had an important meeting, so I went to the airport to meet her. She was all right at the beginning of the visit, but then she changed in a curious way, asked all kinds of questions about the accusations and allegations against her father. You'd almost think she believed those ridiculous charges. The only person she had any faith in was her cousin. Hugh Dixon junior. Every word he uttered was gospel to her. And who was he to wield such influence? A nobody, her father's law clerk who held that position only because he was related. We were afraid she was taking Hughie too seriously.'

'Because he was her cousin? Was that what you objected to?'

'He was nothing. His father, Mr Dixon's late brother, was a shiftless drunk. Many a time Mr Dixon had to pay their rent, buy them clothes and food, beside keeping Hugh senior in an expensive sanitarium up in Connecticut. What does a girl like Gloria need folks like that for? With her looks, Mr Shannon, her charm, she'd only have to raise her little finger. Since she's been a grown-up young lady her father refused even to take her to Washington with him, too many evil influences there, too much temptation. He liked to have her here when Congress wasn't in session. So she fell under the influence of Mr Nobody.'

'Doesn't he know where she is?'

'Hughie's passed,' Miss Price said. The verb showed her origins.

'Dead?'

'Suddenly. It was a terrible shock to all of us.'

'What did he die of?'

'Cerebral haemorrhage. From a fall or blow according to the autopsy. Nobody saw him fall and it isn't likely he'd been in a fight. Hughie wasn't the type.'

'Wasn't there an inquiry? Didn't the police investigate?'

'They said it must have been an accident. He died at home in his own bed.'

'It must have been terrible for—' I caught myself in time to keep from naming Elizabeth—'Gloria.'

Miss Price hugged herself with crossed arms as if someone were about to attack or caress her bosom. Her lips trembled. 'I should've been here to comfort her. I'd gone away that week. To a class reunion at my college, and then for a few days with my sister. When I got home Gloria was gone. Mr Dixon said she was back in England with her mother.'

'Is that where she told him she was going?'

'Probably. I don't know. Whenever I ask about her he tells me to quit nagging. He can't understand that I was hurt when she went away without leaving a message for me. And no letters since. I've written to her several times but got no answers. That's not like Gloria.' Miss Price touched a handkerchief to her eyes. 'I can understand her being shocked, sick with grief over Hughie's passing, but that she neglected *me*, that's unbelievable.'

On the wall opposite me hung an oil portrait of a dark-haired little girl holding a doll. From a silver frame on a table Elizabeth smiled at me. There could be no doubt, none at all.

Miss Price came to stand beside me. In a muted voice she said, 'I phoned London. The butler said her Ladyship and Sir Harry were cruising on the Duke's yacht. He didn't say which duke. I asked for Miss Dixon but the butler hadn't seen her since Easter Bank Holiday when she suddenly made up her mind she wanted to go to America, and had asked him to book a seat for her. On Easter Monday! So then I called the villa at Cap Ferrat. The housekeeper hadn't seen Mademoiselle since Revillon. That's New Year's Eve.'

'Did you tell this to Mr Dixon?'

'He'd bite my head off. And besides,' she leaned over me, 'I think he knows where she is.'

## 6

The picture in the silver frame. A studio portrait by a stylish photographer who commanded the sitter to look up, to look down, to tilt the head a bit more to the left, to the right, to hold the pose, to relax, to look natural. It was unmistakably Elizabeth looking straight into the camera, huckleberry-blue eyes turned black by strong lights and the limitations of photography. What better proof than the comparison of this portrait with my shots of Elizabeth in the Royce's garden? When Miss Price excused herself to follow Emma to the kitchen to answer some question about dinner, I slipped the picture into the pocket of my jacket. I'd have preferred not to take the silver frame but there was no time to remove the photo. When I'd had it copied I'd send it back with a note saying I hadn't meant to steal it but was so overcome with my longing for Gloria that I'd unconsciously pocketed her photograph.

I hoped to get away quickly with my loot. When Miss Price returned I stood up, holding my arm tight against my side to hide the bulging pocket. I thanked her for her co-operation and said I had to leave. She walked beside me through the long hall to the door. A key clicked in the lock. 'He's here!' Her fingers tightened on my arm which she had seized as if for safety. 'For God's sake don't let on that I talked to you. He'll have apoplexy.' She released my arm and scurried through the door of an inner room.

Although he was not aware of an audience Mr Dixon

made an entrance. Probably a habit acquired through years of celebrity. Something of grandeur was lost when he bellowed, 'I'm here, babe. When's dinner?' He started to pull off his jacket, saw me and hastily jerked it on.

'Who are you? What are you doing here, young man?'

To Miss Price I'd represented myself as Gloria's friend, before letting her believe I was a detective. With Dixon I assumed a role more favourable to his interests. Miss Price could not betray me without sacrificing her own secrets. 'How fortunate to meet you, Mr Dixon. I was just about to give you up. Allow me to present myself. Richard Shannon of the *New York Weekly*.' I thrust out my hand.

A politician cannot afford to take chances. He shook my hand heartily. 'New York, uh? What are you looking for? Scandal in the boondocks?' A half smile, a swift wink told me that resentment was not intended, merely understanding of the prejudices of north-eastern critics.

'Have your own papers treated you so fairly, sir?' The first and most bitter attack had been in his home state.

'For the sake of sensation,' he said bitterly. 'How unscrupulously the press blackens an honest man's reputation.'

I played a trump card. 'That's why my editor, our entire editorial board, want your side of the story. The truth from your own mouth.'

'The horse's mouth, uh?' He clapped me on the shoulder. He laughed heartily. 'What are we standing here for? Let's find a more comfortable place for conversation.'

We returned to the sun-room. I hoped he wouldn't notice the absence of the silver frame. Seated on the couch, I leaned against a pillow to conceal the bulge of stolen property. Miss Price came in. She seemed surprised at finding me there.

'Your dinner's ready, sir,' she said in the tone of a good servant.

Dixon said, 'I'd be honoured if you'd join me in a simple repast.'

Protest was futile. Dixon argued that I could interview him as well at the dinner table as in the sun-room, and that he'd enjoy having an intelligent companion with his meal. Moreover the kitchen was tyrannical. Meals had to be eaten when ready. He ordered a place set and food prepared for a guest. Miss Price hurried ahead and disappeared through a swinging door as Dixon ushered me into the dining room. The table was already set for two. My host poured whisky from one of the decanters on the sideboard. 'You'll have a drink with me, I hope. I don't often indulge but with a guest from New York it's a celebration.' He raised his glass. 'It's not often that I'm lucky enough to encounter a reporter who wants the truth. To the truth!'

So we drank to truth in Bourbon of a ripe old age. Dixon asked me not to include this fact in the article I was to write about him. His greatest popularity was in rural areas and among Fundamentalists who regarded indulgence in alcohol one of the deadliest sins. 'I was brought up that way myself. But I've become a sight more tolerant now that I've made my way in the Great World. Not that I'm not revolted by excess drinking. My late brother, alas, forgot the moral precepts of our good parents and allowed the temptations of John Barleycorn to utterly destroy him.'

Dinner was flavoured by much pious talk. The meal was by no means simple. I wondered how they had prepared the food so quickly for an unexpected guest, especially the potato which, according to my mother, cannot be baked in less than ninety minutes. Probably a servant was deprived.

A napkin with a monogrammed silver ring had been forgotten by my plate. This provided the information. 'Babe' had given up her place at the table as well as her spuds.

While we ate Dixon gave the reporter a generous sampling of his views: the Political Poverty of Our Times when Honorable Men were needed to lead our Glorious Country back to the old-fashioned virtues which had made us the Moral Leader of the World; the prevalence of Immorality in general and in particular among young women who had lost respect for Chastity; the peril of the First Step which lowers the bars of Conscious Conscience and leads inevitably to Promiscuity and Adultery.

I was not put off by the oratory. All my life I'd heard the same sermon from my grandfather who was otherwise a wonderful old man. His older daughters, my aunts Matilda and Addie had—although I'd never dared ask—never in their lives been screwed. I used to blame the Church, but during later years had learned that Protestants could be just as narrow-minded. I used to sleep with a Norwalk girl—Methodist—who got down on her knees and asked forgiveness after every session. And a Jewish babe from the Bronx who bawled me out for having tried to make it with a Good Girl who was keeping herself pure for her husband. There is more chastity in this country than New York intellectuals and Woman's Lib would have us believe.

Dixon's eloquence made it easier to understand his daughter. Having that sort of talk drummed in her ears from early childhood would have developed more inhibitions than Freud could have invented. There was solemn conviction in Dixon's every word, also a kind of charm which had probably won the hearts of all his female constituents in the Bible

Belt. Miss Price had said that his daughter had made him her hero, her idol, her God. She had taken His Word literally.

As a matter of fact his diatribes on Lust and Frivolity were far more ardent than his answers to the questions which I asked in order to give credence to my role as a reporter. Dixon answered with generalities uttered as profound truths. His earnestness gave them momentary significance. He declared his life an open book. All were free to read. His record was exemplary, his morals irreproachable. He confessed that he had made mistakes but never intentionally nor for personal profit.

Miss Price joined us for coffee. She leaned close to Dixon as she poured. 'Did Mr Shannon tell you he knows Gloria?'

Dixon frowned. 'So you know my daughter. Where'd you meet her? Somewhere abroad?'

'At a friend's house.' I neglected the last question. 'She's a very interesting girl.'

'A beautiful child. Don't you agree, Miss Price, that Gloria's a little beauty?'

Miss Price agreed. I hastened to add that Miss Dixon was indeed lovely. 'I'm sorry she's not here. Where is she now?'

'In London with her mother.'

'Lady Harrington-Clark is on the high seas. On a world cruise with the Duke in his yacht. There's no one in the house but staff.' Miss Price glanced at me obliquely. My presence had given her courage to contradict Dixon without fear of rebuke.

He swallowed hot coffee and winced. With feigned indifference he asked, 'How is it that you're so well-informed about my ex-wife's activities?'

'I had a letter from her ladyship.'

'Is that so? Do you correspond regularly with her?'

'You may forget that I stayed in her home many times. She drops me a line occasionally.'

'Of course, of course.' He smote his brow. 'Forgive me for forgetting.' Turning to me he explained, 'They're in London so much of the time that I always think of them as being there.' He smote his forehead again. 'How could I forget? You might have reminded me, Lucy. Then she's surely at the villa.'

The sea-green eyes opened wide. 'She is?' said Miss Price.

Why can't people lie simply? Why do they have to add fancy details to their falsehoods? 'I ought to know. I put her on the plane for Nice,' Gloria's father said.


# 7


Holy Mother, what a story I thought as I looked out of the plane's window on to endless banal clouds. I saw a line of type on the *Weekly*'s cover: *AMNESIA VICTIM CON-GRESSMAN'S DAUGHTER, Complete Story by Richard Shannon, page 6*. And on page 6 in the three line blurb under the title: Girl Without A Name Identified by *Weekly* Reporter, Richard Shannon. In my pocket the picture that identified Elizabeth as Gloria Dixon. I felt great. I had a story with all the elements of a great tale: mystery, suspense, beautiful heroine, suspected crime. Perhaps Hollywood would buy the story, hire me to write the screenplay. At an enormous price. Several recent films had been based on actual events.

A stewardess asked if I'd like something to drink. I ordered champagne. Nothing else was good enough to accompany my fantasy. Robert Redford would play Rick Shannon, intrepid reporter. Who else? In the end he'd get the girl. That she was an heiress added glamour to the romance. In old movies heroines were always heiresses.

The wind changed, the plane plunged downward. For a short eternity we suffered jolts and plunges, settling at last to a smooth passage. My imagination had also taken a downward plunge. I saw obstacles and errors in my investigation. With Miss Price I had been too cautious, with Mr Dixon too chicken to ask a straight question.

I hankered to get back to Westport and Elizabeth. How would she react if I walked in saying, 'Hi there, Gloria Dixon!'? Perhaps my information, the straight stuff about her father and Miss Price would shock her out of amnesia. Would the shock be too great? Another neurosis might result. Better to tell her gradually, gently. 'Elizabeth,' I would say, 'darling, I have great news for you.' Eagerness would shine from those dark blue eyes. 'I know who you are, Gloria Dixon. I've met your father, I've been in your home.' She would implore me to tell her more. One by one, gradually I'd reveal the facts. Should I mention Hughie?

I curbed my impatience and stayed in New York overnight. I had to see Dinsmore. Next morning I was in the *Weekly* office before the editor arrived. He had a couple of appointments that could not be postponed and put me off until half-past eleven. Meanwhile I phoned the Royce house twice and got no answer. I was not disheartened. Elizabeth and Kate were probably out shopping. Or playing tennis at the country club. I'd see her that evening.

At last I was admitted to Dinsmore's office. As I'd imagined he was fascinated by the mystery of the girl without a past. That in itself was a story. He was convinced that I'd discovered her identity when he saw my snapshots beside the portrait in the silver frame; impressed when I told him how

I'd followed a slight clue—at my own expense—and found out that she was a Congressman's daughter. 'I wish you'd told me sooner, Rick. We could have run it in two parts.'

A bright idea popped into my mind. 'You still can. Nobody else has the facts.'

'It's worth thinking about,' he said, and scratched his hairless skull. 'I'll talk to the board about it. We've got a meeting . . .' He looked at his watch, gasped, pulled his jacket off a hanger. 'Come back this afternoon.'

'What time?'

Struggling into his jacket, he called over his shoulder, 'Not before four.'

He kept me waiting until almost five. I was greeted by a barrage of questions. Why had Dixon lied about his daughter being in London or Cap Ferrat? Why did he lose his temper and shout whenever Miss Price questioned him about Gloria? What did Elizabeth want so much to forget that she forgot her name? Was she part of some devious plot, amnesia her excuse for pretending she knew nothing?

These questions were no surprise to me. They had ticked in my mind since I walked out of the Dixon mansion. I'd prepared an answer. 'I'm sure Eliz . . . Gloria can tell me. Since she recognised her father on TV she probably remembers—if not everything—a lot that's happened. And when I tell her I've seen Dixon and Miss Price she'll open up to me. I'm seeing her tonight.'

'You think she'll remember?'

'Without a doubt.'

'And tell all?'

'I'm sure she will. She's in love with me.' I spoke with more assurance than I felt. 'I'll tell her my job, my whole future depends on it.'

Dinsmore looked at me through half-closed eyes. 'You were once a Boy Scout. What's happened to you, Rick?'

'Look, Mr Dinsmore, even without those answers you've got a great story. Part One: the mystery of the beautiful unidentified girl. Part Two: search and discovery. Turns out to be the daughter of divorced VIPs. And after I get those questions answered you've got Part Three: the solution. Jesus, man, there are all the elements, Mystery, Search, Solution. If you don't want to give me an assignment I can take it to Jordan.' Nonchalantly I named his deadliest rival.

I got the assignment and an advance to cover expenses. Promised to deliver parts One and Two by next Tuesday. A tough job but I'd written tougher stories in less time. For Part Three I needed details which Elizabeth could provide. I was sure I could worm the necessary dope out of her if I used the right tactics. Her father's face and voice on TV had certainly opened some channels of memory. Talking about my visit to the old Kansas home and my encounters with Dixon and Miss Price would awaken other memories, while mention of Hughie, the dead lover, could shock her to recognition and revelation.

Though he'd given me the assignment Dinsmore had inferred that I was a heel for taking advantage of a girl's tender feelings. I did not like to think of myself as the sort of louse who'd use a woman to advance his career. To absolve myself I sought guilt in her violent objections to having a story written about her situation. Was she concealing something, some dark secret not yet touched upon? Unless she was guilty of an unrevealed crime my story would not hurt her. It might even help her get over the trauma that had caused amnesia.

I had not forgotten that I had crossed my heart and hoped

to die if I wrote about her, but was sure that I could change her mind by promising to show her the script before I submitted it. Flattery, persuasion and kisses would do the rest. Her heart was tender. A hard-luck story would help. I'd tell her what a lean year this had been, how badly I needed money to help my mother and dying grandmother, how a scoop like this could raise me from the ranks of the unemployed to a good solid magazine job. I had my strategy ready when I rang the Royce's doorbell.

# Chapter Seven

# Confrontation

## by Chauncey Greenleaf

# 1

If my mother were still alive and writing her incomparable novels, she would, according to her formula, invent a murder and, through the brilliant deduction and fearless actions of her famous detective, MacDonald Wolfe, reveal the perpetrator and cause of homicide. Since, as I confessed earlier, I lack her creative gift, I am unhappily committed to fact. I am a slave of chronology. Therefore these recollections, still vivid after a year, are recorded as they came to my attention.

Let us then go back to that Sunday, 27 September, when Elizabeth disappeared from the White Lion Inn at approximately five o'clock. I did not know that she was missing until I returned home a little after ten, having driven from Redding after dinner with a colleague, a brilliant fellow in his subject (Roman history and literature), but utterly without social grace. He had also invited a cousin and her husband, a couple so lacking in wit and intelligence that I was stifled by boredom. And after that depressing experience I drove home in the rain and learned that Elizabeth was missing. During the next three hours Kate and I spoke on the telephone four times. I suggested that she inform Pop. Kate refused. Chief Potts was in touch with Dr Jekyll—'no,

Hyde, I always get them mixed up, Jekyll and Hyde'—and it was from him Kate believed that Elizabeth had fled. 'She must have seen him at the White Lion and dashed off. But where to? Why didn't she come back here? Or to you?'

I slept fitfully that night tormented by nightmares and worse, periods of wakefulness given to feckless anxiety in which I saw Elizabeth's body washed up on the shore by the tides of the Sound; saw her dead on the highway, victim of a hit and run driver; saw her bloody, murdered by a gang of rapists. At dawn, exhausted, I fell into a heavy sleep from which my faithful alarm clock failed to wake me. I barely had time to dress and make the 8.04 but could not leave town until I knew whether Elizabeth had come back. Phoning from a too-public open booth at the station, I heard the roar of the incoming train while Kate informed me that she had, at Allan's command, informed Chief Potts that Elizabeth had disappeared, and Pop had said he would inform the State Police.

Another dreary day passed. Neither Pop's office nor the State Police had any trace of her movements. On Tuesday evening Kate asked me to have supper and spend the evening at their house so that we could worry together. Efforts to talk of other things proved useless. Allan retreated to his study to brood over architectural problems while Kate and I played Scrabble. Another storm started. The beat of rain on the roof affected our humour. Kate accused me of making up words while I told her she ought to go back to school and learn to spell. I yawned through two oppressive games and left with the excuse that I needed a good night's sleep. The storm worsened, rain fell harder, wind howled through the trees. Depressed by the thought of one more lonely night in that unhappy house, I mounted the stairs in the mood of a child certain that a bogy man waited in the dark of the floor above.

I had barely fallen asleep or so it seemed when I was awakened by a series of sounds like the warning thunder of a September hurricane. At first I thought this the extension of a nightmare, then recognised the clamour of the old brass knocker on the front door. With slippers flapping and bathrobe floating from my shoulders, I hastened down the stairs.

On the doorstep, pallid, wet and trembling, stood Elizabeth.

'Good God, child, where have you been?'

'May I come in, please?'

I seized her by the shoulders and pulled her into the hall. She crouched before me like a suppliant. 'I'm sorry if I woke you, Chauncey. I have no idea of the time.'

'Where have you come from at this hour?'

A nod indicated the west side of the house. 'There.'

'Where's there?'

'The shed.'

'The woodshed? Why? Why?'

'You weren't home when I got here and it was raining. I'm hungry. May I have something to eat?'

I suggested that she call Kate and say she was safe. She asked if she could not wait until morning instead of waking them up at an ungodly hour. 'I'll call first thing in the morning. I did want to let her know but I . . .'

'Tell me later. Go take a hot shower. I'll try to find something dry for you to wear.' I went to the kitchen to put water on for tea. Elizabeth followed to tell me she had had no dinner and was starving. Her appetite was startling. She ate before and after her bath. I laid out my silk pyjamas for her and a Paisley robe from Liberty's of London. She looked small and sweet in garments far too large. I drank a cup of tea while she ate. Leaning across the table I wiped buttery crumbs from her mouth and kissed the soft lips. In return they grazed my unshaven cheek.

'Oh, Chauncey, you're such a good man.'

I enjoyed the compliment but would have preferred a more ardent adjective. When she had finished eating I suggested that we go upstairs and try to get some sleep before day made its demands. We were both too exhilarated to retire. We moved into the library where a fire had been laid. Elizabeth settled herself in my mother's favourite chair. At once I started questioning her. 'Now tell me the meaning of all this. Where have you been since Sunday and why did you hide in my woodshed?'

'It was raining cats and dogs when I got here and you weren't home and the house was locked and that was the only dry place. You see?'

'Logical but not revealing. Why didn't you come in when I got home? I got in quite early.'

She had been tired, she said, and it had begun to rain. The woodshed had offered, as well as shelter, a couch and a blanket. With nothing to do in the dark shed she had fallen asleep. Lest this seem incredible to the reader, let me explain that ours was a family that threw nothing away. The detritus of generations was piled in the woodshed; old furniture, old pots, old rugs, towels, worn bedsheets and books, thousands of books yellow and mouldy, forgotten best sellers by forgotten authors; wash-tubs, a mangle, cans of dried paint, trunks filled with garments long out of fashion, tyres and tools from a Ford, a Packard and an Oakland; boxes filled with letters from the dead, files of receipted bills, umbrellas with broken ribs, grandmother's corsets, golf clubs, roller and ice skates, tennis rackets, the rusted wickets and broken mallets of a croquet set, lamps and shades, sleds, bound copies of *Scribner's Magazine* and the *Atlantic Monthly*, tattered flags, lawn furniture, paints and paintings by my Great Aunt Julia, crutches reminiscent of my father's broken leg. And more and more and more. At least twice every year I vowed that I would clear the woodshed. Some objects might even be sold as what so-called antique shops refer to as 'collectibles', the pseudo-art of the past fifty years. Nothing was ever done and the woodshed today contains relics of a family that has occupied the same house for five generations.

On my grandmother's old couch Elizabeth had slept covered by what my mother called 'the buffalo robe' with which ladies who had preceded her had wrapped around their legs while driving in their carriages in cold weather. The leather couch smelled of moulds, the buffalo robe was frayed and punctured with moth holes. None of this had disturbed Elizabeth who had slept as soundly as on a well-advertised inner spring mattress. She had awakened in musty darkness, looked out of the small window to see that my house was dark except for the light burning in the hall. After worrying about disturbing me she had decided to knock at the door. 'I was so hungry, you see, and I knew you wouldn't mind being wakened when you found out it was me.'

'Where have you been all this time? Now don't tell me you were in the woodshed.'

'Don't be silly.' She smiled coyly.

'Where were you?'

'At the Waldorf Astoria.'

'Don't tease. Where were you? Tell me the truth.'

She stared straight into my eyes. 'That's the truth. At the Waldorf in a seven-room suite.'

'I don't believe you.'

Nor was I completely convinced after she had told a weird story of having been at a table in the White Lion Inn while Dr Tisch was telephoning; of having seen that awful Dr Hyde go into the bar; of rushing out to escape his notice; of running along the road when a beautiful silvery-grey car passed and stopped ahead of her; of the tall handsome man who jumped out to block her path and with outstretched arms cry that he had found his 'Claire'.

'You're not Claire?' I said.

'Never heard of her, nor of him either.'

'Are you sure that's not your name?'

'I am not Claire Margaret Ravage Foster.'

'How do you know her string of names?'

'I heard it enough in the last couple of days.'

'At the Waldorf?' My tone was less credulous than indulgent.

'At the Waldorf.' She was grave.

'All right. What did the tall handsome man say when you told him you were not Claire.'

'He thought it was amnesia.'

'Go on with the story. What happened?'

The man had asked if he could give her a lift. She was grateful as she had walked a long way in the rain. He had been very gallant, had taken off his jacket and given it to her. He had asked a lot of questions about things she was sure she had never heard of and the time had passed so quickly that they had long passed the road to the Royce house before she noticed that they were on the road to New York. He had paid no attention to her protests but gone on promising her all sorts of things and saying that he would get the greatest psychoanalyst in the country to cure her of amnesia so that she would recognise herself as his beloved Claire.

At the Waldorf she was given a big beautiful room in the suite. The telephone was taken out so that she could not tell anyone where she was. A guard was kept in the corridor outside her door when Mr Hildebrandt and the lawyer who was with him, Mr Abel, were out on business.

'Hildebrandt,' I interrupted. 'What's his other name?'

'Gordon.'

'Gordon Hildebrandt for heaven's sake. Do you know who he is?'

'A millionaire. He was engaged to Claire and has spent a fortune trying to find her.'

A wave of jealousy rose up in me, envy of the millionaire who could give a fortune to the search for a lost love. I regarded Elizabeth sternly. 'Are you sure you're not Claire?' She shook her head in fierce denial. 'Are you Grace Dearborn?'

Tremors betrayed her effort to keep her voice level. 'You know about Grace Dearborn?'

'Are you Grace Dearborn?'

'No. No!' The little chin was tilted at an angle of defiance, the arms of the chair beaten by angry little fists.

Violent protest aggravated suspicion. I sensed madness in the contradictory tales; Grace Dearborn who had escaped from a madhouse might invent a wild fiction about having been held captive by a millionaire in a suite at the Waldorf. She spoke too hastily, too breathlessly about locked doors, guards and finally of this man, Mr Abel, who had taken her to Grand Central and given her money for a taxi to the Royce's.

'Why didn't you go there? Why did you come here?' I asked, secretly gloating that this had been her choice.

'I was afraid.'

'Afraid of what, Elizabeth?' I used that name as a charm against the evil spirit of scepticism as I did not want her to be transformed into Claire or Grace Dearborn.

'Afraid Kate would think it was her duty to send me back to that place,' she shuddered. 'Allan doesn't go to church, but he's got an awfully Christian conscience about right and duty.'

'What place? Dr Hyde's sanitarium?'

'I'll die before I go back. It's a ghastly place. Do you think I'm crazy?'

She was in a state approaching hysteria. To soothe her I spoke gently. 'I've found you quite sane and very sweet.'

'With amnesia though . . .' She could not go on. Firelight showed all too clearly the countenance of a disturbed soul. Her lips moved but no words sounded. A sigh was bitter. For an instant she remained quiet, her head bowed, then straightening she sprang out of the chair, moved off and turned her back to me before she spoke. 'Amnesia isn't insanity. Or is it? But I didn't have it when I was in Dr Hyde's hell. Oh, no, no sir, my memory was too good, too dangerously good. They wanted me to forget, they gave me shots to make me forget, they used electricity to make me forget. And the lies they told me, oh God!' She whirled around to face me in such rage that I might have been the enemy. The fire cast its red glow upon her. In that hell-fire light, with dark hair flowing over her shoulders, and in the oversized Paisley robe, she had lost all resemblance to my gentle Elizabeth and had become a figure of fury from a Gothic tale of the Eighteenth Century.

'You remember it all now?'

She shuddered.

'Would you like to tell me about it?'

'Not now, Chauncey. Please not now. Let me stay Elizabeth a little while longer.'

'As you wish, Elizabeth.'

'Elizabeth X, the unknown quantity.' In her laughter there was harsh irony but when she turned from the fire, the changeling became again the lovable girl. Of her own volition she came into my arms, tightened her body against mine, raised her face for a kiss and left with footsteps so light that she might have been a phantom.

Long after she was asleep I sat before the fire pondering the folly of my love for a girl who was, if not mad, a sham, an opportunist, a liar? An aberration of the heart, a contradiction to sanity, love is the classical enemy of rational man. Indeed, though she might be sham, opportunist, liar or lunatic, I would happily keep her in my house and my heart.

# 2

Waking the next morning I heard the unlikely sounds of another person in my lonely house. I had slept late as I had no classes in New York that day so had failed to set the alarm. For a few minutes I thought that Mrs Maple had come in for her weekly attack on dust that had accumulated, but then recalled that it was not her day. Gradually achieving clarity I remembered my house guest, sprang out of bed, pulled on jeans and a sweater and raced down the back stairs to find Elizabeth eating cold cereal and drinking milk. When she declared that she was dying for a cup of hot coffee I asked why she had not made a potful. She said she had hunted in vain for a jar of the instant variety, and as she did not know how to make real coffee had waited for me. I could not believe her. There was the coffee, there the filter pot; how could she be so ignorant?

'No one ever taught me. Please, may I have some eggs and bacon?'

We lingered over breakfast. It was pleasant to have a woman opposite me at table. After seven bachelor years I treasured every moment of the domestic scene. Elizabeth told me she had phoned Kate who had 'swooned with joy' at the news of her return. As soon as she had tidied the house, bathed and dressed, Kate would come over. Meanwhile my house needed tidying. Elizabeth had made her bed and offered to do mine. 'Even if I don't know how to make coffee I make a beautiful bed. You'll be surprised when you see my corners. I was taught by a very strict lady who wouldn't let me get by with anything that wasn't perfect.'

'My corners aren't bad either. My teacher also demanded perfection. The Army doesn't let you get away with anything.'

So we made my bed together and I knew I would sleep peacefully between sheets smoothed by Elizabeth's hands. She regretted that she was not accomplished at any other household task, but followed me about, trying to help. Our talk was trivial. We laughed overmuch, nervously, both aware that mirth was a way of postponing a painful discussion.

Presently Kate arrived. There was much hugging and kissing and exchanging of endearments. Now that she had been found unhurt and safe Kate, relieved of anxiety, wept.

Elizabeth was also moved to tears. While I can endure, even derive a kind of pleasure in having a lovable woman weep in my arms, two crying females are two too much. I retreated to the basement for a bottle of champagne to celebrate the reunion.

Elizabeth begged forgiveness for having been the cause of anxiety. She had wanted to let Kate know where she was but the telephone had been taken out of her room in the Waldorf Astoria.

'Waldorf!' exclaimed Kate in much the same amazement I had shown when Elizabeth told me the incredible fact. 'How did you get there?'

With the coy smile she had worn when she answered the same question for me Elizabeth said, 'I was kidnapped in a silver-grey Mercedes . . .'

'By Gordon Hildebrandt!' exclaimed Kate.

'You knew about him?' I snapped at her. In one way I was glad to learn that Elizabeth had not invented the improbable adventure, in another, resentful of Kate's superior knowledge.

'Oh, yes. I spoke to him on the phone several times and he came to the house on Sunday. I wondered why he never came back.'

'Why didn't you tell me?' I demanded. 'You'd have saved me hours of anxiety.'

'How could I know she was with him?' asked Kate, made petulant by my ill humour. 'It never occurred to me, and even if it had, how could I have known where they were?'

'If you two would stop quibbling and listen to me,' said Elizabeth, 'you'd find out a lot of things.' She started at the beginning of the tale, with her shock at having seen Dr

Hyde at the White Lion. Kate with a kind of *Ladies Home Journal* nobility forgave and declared that, after visiting Shady Oaks, she could not blame Elizabeth for having tried to escape the notice of that awful Dr Jekyll.

Elizabeth told her story without order or coherence. Kate swallowed every dubious word. Having become acquainted with Mr Hildebrandt and his lawyer she listened to Elizabeth's incredible story like a woman panting over a romantic film; expressing disappointment each time Elizabeth declared that she was not the millionaire's fiancée. Raised eyebrows and surreptitious glances in my direction showed quite clearly that she believed the anguished denials to be evidence of continuing amnesia.

Kate was put out when she learned that Elizabeth had chosen to stay at my house rather than hers. The explanation that Dr Hyde might again pay the Royces a visit could not satisfy her. She promised that if he should come again she would pretend not to know where the girl was living. 'Do you think it wise for her to stay here with a single man?'

Elizabeth laughed. 'She thinks I ought to have a chaperone.'

'I didn't expect you to be conventional,' I told Kate. 'Do you think I have dishonourable intentions?'

Elizabeth assumed a look of coy discretion and bent her head to study the intricacies of the Persian rug. She soon returned to her obsession begging assurance that we did not consider her insane.

We both hastened to assure her of our belief in her sanity. As I had given my promise to let her 'stay Elizabeth' I asked no questions. It was Kate who demanded an answer. 'Why were you committed to that asylum?'

In the fireplace dry wood crackled. My grandfather's clock ticked aggressively. We waited. Finally Elizabeth, still contemplating the whorls and arabesques of the carpet, pleaded for time. 'I'm still confused, I can't remember everything. Let me get things straight in my mind before I talk about it. Please.'

It was another day, and after a terrifying ordeal that Kate's question was answered.

# 3

At that moment as I recall the telephone had an ominous sound. This, of course, may be an afterthought conceived as a prelude to the writing of a scene ill-fitted to the atmosphere of my quiet library, a scene more appropriate to my mother's tales of intrigue and violence than to the home of a bachelor of academe. The phone call was for Kate from Mrs Maple who informed her that two gentlemen had arrived a few minutes before and asked for the young lady. In her happiness over Elizabeth's return Kate had given the good news to the cleaning woman. And Mrs Maple quite naturally told the visitors that both Mrs Royce and the young lady were at the professor's house just down the road.

'Why did I have to tell her?' groaned Kate. 'They'll be here any minute now.'

'Who?' asked Elizabeth.

'She didn't say. Probably that wretched Dr Jekyll. What should we do, Chauncey?'

We heard the crunch of tyres on the drive, the slamming of a car door and the thud of the knocker. Elizabeth had turned pale. She clutched the arms of the chair with such tension that her knuckles shone white.

'What do you want me to do, Elizabeth?'

The knocker sounded again. Elizabeth slid backward in the chair, pressing her spine against the leather cushion. She raised her head in defiance of the approaching 'enemies'. 'Let them in, Chauncey. I will not go back there whatever happens.'

'Don't go to the door,' pleaded Kate. 'We can't let her go back to that awful place.'

'I said I wouldn't go. Didn't you hear me?' asked Elizabeth haughtily. The knocker sounded again. 'Go to the door, Chauncey.' The change in her was startling. When, where, how had the transformation occurred? She had claimed the return of memory, the discovery of identity; had this turned the shrinking child into a resolute woman? My admiration was diluted by regret: I had lost my heart to the child. Kate, I noticed, resisted as firmly the loss of her surrogate baby.

She tried to bar my way to the door. I pushed her aside and hastened to admit the callers. It was not the bearded doctor who greeted me but the tall, blond, handsome Gordon Hildebrandt. I recognised him, of course, from Elizabeth's description, and immediately acquired an unreasonable prejudice because of his height. It is not that I, standing an inch under six feet, am a small man, but this long drink of water, six foot four at the least, could sneer down at me. At the same time I warmed to Mr Abel, not only because he had rescued Elizabeth, but because I could look down upon him.

'Where is she?' demanded Hildebrandt.

'What are you doing here?' Elizabeth had come out into the hall.

'Claire, my sweet.' Hildebrandt approached her with open arms. She backed away.

'Come in, gentlemen.' I led them into the library. The encounter would not be pleasant, I knew, but I hoped to keep it civilised. Hildebrandt tried again to embrace Elizabeth who again eluded him. Kate, Mr Abel and I remained in the background as audience to a game of attack and defence played by an angry girl and a reproachful man.

'Claire, Claire, why did you run away from me?'

'Why did you have to keep me locked up like in jail?' she asked.

I deplored her grammar.

'Come now, sweetheart, you were never uncomfortable. I spent as much time as I could with you. In the midst of one of the most important deals in my life. I'd have given you anything, anything you wanted if only you'd given me a bit of time.'

'I wanted to be free. Couldn't you see that? Didn't you care that I was unhappy?'

'You certainly didn't act unhappy. Didn't we have nice long talks at night?'

'And those nice long fights when I wouldn't get into bed with you and do those—'

He hastened to silence her. 'But you seemed glad to be with your lover again.'

'Did I fool you!' She knew she had and was bragging. 'It was only to get around you. I hated every minute of it. I hate you, too.'

'Now, darling—'

'I am not your darling. I am not Claire Foster.'

Hildebrandt turned to the audience to announce in a half-whisper that insolence and denial were the product of a disturbed mind. 'As soon as I've got her back in California I'll have her treated by my analyst. Dr Eisenbaum is acknowledged as the greatest.'

Scornfully Elizabeth said, 'I will not talk to your Eisenbaum and I'm not going to California either.' The venomous tone suggested a long history of enmity rather than a three-day war. Hildebrandt, assuming a mourner's face, turned to us again for confirmation of his diagnosis.

'What are we standing up for? Let's sit down,' I said.

The audience found seats while the players continued to stand. 'I wish you'd go away,' Elizabeth said.

'Not unless you come with me.'

Mr Abel cracked his knuckles.

Elizabeth's laughter mocked Hildebrandt's arrogance. There was no joy in it, none of the pretty glee, the child-like delight that had made us love Elizabeth's laughter. Watching her closely I became aware of controlled tremors. 'I am not Claire Margaret Ravage Foster. I do not have amnesia any more. I know who I am and where I come from.'

The declaration caused a variety of reactions. 'Not Claire!' cried Kate, disappointed at the collapse of romance. Mr Abel, pleased by the declaration of a belief he had never dared express, smiled and nodded. I marvelled at her firmness yet the quick alteration of character brought suspicion into my mind. Methought the lady did protest too much. Could it be that she was Claire Foster who had fled into forgetfulness of a mistaken love affair?

'Poor girl,' sighed Hildebrandt, 'without memory how can she ever know the truth?'

'Don't you pity me.' Her voice rising out of a throat whose cords thickened the lovely neck, she shouted: 'If anyone's lost his memory, it's you. You're crazy. You knew from the first night when you couldn't get me to do whatever she had done with you that I wasn't Claire. But then you wanted me so much you had to pretend—'

'Delusion,' declared the man smugly.

His calm aggravated her rage. She whirled around to show us a face contorted by anger but wearing a look of cunning that hinted of depths beyond the display of fury. I was favoured with a wink that sought to claim me a partner in the violence. Swinging around towards Hildebrandt again she called him a bastard, a lecher, a pervert and further a string of epithets such as I hear on New York streets or see written on walls of lavatories. I shall not, I cannot write words which dishonour our beautiful language and shall leave them to the reader's imagination.

Complacence was shocked out of Hildebrandt. He claimed that nothing she said had a word of truth in it and commanded her on the threat of death never to make such allegations again whereupon she retorted that unless he quit pestering her she'd tell the world everything she had learned about him at the Waldorf.

'Be quiet now. We've had enough of your nonsense.' He seized her by the shoulders. 'You're coming with me.'

In a voice surprisingly mild she begged to be let go. He tightened his grip. I ordered him to take his hands off her. He looked down at me with a supercilious smile. Elizabeth tried to wriggle free while he started to drag her towards the door. 'Come along now,' he ordered in the voice of a dictator.

Mr Abel sprang up. 'No, don't.'

I thought this was a warning to Hildebrandt, but saw with astonishment that the smaller man was trying to pull Elizabeth out of the other's clutches. Hildebrandt snapped, 'Hey, Abe, what are you doing? Help me get her to the car.'

I aimed a blow at Hildebrandt's jaw. He ducked his head so that my futile fist struck nothing more substantial than air. I seized one of his arms, Abel took the other. Kate ran towards the phone, saying the police should be summoned. I begged her not to cause a public scandal. The air in the room had a strange smell, sulphurous: brimstone, no doubt. And while no word was spoken the room was alive with sounds; in addition to the solemn ticking of the old clock there were gasps, snorts, pops and squeaks as though offended wood remonstrated against the unwelcome commotion in its quiet home.

A change as swift and electric as the coming of light when a switch is turned had come over Elizabeth. Her struggles ceased and her face, no longer disfigured by anger, came alive with its familiar charm and innocence. In a voice as bland as cream she said, 'Gordon, are you going to kidnap me again?'

Hildebrandt relaxed his hold of Elizabeth although he kept his hands with less tension on her shoulders. He spoke smoothly. 'I'm going to take you home, my dear, and get you cured of this wretched illness.'

'I am cured. I told you, Gordon, I know who I am.'

He sighed and shook his head, asking the audience for sympathy.

In the softest voice and with the sweetest smile Elizabeth said, 'He wants to believe I'm Claire with amnesia. He wants it so much that he's got to pretend to himself that I am. Like crazy people in asylums believe things that aren't true.'

Hildebrandt's face darkened to a reddish purple. His

hands slid off Elizabeth's shoulders. 'Are you saying I'm crazy? What do you say to that, Abe?'

As pious as a preacher, Abel said, 'He's one of the sanest men I've ever known.'

'Tell them about the deal I've just put across, Abe. Let them decide for themselves if a man not in his right mind could have pulled that off.'

Abel scratched at thinning hair combed over a bald spot, cleared his throat and began what would, no doubt, have been a speech of excruciating boredom had not Elizabeth declared, 'I didn't mean it that way, Gordon. I mean—' she hesitated while she combed the snarls out of her tangled mind—'what I meant is . . . is . . . lots of people not in asylums think something's real that isn't or that something that's not real is.'

'If you aren't Claire, who are you?' demanded Hildebrandt. 'Do you know?'

'I am Grace Dearborn, I'm an incurable schizophrenic escaped from the loony bin.' Hildebrandt shook his head to show disbelief. Elizabeth cried angrily, 'Ask Dr Hyde at Shady Oaks in Newbury. He'll tell you it's true.'

We were shocked by the declaration, stripped of illusions. 'No, no,' cried Kate, unaware that she spoke aloud. Abel, having known the girl for only a few days and been charmed, sighed mournfully. For the moment Hildebrandt gave no sign of having heard the news. As for myself, suffering the delusion of love, the immediate response was disbelief. Like all those poor souls locked up in institutions like Dr Hyde's and worse, I rejected reality. To my mind it was not possible that Elizabeth could be deranged. Although I knew that the schizoid patient could be, to use a word precisely defined, normal for periods between maniacal attacks and that I had, within that hour, heard her shriek like a guttersnipe using words I would not have believed she knew, I discarded logic to console myself with the conviction that what she had said was not true.

With great formality Hildebrandt bowed as he asked us to forgive him for the annoyance he had caused, kissed Elizabeth's hand and Kate's. 'You found the cheque?' he asked.

'Oh, yes, but you paid far too much for it.'

'So long as you are satisfied it does not matter.'

None of us knew what this exchange meant; later Kate told me that Allan was delighted as he had always disliked her Peruvian god. Mr Hildebrandt then departed with Mr Abel who had received a farewell kiss from Elizabeth.

While the wheels of their car could still be heard on the gravel of the drive, while Kate muttered something about Grace Dearborn having been the name of the girl who had escaped from Dr Jekyll's place, while I indulged in the denial of reality, Elizabeth danced around the room like a creature possessed.

'I was great, wasn't I? The mad girl of Westport. Maybe I ought to be an actress.'

Kate and I sat as still as stone figures on a tomb. Was Elizabeth's wild glee a manifestation of schizophrenia? Would she descend from euphoric ecstasy to manic fury? The dance ended as suddenly as it had started. Kate and I exchanged covert glances. Elizabeth kissed Kate, then came to stand before me with bent head and hands clasped as in prayer.

'You're angry with me, aren't you?'

'What makes you think I'm angry?'

'You're too quiet. It's not like you to sit like a mummy. You don't love me any more, do you?'

'Why do you say that?' The tone was harsh, more like a schoolmaster than a lover.

'The way I acted, yelling and screaming and all those dirty words. But I had to, don't you see?'

'See what?' I thought Kate's tone unnecessarily sour.

'Suppose he'd found Claire and she was a raving psycho, what do you think he'd have done?' She ran her tongue over smiling lips. 'A kiss on the hand and goodbye, sweetheart? You wouldn't do that to someone you loved, would you, Chauncey?'

I wished to show her that I was not to be teased out of disapproval and asked sternly where she had learned the execrable epithets she had flung at Hildebrandt.

'Why are you shocked? You must know that those words are in all the popular novels, and don't forget either that I had a liberal education in the lunatic asylum. How do you suppose I learned the schizo act? Some of my best friends are psychotic.'

'Elizabeth,' Kate began, 'or should I call you Grace?'

'Call me Elizabeth. I am not Grace Dearborn.'

Not Grace Dearborn! Kate and I exchanged bewildered glances. Not Grace Dearborn! We could not blame her for getting rid of Hildebrandt with a lie, but hadn't she just told us, to whom she owed the truth, that she had been confined in an asylum? And hadn't a patient named Grace Dearborn escaped from Dr Hyde's refuge for disturbed adults? Our beloved Elizabeth was either a madwoman or a cunning liar.

# 4

As we lingered over our coffee that night, Elizabeth used every female trick to charm me out of my uncertain humour while I exercised strict control to resist the pretty wiles. If our eyes happened to meet there shone on me a smile of such radiance that I could not continue to show indifference. The fire shed a rosy glow upon her. In its light she was, more than a merely attractive girl, 'a vision of delight', an angel draped in Paisley silk, a Rossetti saint with a long pre-Raphaelite neck and dark hair framing the delicate oval of her face. Her movements were pleasing to the eye. She poured coffee with grace, handed me the cup with the elegance of an actress in a drawing-room comedy.

Please forgive the hyperbole. I was a man in love.

Our dinner had been perfect. This boast must also be forgiven. Since my wife had left me, I had made a serious study of cookery books and acquired some skill in the arts of the kitchen. Not a stylish chef, I could prepare a simple meal for myself and not more than three guests. Elizabeth marvelled at a man's, a professor's, ability to fold in the beaten whites. Her admiration provided satisfaction as well as stimulation. I was more of an exhibitionist with my salad than with my conversation. Over a table laid with my mother's porcelain and my great-grandmother's silver we chatted like a man and woman on their first date: discovered common tastes and, what makes for even closer understanding, common dislikes. Both spoke enthusiastically of our antipathies and grudges, laughed together over the folly of our prejudices. I saw Elizabeth as she must have been and could again be when she was free of the horrors that had sent her to Dr Hyde's sanitarium.

Inevitably we came to this unwelcome subject. She approached indirectly. 'Chauncey, you once said you'd marry me. Do you remember?'

'At any moment you choose, dear.'

'Would you still . . .'

In the silence that followed the mood changed. A moment before her unfinished question we had been cosy in the library with the flames throwing their rosy glow on the silver coffee pot—on Elizabeth's cheeks and eyes. Now the fire died down, the glow faded, shadows fell upon the room and the girl. Her mouth was drawn in, her flesh hardened over jutting bones, the radiance gone from eyes that stared at some phantom of the haunted past. 'How would you feel about me, Chauncey, if someone told you I was a murderer?'

'I wouldn't believe it.'

'Suppose a man, a well-known and respected person, should come here and tell you that I killed a man?'

The scene had changed from drawing-room comedy to melodrama. I walked to the window to close the curtains, not so much to shut us in as to give me time and solitude to consider the dreadful possibility. With my back to her, I asked, 'Did you?'

'I don't know.'

'You don't know! Is that possible?' I whirled around to show her the face of incredulity.

In a voice too bland for the subject it embraced, she said, 'They say I did. And after all that's happened, I'm not sure of anything.'

'Who are "they"?'

'Daddy. And Mr Dearborn. And that doctor, he was the worst. Over and over again.' Bent over, she rocked back and forth like a distraught crone. 'He says if it ever comes out, he can say I'm crazy.'

'If what ever comes out?'

'How he died.' She breathed heavily, her hands protecting her heartbeat.

'Who died?'

'Hughie.'

At this inopportune moment someone knocked at the front door. Allan had brought a paper shopping bag with Elizabeth's clothes. 'There's not much but Kate thought she'd need them.'

Allan's presence and the contents of the shopping bag changed Elizabeth's mood. Took, Chauncey, my entire wardrobe. Mother should see this. She's always buying me stuff in Paris—Balmain, St Laurent, Courreges—that's her idea of maternal love.' Her laughter was high, sharp, unlike the artless glee of the childlike girl who had no previous life to remember and had looked upon every thought and sensation as new and dazzling. With the return of memory, innocence had departed.

When Allan had gone, I asked her to go on about this Hughie, the cause of whose death had not 'come out'. For a moment she was quite still, reproaching my curiosity with silence; then she sprang from the couch to pace the floor with ill-contained energy. With her back to me, at last, she said, 'I don't care to talk about it now.'

'You can't do that to me, Elizabeth. I was shocked by what you began to tell me. It's unfair of you to stop. So go on, tell me. How did Hughie die?'

She whirled about and came towards me with a straight

back and firm footsteps. 'You wouldn't believe me. It's too weird.'

'If you promise me it's true, I'll believe you.'

'Swear it.'

I gave my pledge, and having my assurance that I would accept her every word as truth, she murmured, 'My father . . . Daddy . . .' and failed at the next word, her lips working without sound as though she were telling herself a sacred secret. I tried as gently as I could to assure her of my sympathy.

'No, no, I can't, don't ask me.' She burst into a sudden unaccountable tantrum. A small brass Buddha, souvenir of my mother's first world tour, was snatched up and hurled at the far wall. This was a new Elizabeth. I had seen her beat a table or the arms of a chair in futile wrath, but had never witnessed a display of violence. 'You've got no right to ask me,' she cried, flung herself out of the room, and stamped up the stairs. In the guest-room above the library, the old boards groaned under the pounding of passionate feet.

I waited for her temper to cool before I knocked on her door to bring her a cup of hot chocolate. 'To help you sleep,' I said.

'Thank you, dear Chauncey, thank you and please forgive me for that awful scene I put on.'

'You needn't say anything until you feel like it. And I promise to believe you.'

She snuggled against me, warm and soft as a kitten. 'You're such a dear man, you make me ashamed of my awful temper.'

Waking early the next morning, my first thought was of the girl asleep in the guest-room. I hoped my alarm clock had not awakened her. There was no sound from behind her door as I passed on tiptoe. Less than five minutes later, while

I poured boiling water into the coffee pot, I looked up and saw her at the kitchen door. She ran across the kitchen to lean over the steaming pot and planted a light kiss on my chin. 'Have you forgiven me?'

'Be careful when you kiss a man with a steaming pot in his hand. Did you sleep well?'

'Look.' From behind her back she drew a sheaf of paper. 'Look what I've done.'

Sunshine slanting through the east window gilded the checked tablecloth and enriched the cream in the china jug. Elizabeth had combed her hair and touched up her lips before she came downstairs to wave her papers in my face. She seemed as fresh as morning air, as wholesome as the wheat bread in the toaster, as tempting as the aroma of good coffee, as I stood there like a love-struck dolt. The smell of burning crusts distracted me and I hurried to rescue the toast.

'Aren't you going to ask me what this is? I've been up and writing since three o'clock.'

'You didn't sleep?'

'Sleep's ghastly. Like being alone in a strange country where you don't know the language. This,' she brandished the scribbled pages in my face, 'is better therapy than sleep. Dr Tisch said so, she said I should write down everything in my mind. Everything I think of. This is what I couldn't tell you last night. May I use your typewriter?'

As I had an early class in New York, it was necessary that I catch the 8.04. Elizabeth was not disappointed. She had not expected me to read her story at once, but merely to admire her zeal and industry. When I returned in late afternoon, she would not come downstairs until she had finished the job. Not until we had finished dinner and cleared up in the kitchen was I given the script. While I read she pretended to be engrossed in *The Egyptian Tomb Mystery*, but I did not have to lift my eyes from her script to know that she was watching me through her lashes. There was good reason for her tremors.

# Chapter Eight

## Confession

### by Elizabeth

So that the reader may share the drama and suspense of Elizabeth's tale, I am presenting it as it was unfolded to me, in two parts, rather than as consecutive narrative.

C. J. G.

## 1

What is amnesia . . . what was it like? What do I remember of that strange time? People probably think of it as blankness, the inside of a vacuum. To me it is like a dark theatre before the curtain goes up on the last act. You know something has happened and you try desperately to find out what it was. At last the curtain rises. The stage is seen . . . dimly, gradually . . . by the glow of an offstage lamp . . . a light behind a screen . . . closed curtains in a dark room. Then the actor enters. Muffled in heavy robes. Slowly the screen slides away . . . the lamp shows a room . . . curtains open. The sudden brilliance confuses you. You are the actor but you have forgotten your lines. Where am I? Who am I? You babble words, anything that pops into your head. You are not you but someone that other people want you to be.

When I was at the Waldorf with Gordon my memory was coming back . . . not whole but in shreds and tatters. I heard familiar voices, caught glimpses of faces, remembered bits of incidents. But this, this grasping after memory was upset when Gordon kept calling me Claire. For moments I wondered . . . was I Claire? He would talk about tennis, tell me I was the only woman who had beaten him . . . my memory brought back a tennis court and just beyond it my magnolia tree. Gordon was never in that picture . . . it was another man. Hughie. And what about the ring Gordon kept talking about? Gordon said my fingers stroked the wrong hand. I had worn his ring on my left hand, an engagement ring. The place that felt empty was on my right hand. I remember a ring, a star sapphire in a velvet case that Daddy gave me on my twentieth birthday. I could not remember the large emerald cut diamond Gordon kept talking about. Gordon gets up-tight if anything he ever owned is lost. Everything of his is precious, everything his money buys is extra valuable. Whenever he has the slightest desire for anything he must have it at that moment and he will never let it get away from him.

This was very confusing to my muddled memory. On Saturday night when I saw his face and heard HIS voice on TV . . . things started coming back. Then on Sunday Gordon came and told me I was Claire. I thought maybe I was and the other was just something I imagined. That was when I became afraid I was crazy. I found myself talking French fluently. Gordon had made a phone call while I was allowed in the living room. He was speaking French to the Swiss banker. When he hung up I spoke to him in French. And I did not even know I knew French. Could Claire speak French? Gordon was surprised. So was I but I saw Mother and the hotel was not the Waldorf. It was the Plaza Athenée in Paris. Pricey was there. Pricey! Another association, a terrible one. I shrank from memories. Gloria Dixon! She came back that night I saw HIS face on TV. Too many associations . . . I could not answer the questions Rick asked. Saying things would make them real.

Flashes of memory came faster and faster. The lights on the stage were too bright. The audience was watching me. Amnesia was the name of the drama. I know my lines now. Horrid, scary lines. I will have to say them loud and clear.

Tonight when I was so horrible to Chauncey it was because I couldn't go back to the beginning and tell the audience what happened in Act One. I am not in that first act. It is about my parents and takes place before I was born. Or even conceived.

My father was a twenty-six-year-old virgin. My mother was a nineteen-year-old heiress. They were *desperately* in love. A poor young lawyer but so handsome that the heiress swooned at the sight of him and would have done anything he wanted, but all he asked for was a chaste goodnight kiss. He had come from a small town in central Kansas where his father was a minister. She had three début parties: one in Topeka, one in Kansas City, and one in Chicago.

Their wedding night was a horror. He had kept himself pure for his bride. She had not. The blow to his pride and the shock to his principles turned love to rancour. They lived together respectably for five years. In separate bedrooms. When he came to her bed he was so ashamed of his carnal desire that it was like raping a stranger. He cursed the 'sinful woman' and called her names out of the Bible.

So Mother took a lover and flaunted him in Daddy's face. He could have sued her on grounds of adultery, but avoided a scandal by letting her divorce him. I was four years old.

That is Act One. I heard about it from my mother who is never ashamed to talk about anything. She had four husbands after Daddy, lovers too. Whenever I would leave her to stay with him she would tell me to be sure to let Daddy know about her wicked life. She is not a mean woman but can never forgive him.

When you are four years old it is a terrible shock to be taken from your home and father. I don't remember much about that time except what Mother and Pricey have told me . . . that I cried every night because Daddy did not come to hear me say 'Now I lay me', and hug and kiss me. Mother had me for nine months of the year—why nine months, the period of gestation—Daddy for three.

Mother tried to explain it to me, but how could a little girl of four understand that a court decree had dictated the shape of her life?

Mother took me to live with her in England and the Continent. Hattie, my big soft black nurse, did not want to leave her family and live abroad. For the first few weeks Mother took care of me herself. In Paris she hired Mademoiselle who was to teach me to speak perfect French among other things. I have been told how pitifully I wept and how I refused to speak her funny language. Since then I have had screaming tantrums, stamping and breaking things. Once I threw a fine Sèvres piece through a window shattering the pane and decapitating the shepherdess. After that Mother hired a refined English nanny. She was told never to hit me, but she spanked me secretly so that I was afraid of punishment and learned to control my temper except in extremity.

After the first nine months the nanny brought me back to Daddy. He has often told me that I was so happy to be home that I kissed chairs and tables. He hated the stiff Englishwoman as much as I did and she returned the compliment by leaving without notice. Hattie had gone to live with her son in Harlem and that was when Miss Price was hired as my governess. She was strict about lessons and manners and morals but she never hit me.

Pricey is a white black woman—very beautiful, with eyes the pale green of peridots. Members of her family would come to visit her in our house. This is how I learned that she was not a white woman. I loved her dearly and still do in spite of what I discovered about her secret life. When I was little I would cough and moan pretending I had TB. I wanted Pricey to love me as much as she loved her little sister who had consumption.

When Daddy's three months were up, Pricey took me back to my mother who was living with her second husband in his house in Sussex. Mother was glad to have a dependable woman to take care of me and kept Pricey on. When I was old enough to go to boarding school, Pricey stayed to help Mother run her various houses and do the mending. When we stayed with Mother in Paris or the house in Cap Ferrat, Pricey and I studied French together, and I learned to love the language I had hated so much at first.

Mother still has the house in Cap Ferrat and the one in Wilton Crescent in London. She keeps her houses longer than her husbands. I am devoted to my mother although I was taught to despise her.

*

Before I knew the meaning of the word I was told that my mother was a whore. The Whore of Babylon, Daddy said, and read to me out of *Revelation*, Chapter 17, I knew it was a naughty word so that I did not dare mention it and was even ashamed to ask Pricey. I think it was the first word I ever looked up in the dictionary. '*A woman who practises sexual intercourse for hire*,' it said. I had to look up 'sexual' and 'intercourse' too. The dictionary definitions did not explain it satisfactorily. Mother never had to do anything 'for hire'. She was richer than any of her husbands except the Greek with the English name.

I looked up other words of Daddy's too: harlot, prostitute, vicious, impure, carnal, depraved, corrupt. The older I got the more confused I became. In my mother's houses casual sex relationships were commonplace, expected, often a topic for gossip. Dying for knowledge I would hide behind doors or drapes to hear what grown people were saying. Mother was frank but never indiscreet. She spoke carelessly about affairs and lovers, but never let me see or hear anything crude. Falling *desperately* in love was the excuse for her affairs and marriages.

Carnal lust was what Daddy called them. He never stopped telling me not to become a whore like my mother. The worst thing a girl could do, the very worst, was to lie with a man who was not her legal husband. Letting a boy kiss or touch me would be a fatal step on the road to prostitution. With the blood of a harlot in my veins I must practise the utmost self-control in avoiding all temptation.

Can you believe that these warnings influenced a modern girl? Everything I read in the sex books girls sneaked into the dormitory taught just the opposite. And modern novels are overflowing with sex. In boarding school I knew girls from good families who had had intercourse at fifteen. But I could not lose my inhibitions. In college I was so ashamed of being a virgin that I would slip out of the room when girls talked about sex.

When a girl gets older and goes out with boys it gets harder to practise self-control. In Topeka with Daddy I was never allowed to meet boys because he thought this whole generation lacked moral principles, and the only male of my age that I knew was my cousin Hugh. He was four years older and had always come to play with me when I was a little girl.

It was different in Mother's houses. On school holidays the nephews and cousins and sons of her English friends were introduced to me at teas and tennis and cricket matches. On neighbouring estates in the South of France there would be sons and nephews too and American relations hitch-hiking or seeing Europe in old dilapidated cars. There was not much difference between them. Long hair, blue jeans and dirty fingernails were the style on all continents. All of them tried to tempt me to the first fatal step on the road to prostitution.

I had to grit my teeth and stand still while I learned to let a boy kiss and touch me. I tried not to think of Daddy and what he would say if he knew. But Daddy was always there. I could never escape the sound of his voice in my head or the hurt look in his eyes. Sometimes I would pull away and run off and hide. Then I would stay awake all night and worry about being frigid. I longed to be an attractive passionate woman but I was afraid to give in to carnal lust and become a whore.

Most of all I wanted to love and be loved.

*

But I cannot say I was an unloved child. Whichever parent I was with tried to make me love him . . . or her . . . more than the other. Mother petted me and dressed me in the most exquisite clothes and had me brought downstairs to be exhibited. Pricey was always angry with the guests for stuffing me with sweets and giving me canapés when I was shown off at cocktail time. She said that such unwholesome foods would ruin a child's stomach. At a very early age I learned to appreciate caviar and pâté. When I was old enough to join the dinner guests I was displayed like a fine piece of porcelain or a rare antique.

I was an antique . . . sexually.

Ashamed and afraid.

Daddy showed his love by keeping me for himself. My three months with him could not be shared. Summers in Kansas are unbearable, but I had to go there during school holidays as he preferred me with him when Congress was not in session. He took me to Washington only once. He said he did not want me subjected to influences of that corrupt city.

He treated me like a grown-up lady. When I'd come to America, Daddy would meet me in New York. We'd have a beautiful time together, going to the theatre, eating at the most popular and elegant restaurants, and after I was sixteen to night clubs. He is a better dancer than any of the English, French or American boys I've known.

He was very handsome and I was very proud.

Sometimes he was kept in Washington on important national business. Then Pricey would come to meet my plane, and when I left she would fly back to New York with me. When I no longer needed a governess she became Daddy's

VERA CASPARY

housekeeper. Last winter when I came to spend Christmas with my father in New York, Pricey was with him. She did not look like a governess or housekeeper but like a woman of fashion in chic, expensive clothes. Her mink coat was magnificent.

This is not as irrelevant as it sounds. Later you will know why.

I had not intended to come to America this summer. Eighteen months ago I became of legal age and was no longer bound by court decree to live nine months with Mother, three with Daddy. I could live where I chose and do what I wanted. I was free! The Waterfoot inheritance will not be mine until I am twenty-five, but there is a sort of freedom in not having that money to make decisions about and I do have a nice little income from a trust fund left me by my grandmother. I had finished my four years of college and had my B.A. Which was still another kind of freedom. I had to decide what I wanted to do next. I was dizzy with freedom. I thought of going to graduate school but could not decide which college, or in what country, or what I most wanted to study. Etymology or art history? I also dreamed of going to the Cordon Bleu and opening a charming little restaurant somewhere. While I thought about these things I had to choose between accepting an invitation to spend a month or two at the estate of a friend's grandmother in Scotland, or going with Mother and Harry—Lord Harrington-Clark—on a cruise somewhere in someone's yacht.

The decision was made for me by something I heard on the radio. I was always hoping to hear about Daddy on American broadcasts. One night a news item shocked me so that I shouted at the radio . . . kicked and screamed . . . lapsed into a temper tantrum like the naughty little girl I used to be. 'It's not true, it's a filthy lie,' I shouted in the empty room and picked up the radio and threw it to the floor. Then I grew angry with myself for having broken it. The little transistor had come in a green antelope case with my monogram in raised gold letters. Harry had given it to me as a bridesmaid gift after I stood up for Mother when she insisted on marrying him in a registry office.

With the radio broken I could not hear any more of the accusations against my father. He was said to have got special privileges for corporations that had paid him large amounts of money *secretly*. Bribery. My father! And now the income tax department was reviewing his returns . . . suspecting him of cheating the Government. I refused to believe a word of that report. I would have to hear it from him in his own voice before I would believe it to be anything but a rumour spread by his enemies . . . people supporting a rival candidate for senator. I know something about the evils of politics. I had listened to talk among visitors in Daddy's house.

That very night I was on a plane, the next day in Kansas. I had telephoned to warn them of my coming. Pricey met me at the airport. It was a great surprise to have me there, she said. Daddy would be grateful for my support, she said. I asked how he was taking these wicked rumours, and she said it saddened him that people should think evil of him. But his spirit had not been conquered.

'Your Daddy is a brave man,' she said. 'He is going to every town and village, to every crossroads in this State, to clear his name. In a hired plane. In the end truth will out and his enemies be vanquished.'

I laughed. The words and tone and even the rhythm of her speech were exactly like Daddy's.

The rented plane was piloted by a man both Pricey and I loathed—Charlie Dearborn. He had been a pilot in the Second World War and would have liked to stay in the Army but had grown too fat. He was part of Daddy's office staff in Washington, but often came home to do all the inconvenient little jobs for the Congressman.

Daddy was not there when I arrived home. At two in the morning he and Mr Dearborn arrived. Without notice and within twenty minutes Pricey had supper on the table. Daddy seemed older and more nervous than I had ever seen him. He was glad I had come home. 'My angel, my consolation, a ray of sunshine in a dark hour,' he said. With his usual eloquence he assured me that the evil rumours were entirely without foundation . . . 'manufactured by my enemies'.

'No sane person could doubt your father's probity,' said Dearborn. He seemed proud of that word, 'probity'.

I certainly had no doubts of Congressman Dixon's probity.

The next morning . . . it was Sunday . . . we went to church, Dearborn driving us in a new Lincoln, Mark IV. Members of the congregation offered kind words that showed complete faith in Daddy's probity. I was happy that morning. I believed my father to be the most honourable man in the world, incapable of sin, the very heart and soul of goodness. I was glad I went to church with him and felt clean and pure and happy because I had never let a man get familiar.

*

Tears crowd into my eyes when I think of Hughie. He was my cousin. As children we loved each other. Whenever I came to stay with Daddy, Hughie . . . he was four years older . . . would come to play with me. I thought him a romantic boy because he was poor and lived with his mother in a squalid flat on a seedy street. His father, my father's brother, drank. An unregenerate drunk, Daddy said. He had undergone the cure twice in an expensive institution in Connecticut with Daddy paying the bills, but had never had the willpower to stay 'on the wagon'. Daddy had also paid for Hughie's education and given him a job as an aide in his Washington office.

Pricey told me that Hughie had been fired. He was disloyal, she said. Daddy called him ungrateful. Hughie had not been told that I was in town, not invited to have Sunday dinner with us. I was afraid to mention Hughie's name lest Daddy forbid me to see him. Would I have obeyed? This story would be very different if I had.

Daddy always took a nap on Sunday afternoons. He never worked on the Sabbath, not even when he was standing for office. While he slept I came to the decision that I was a free woman, going on twenty-three, and did not need permission to make a phone call. Since Hughie had lost his job in Washington, I phoned his mother to ask where to find him. He answered the phone. His voice became happy when he learned that I was in the city.

'Are you free? Can I pick you up and take you for a drive in my old bus?' he asked.

'Why don't we stay here and swim in the pool?'

'I don't think Uncle Claude would care to see me,' he said.

Daddy was still asleep when Hughie drove up in his yellow Volkswagen. I felt like Juliet stealing out to meet Romeo as I dashed downstairs and out of the house. At first Hughie and I babbled with joy at being together, but before long I asked questions I had not dared to ask Daddy or Pricey. Why had Hughie been fired? Why had Daddy called him ungrateful and disloyal? Had it anything to do with the frightful things I had heard on the radio? Hughie said I might not want to hear the truth. I remember saying, 'I want the whole truth and nothing but the truth.'

The truth smelled of Kansas heat and gasoline fumes on a crowded road. Long lines of traffic crept along like cripples on parade. Hughie suggested that we find a place where he could talk quietly without having to concentrate on the car ahead. In our favourite ice-cream parlour where he used to take me for hot fudge sundaes and banana splits, a big old-fashioned fan whirred above our heads. When I think about what he told me in the ice-cream parlour I hear whirring like the wings of hawks and vultures. I was eating a chocolate mint soda when my idol began his fall from the height of righteousness to the depth of iniquity.

At first I could not believe Hughie was telling the truth. I said he was a fool, a stupid gullible fool to believe unfounded rumours. I asked how, when Daddy had been so good to him, so generous to his mother, he could side with the unscrupulous liars who were spreading malicious lies so that their candidate could win the election. 'I don't like you any more, I hate you,' I said. 'Take me home.'

I could not finish my soda. The ice-cream tasted sour.

Hugh put his hand on mine. 'I don't like telling you this, Gloria, but you asked for the truth.'

'It's not the truth, it's a pack of dirty filthy lies,' I said. 'I'm shocked at you believing them. And I never want to see you again.'

'Listen to me, Gloria. Or are you afraid to know?'

I listened but could not believe that the accusations were true ... that Daddy had used his influence with Congressional Committees to obtain favourable rulings for corporations that paid him big bribes. This was not the first time. Hughie had a key to locked files. He had not been given the job out of generosity. Daddy had taken his nephew into his office thinking a member of his own family, who should have been grateful to him, would never betray him. Earlier in the year Hughie had been asked to work out the conditions of an illegal transaction. When he questioned the ethics of the deal Daddy had been enraged. When the facts were exposed, Hughie had been accused of 'leaking' information.

'Did you?' I asked.

'Gloria, how can you say that? You know me too well to think I'd do such a sneaky thing.'

'You cannot make me believe my father's a crook and a liar.'

'He needs money badly for this campaign. Contributions aren't coming in the way they used to. You know what that plane costs him? He's crazy to get into the Senate. This is your Daddy's last chance.'

'I don't believe anything you say. I refuse to believe you.' I sobbed so noisily that we had to leave the ice-cream parlour.

Hughie said he had proof: memos and the numbers of Swiss bank accounts which no one else knew about. He had been entrusted with these numbers so that if anything happened to Daddy, the bankers could not keep the money, as they did when people died suddenly without having given their heirs or their lawyers the numbers.

'If he's ever questioned about it, he'll say it's interest on the hundred thousand he got in the divorce settlement. But why in a Swiss bank? Doesn't he trust America?' Hughie said.

'He got money in the divorce settlement! From my mother?' I said with amazement.

'Has he ever been divorced from anyone else?'

'Why do you ask such silly questions? You know he hasn't,' I snapped. 'I don't believe my father got money for letting Mother divorce him. He was a perfect gentleman and let her sue him when she was the one who'd sinned.'

'Where do you think he got the Waterfoot mansion? They didn't want it. The old couple were living in Florida and your mother said she was never coming back here. No one ever told you?'

'I don't think you know a thing about it, Hughie, and I will simply not believe anything you say. I'd like to go home.' I tried to show dignity, but my nose was running and I had to borrow his handkerchief.

The heat was terrible. I sweated as much as I cried. It was hell fire all the way home. Jolting along in the Volkswagen Hughie said he loved me and felt it his duty to tell me the truth before I learned it from other sources. I was haughty and pretended not to listen. At the front door he asked when he would see me again.

'Never,' I said. At that moment I meant it. I tried to hate him, to think of him as an enemy, to believe he had started the rumours. Suppose he had been fired for inefficiency, for laziness, talking indiscreetly, seeing the wrong people and in revenge 'leaked' false information. Before the thought was finished I saw how silly it was. Hughie could be angry but he was never malicious. Why should he have told me the accusations were true if they were not?

I saw him the next day and the next and the next. Unwilling to believe what he told me, I begged for more—facts, dates, documents, proof. When he failed to answer a question I was furious, worse when his facts convinced me. All at the same time I believed and disbelieved . . . wavered, swung from doubt to trust like a monkey on a trapeze . . . from hate to love. Between arguments we kissed and snuggled. I was whirling on a carousel, the world whirling with me.

But that was not the worst.

We left the cinema before the robbers got away with the stolen money. The film was atrocious. Hughie had been yawning all evening. 'What would you like to do now?' he asked. We were sitting in his Volkswagen. He had not started the motor. It was early, just a bit after ten. He suggested another film, a drive, a bar with a jazz pianist.

'Let's go where we can talk quietly,' I said. 'I want you to tell me—'

'No, no, we've had enough of that,' he said. He was cross and nervous, having been served with a summons to appear before the Grand Jury.

'All I want to know is what you're going to tell them,' I said.

'The truth. What do you expect?' he asked angrily. And yawned again.

'But not against Daddy!'

'The truth. I told you, Gloria. Stop pestering me.'

Knowing him well I recognised his petulance as exhaustion. He was working hard at his new job in the office of a

223

local law firm. So I said that I was tired and suggested that we call it a night. At the front door he begged my pardon for his bad temper, kissed me and drove away.

The house was dark and quiet. A sliver of light under Pricey's door told me she was not asleep. It was not unusual for me to visit her at night, to tell her where I'd been and what I'd seen and what I'd had for dinner. I burst in without knocking.

I cannot write about what I saw. Daddy and Pricey! The Congressman and Miss Lucy Price . . . like an illustration in a sex book. I see them still . . . I am haunted . . . I wish I could forget. I tried to imagine a giant eraser wiping my brain clear of the scene. Must I carry it till the day I die? If I had seen anything like that in my mother's house I would have run to my room, buried my face in a pillow, thought about immorality, depravity and all the sins my father had warned me against.

I did not run to my room and hide my face and cry. I closed the door quietly, I held my head high as I walked to my room. I washed, I brushed my teeth, I undressed and turned out the light. Later Pricey opened my door a crack to see if I had come home. I lay still until she went away.

In the morning I forced myself to go down to have breakfast with them. I tried not to show my feelings. Pricey's 'good morning' was answered in a tiny voice. I submitted to Daddy's kiss.

'What's the matter?' he said. 'Doesn't my little girl love me any more?'

I drank my orange juice.

'Her head's in the clouds. She doesn't pay attention when you talk to her,' Pricey said.

Daddy was to fly to Washington for a committee meeting. 'Give me a nice kiss, pet. You won't see me for a few days.'

You won't see me again ever, I thought, and submitted to his caresses. My one thought was to get away before my self-control collapsed. As soon as he was out of the house I phoned Hughie at the law office and asked him to meet me for lunch. Then I took the Buick and drove off. Pricey ran out to ask where I was going. I waved goodbye without answering.

For the first time in my life I was independent. Overnight the spoiled child had grown up. In my pampered protected life I had never done anything for myself. There had always been a governess, maids, chauffeurs, secretaries, lawyers. When I was given papers to sign, I signed without bothering to read them. When I saw something I wanted I charged it. In England or France Mother's secretary paid the bills, in Kansas someone in Daddy's office wrote the cheques.

Independence was an adventure. I wrote and cashed a cheque at the bank, went to an airlines office and booked seats on planes to New York and Nice. I was ten minutes late meeting Hughie and vowed that in my new independent life I would overcome my besetting sin of tardiness. This was not the first time I had met a man for lunch but it was different. I felt mature, free. I drank a Martini cocktail and flirted.

First I begged Hughie's pardon for having doubted him. 'Tell me everything about the bribes and corruption,' I said. It seemed important that I found out everything about my father's double standards. I also told Hughie about buying the plane tickets and my intention to leave two days later.

'Why so soon?' he asked.

'I can't stay in that house any longer,' I told him.

He stared at me as if I was wearing a false nose or my face had turned green. 'There's something different about you, Gloria,' Hughie said. 'What has changed you?'

'I've grown up.'

'Since yesterday?'

'I'm free.'

'What does that mean?'

At that moment . . . eating avocado stuffed with shrimp salad . . . I knew as if a dazzling light had been turned on inside me, that freedom had another meaning. My father's disapproval could not matter to me any more. A kiss was not the first step on the road to prostitution. A harlot's blood was not running in my veins. I did not have to keep myself pure for the man I would marry.

Hughie said, 'What's on your mind? You haven't heard a word I was saying.'

I begged his pardon and asked what he had said. He begged me not to leave so soon. My visit had been too short. We had not seen enough of each other. 'Stay for my sake,' he begged.

'I can't. I've got to get away.'

'I love you,' he said, 'I've always loved you.' His voice shook. These were not the conventional words of a cousin . . . this was the passionate declaration of a man in love.

The restaurant was filled with Musak and loud voices. Definitely not a place for tender feelings. Yet Hughie and I seemed alone on a remote island. Joy sparkled like fireworks within me. Last night I had lost a father. Today an honest man offered love and protection. 'If you weren't so rich I'd ask you to marry me,' Hughie said. Last night the muscles of my heart had become hard and tight. Today in a noisy restaurant the effect of the shock began to wear off. My lover's hand stretched across the table to touch my wrist. I bent down and laid my lips on his hand.

'How do you feel about me?' Hughie asked in a shy boyish voice.

The music died away, the voices took over . . . gossip, boasting, business talk. The clatter confused me. I loved my cousin but was not *desperately* in love. The economy was sure to improve, said a bald man on the other side of me on the crowded banquette. Musak offered another tune. 'Hughie dear,' was all I could think of to say.

'Don't you care for me at all?'

'Money has nothing to do with love,' I said.

His eyes were big and brown, as soft as the eyes of a cocker spaniel I had once loved. The gardener's wife poisoned him. I said that this noisy restaurant was no place for intimate talk and asked him to come to the house for dinner. Daddy would not be there, I promised.

Pricey was not there either. I got home just as she was leaving for a reunion of her college class and a short visit to her married sister in Mississippi. 'Emma will take care of you,' she said. 'I'll see you in a week.' I said nothing of my plan to leave before she got back. Pricey was no more to be trusted than my father. It was a relief to know that she would not be in the house watching me as if she were still my governess.

The dinner was to be my first exercise in freedom. I went to the kitchen to discuss the menu with Emma, I changed every dish Pricey had ordered. To celebrate I brought a bottle of Dom Perignon from the cellar. I took a long foamy bath, I washed my hair, I chose my sexiest dress. In the tub I thought about my change of status. If my father and Miss Lucy Price could make love in the position of an illustration in a sex manual, I could experience *normal* love. Hughie was handsome and masculine. He loved me. And I . . . well, when he kissed me, I felt a definite throbbing in my vagina. Not that I wanted to marry him. Or anybody yet. Before I settled down with a husband, I wanted to be on my own, to have experiences, to know life!

This is what I told Hughie while we drank champagne. I was coy and flirtatious. I do not think I was completely carnal and selfish in my desires. The spaniel eyes showed a need for consolation. To let him take me with love and without guilt would in a way comfort him and build his ego. What would happen after? I might fall desperately in love and marry him after all.

I led him on. Boldly. He tried to hold off for moral reasons. I was his cousin. In the middle of an ardent kiss he broke away and crossed the room and stood with his back to me. I followed on tiptoe and surprised him by putting my arms around him. 'Oh, God,' he moaned in a voice that made me think of sin and pain and the Book of Job.

'Hughie darling,' I whispered with my lips almost touching his ear, 'I want you as much as you want me.' He whirled around. The next moment I was in his arms being carried to the couch.

Emma had gone home for the night. We were alone in the house. Hughie forgot scruples, I forgot fear and ignorance, ready to yield myself with all the fury and ardour kept in check for so many years.

That was when Daddy walked in.

Chauncey: I cannot write any more now. I have relived so many old emotions that I am utterly exhausted. The worst part comes next. Thinking about it makes me almost wish I had amnesia again. I will try to write about it tomorrow.

# Chapter Nine

## Consequences

### by Chauncey Greenleaf

'Well done,' said I, laying aside the script, 'and brave of you to write so frankly about painful experiences.'

Crouched in the wing chair, small and nervous as a cornered rabbit, Elizabeth bore little resemblance to the image created by her confession: of a defiant young woman flaunting new-found independence with the man who was to be her lover and her prey. 'The writing's no good,' she murmured. 'I was never good at writing.'

'You write clearly. That's a great virtue in writing. Many successful writers, indeed the most popular of our contemporaries, never achieve clarity.'

'I wanted you to know about me. Even the bad things.' Apprehension shadowed her eyes. Through the curtain of dark lashes she measured my mood. Had I become an enemy like those so often referred to during amnesia? Had frankness and clarity shown her unworthy of my affection?

To assure her of my sympathy, I exclaimed, 'What a childhood! With all that contradiction and confusion. And then that shocking climax. I don't wonder that you sought escape in forgetfulness.'

'That wasn't what caused it.' She shook her head violently as though rejecting shadows of the past, crouched lower in the chair. 'What happened after was worse, the worst thing that could happen to anyone.'

Eager as I was to hear the rest of the story, to know what dire circumstance had caused the past to be so completely erased that she had lost the memory of name and home and the faces of her parents, I could not then put her to the strain of reliving the most painful incident. She had already told me that Hughie, her hero and victim, had died, and that she was not certain of her part in the tragedy. Amnesia is said by psychologists and their breed to be caused, in whole or part, by guilt.

In a small voice, barely more than a whisper, she asked, 'Do you despise me?'

'Despise you, dear? Whatever gave you that foolish idea?'

She nodded towards the sheaf of papers. 'That. It shows what an awful bitch I am: stupid and selfish and spoiled and smug and whining and pitying myself and never thinking about people whose lives are really hard.' She had grown aggressive, slightly shrill, in self-accusation. No longer the Elizabeth I had first known, innocent of her past, childish in her delight in a world newly discovered. Now an adult, she was like the rest of us, the captive of relentless memory.

'Aren't you exaggerating? You've got faults, everyone has, but you can't blame yourself for everything.'

'I despise myself,' she declared, rising and coming towards me defiantly, as though she took pride in her failings. 'I'm twenty-three years old and I've never in my life done anything good for anyone.'

Perhaps it was youth that gave sweetness to her rue. She stood so close that I became aware of the fragrance of her body, rejoiced in the sight of pearly flesh in contrast to the darkness of brow and lash, observed the softness of tremulous lips, watched the delicate colour rise in cheeks heated by emotion. Or maybe it was lust that was inspired in me by what I had just read of a girl's craving for a lover. I had also begun to tremble.

During these silent moments we heard but did not heed the insistent clamour of the knocker. Elizabeth sighed, moved away and curled up in the wing chair. I closed the library door as I went to confront the intruder.

# 2

Under the entrance lamp which gave the effect of a halo to his copper-bright hair stood the young man, the 'snooper', whom I had met with Elizabeth in a cinema and inadvertently unmasked as a writer (rather than the detective he had pretended to be) for the *Weekly*, a magazine which I look into occasionally because a former student, now on its staff, had had my name put on its free subscription list.

'Sorry to disturb you, sir, but I've got to talk to Elizabeth. Allan told me I'd find her here.'

'Come in, Shannon. I'll tell her you're here.' The invitation was cool. His deference and the word, sir, had offended me by its implication of advanced age. I was not to become fifty until Christmas Eve. I offered him a chair in the living room where he was to wait while I warned Elizabeth against the wiles of a reporter for a sensational journal.

This opportunity was denied me. Having heard the fellow's voice, Elizabeth hurried out to greet him. 'Rick, Rick,' she cried rapturously, 'I was afraid you were angry with me.'

He took her hands, urged her towards him, kissed her lightly, the discretion due, no doubt, to my presence. Using the trite excuse that I had some letters to go out in the early morning post, I made what to them must have been a welcome departure. On the way to the library I had to pass the baroque mirror my mother bought when she had finished *The Venetian Glass Murders*. Ordinarily I see myself as the typical New Englander: austere of feature but gentle of expression with humour in the mouth; too lean for my height perhaps, but this slenderness along with horn-rimmed spectacles and a touch of grey at the temples gives refinement and a certain distinction to my appearance. Or so I thought until that unfortunate moment when the mirror cast back the image of a cliché, the older man seeking a return of youth in the love of a young girl.

Behind me the two young people chattered eagerly. I retreated to the library. The closed door could not shut out the hum of their voices. For all the control I attempted, I could neither write letters nor concentrate on a book. Lest curiosity overcome decorum, I put myself out of the way of temptation by carrying the coffee pot and cups to the kitchen where I fed our dinner dishes to the machine. Its sound and fury which ordinarily drives me to distraction now provided an appropriate accompaniment to the dramatic excesses of my imagination. Restlessness was not relieved by the kitchen's petty chores. These accomplished, I returned to the library for the book I wanted to carry up to my bedroom.

The voices in the living room had grown louder, harsher, the rhythms faster, the tones belligerent. Here I must confess that I allowed curiosity to overcome scruple. Guilt determined my gait. It was not necessary to walk on tiptoe on thick carpets, yet I moved with the caution of a burglar to the double doors, and for the first time since I was sent to bed without supper for listening to neighbourhood scandal, I became an eavesdropper.

Elizabeth's voice quavered with fury. 'But you promised, you crossed your heart and hoped to die.'

The fellow thundered, 'Listen to me, will you. I told you I hadn't written it yet.'

'You will. If it means all you say it does, you'll write it.'

'I thought you'd understand what that job means to me. My living, my future, everything that—'

'I know, I heard you the first time.'

'Was I wrong in expecting a little sympathy from you, love?'

'Don't call me love, you traitor.'

'Gloria—'

'Don't call me Gloria either.'

'Okay, Elizabeth. If it hurts you so much, I won't write it. I'll phone Dinsmore and say the deal's off.'

'You mean that? Really and truly?'

'Would I say so if I didn't?'

'Then you won't get the job?' Elizabeth's voice had softened to sympathy. 'And you'll have to scrounge around for assignments and—'

Shannon interrupted, the tone strong and manly. 'Don't worry about me. There'll be another good story sometime. Maybe.'

'Don't look so sad, Rick. You make me feel so cruel.'

'I can't say I'm not disappointed.'

'Oh, Rick, dear Rick, I'm so sorry. I'd love to help you—'

'Don't cry, love. You mean a lot more to me than any job.'

'Do I? Do I really?' Her voice rose to rapture.

'My sweet love,' the fellow muttered.

I imagined the tender scene; his wrapping her in his arms,

holding her close, patting her back, kissing her tear-stained face while convulsive sobs became faint whimpers. How, I wondered, could she allow the rascal's caresses? How could she be consoled by the cheat? All I knew of the situation was that he had broken a promise not to write about her and had then gone to an editor who had evidently offered him a steady job as reward for bringing in a sensational story. My mood was murderous. I longed to burst into that room, assault Richard Shannon and offer Elizabeth honest consolation.

This I could not do without confessing to the sin of eavesdropping, and so I remained with my ear to the keyhole and was punished for my wickedness by an acute pain in the back—the result of remaining in that stooped position—but worse, by having to listen to silence, and suffering the pains inflicted by an over-active imagination. Oh, the ardour my jealousy conceived, the visions of caresses, the passion burning in the fertile brain, the arrows that pierced my heart. I decided never again to caress her, never to hope, never to allow her beauty and her sweetness to affect me. I called myself a fool for having permitted myself to believe that this young and lovely creature could care for a skinny professor twenty-odd years her senior.

And so I straightened my protesting back, refrained from sigh or groan, and as cautiously as I had come to it, abandoned the keyhole; again on tiptoe crossed the library and mounted the stairs to my lonely bedroom. Sleep did not knit the ravelled sleeve of conscience. I woke often, haunted by fragments of nightmares, listened for the murmur of voices, stupidly, because the walls and ceilings of the old house reject all but the loudest intrusions. Silence gave rise to unwelcome visions. In my dark bedroom I saw the two celebrate their youth on my mother's velvet couch: and then I saw ecstasy interrupted by a ghost. Hughie! Had she told Rick that she was haunted by the memory of a murder which she was accused of having committed? If truly in love, she might have refrained from the question she had not been afraid to ask me. In love with her myself, I was unwilling to accept the probability, thinking it as no more than the concept of a tortured mind.

Perhaps I slept again. It seemed that an entire night had passed when I looked at the illuminated dial of my bedside clock and discovered the time to be not quite 1 am. Had I to suffer the hell of sleeplessness another six hours? Although I disapprove of sleeping pills I swallowed two of the pellets Dr Greenspan had prescribed during a bout of sciatica.

In the morning, heavy-eyed and slow of movement, I stumbled through necessary chores. While shaving I recalled the resolution never again to caress, nor speak to Elizabeth of love, yet could not escape subliminal flashes; her tender lips pressed against mine, her body warm beneath me. I was angry with the wench, indignant that she should have permitted the embraces of a scoundrel who had broken his word to her, lied, betrayed her trust.

To rational man no mystery is so incomprehensible as the female mind. One never knows what to expect of a woman. The duality, the contrariness, the cunning, the sincerity with which they disguise guile, the ease with which they twist reason to fit their whims are beyond masculine intelligence. Once before I had been misled by a woman's charms. I knew that it was my fate to suffer a repetition of the anguish.

# 3

Pacing the platform as I waited for the 8.04, I knew that classroom discussion would be dull this morning. While the anxieties of the previous night continued to vex me, I would not be able to arouse much fervour in analysing the works of Sterne and Richardson. How inane the mischief of Tom Jones when compared with the misbehaviour of Richard Shannon; how lacking in drama the amours of Clarissa Harlowe in contrast to Elizabeth's involvement with the men who loved her. Yet more worrisome than these distractions was the fear and suspense aroused by a conversation on the train.

Allan Royce had spied me on the platform just as the train was about to pull out, had jumped on to the rear car and worked his way to the carriage where I had settled myself in a window seat and opened *The Times* in the hope of finding some hitherto unrevealed Washington scandal to exorcise personal distress. Without the courtesy of a greeting he settled beside me and said, 'I've got news for you.'

'Good morning, Royce.'

'Our mystery girl's no longer a mystery.'

'Yes, I know. She's recovered remembrance of things past.'

He let the allusion pass without so much as smile. 'Then she's told you who her father is?'

'Has she told you?' I was irked because she had not mentioned Daddy's name to me.

'Weren't you shocked?'

Unwilling to show ignorance, I shrugged.

'It's not so shocking,' Allan went on. 'Many prominent people have difficult children. But you'd never think that

that holier-than-thou Dixon would have trouble with his daughter.'

I confess to shock. Elizabeth the daughter of Representative Dixon! That most articulate, combative, righteous member of the House. A man with the ability to twist any point to the benefit of his views, he was constantly in the news. Handsome and colourful, he appeared to advantage on television where he was wont to call upon the Almighty to endorse his disapproval of bussing, abortion and equal rights for ladies who would be better served upon the pedestals of their grandmothers' day than in the rude world of law and commerce. In no appearance did the Congressman neglect to deplore contemporary standards which tolerated the defilement of womanhood by premarital intercourse.

My shock lessened as I compared his opinions with the father Elizabeth had described: a hypocrite, a liar, a whited sepulchre she had called this pillar of rhetorical righteousness. Discovery of his corruption, disillusion with the idol, disavowal of his values had plunged her into heresy and the arms of her cousin. The pieces of the intricate jigsaw had begun to fit, the picture to emerge.

I said nothing of this to Allan, but stared out of the window at the changing colours of September foliage while I mused on the contradictions of the human beast. The splendours of nature, the sordid acts of man have been in conflict throughout the history of civilisation.

'They're coming for her today,' Allan said.

I turned from the colours of autumn to face him. 'Who? Her father?' I demanded in a voice inappropriate to the issue and the place. A man in the seat ahead turned around to see who was bellowing behind him.

'And Dr Hyde from that loony bin.'

'You don't think they'd take her back there?'

Allan did not know where they meant to take her, only that they were coming this day. Dr Hyde had telephoned him early that morning to ask if she had returned and Allan had said that she was at my house. I could barely control my rage at his having given out the information.

'Have they the right to take her if she doesn't want to go?' I asked.

Allan could not answer this either. He supposed that a patient escaped from an asylum could be forced to return.

'If unwilling?' I asked.

'Why the devil was she sent there in the first place? She's not insane,' Allan argued as though I were the culprit who had committed her, and added that while she was a guest in his house, she had not only behaved with sanity, but had been welcome company. 'Helped Katie a lot, you know. Got her out of that depression and made her take an interest in life again. Except for that amnesia, Elizabeth seemed a lot more normal than most people. Maybe amnesia was a symptom of—' He tapped his head. 'Can you believe the kid's nutty?'

Doubt assailed me. Could the confession of murder have been the fantasy of a deranged mind? After the arrival in New York, the question pursued me while I rode the subway, walked on the street, ascended the stairs to my classroom. From a public booth I telephoned my home, told Elizabeth to stay inside, lock all doors, pull down the shades as though the house were empty. She was not to open the door to anyone nor answer the phone. There was plenty of food in the refrigerator and pantry and enough books to keep her occupied for fifty years.

'Suppose Kate comes to see me,' she said.

'Kate will understand if you phone and tell her why.'

'You haven't told me why.'

'You're in danger. Isn't that reason enough?'

'I wish you were here, Chauncey. I'm scared.'

'Be a brave girl, do as I say and you'll be safe.'

As I had anticipated, my morning classes were dull. Certainly my students were not inspired with a passion for the English novel. At noon I informed the dean's office that I had been called away by an emergency. There was no train before the 3.34 so I hired a car and, in an excess of nervousness, exceeded the speed limit. Fortunately I was not stopped by the police.

# 4

A long black limousine of the kind that carries politicians to rallies and mourners to cemeteries was parked beside the picket fence. As I turned into the driveway, two men jumped out and hurried to bar my way to the front door. Claude Dixon, victim of his publicity, was instantly recognisable. Handsomer than his television portraits with his silver mane and black brows, broad shoulders and broad carriage, he was the very image of the successful political figure. His companion was also symbolic of his calling, the bearded physician who recommends this or that brand of toothpaste, vitamins and laxatives.

They introduced themselves, told me they had been waiting since noon and asked if Dixon's daughter was in my house. 'We've rung the bell several times and phoned from down the road. No one answers.'

With closed curtains and drawn blinds, the house looked empty indeed. 'She's probably out,' I said.

They had also sought her at the Royce's. Mrs Royce had told them that she had no idea where Elizabeth might be. I was tempted to retort that she may have been warned that Dr Hyde and her father would come for her and, as on Sunday, had run away. Better not to be flippant, I decided, better to assume an air of serious concern lest they suspect me of putting them off. I led them into the house and in the entrance hall said, 'If you gentlemen will excuse me, I'll go upstairs and see if she's there. She may be sleeping.'

'Wake her,' commanded her father.

I found her curled on the bed with the writing pad and sharp pencils idle on the table beside her. 'I couldn't write this morning,' she said like a student who has neglected to prepare the lesson. 'I can't concentrate.'

'Quiet,' I commanded. 'I don't want them to know you're in the house.' Whispering, I bade her stay in her room while I tried to get rid of the visitors. Should I find it necessary for her to appear, I'd whistle a few bars of the *Flute* motif; she was then to go down softly by the back stairs and come in from the kitchen as though she'd entered by the back door.

'Must we lie?'

'I don't mind telling a convenient lie but I hate being caught. It won't help to let them know we've been conniving.'

She scowled. 'Why can't I just come down and face them and tell them what liars they are?'

'Do you think it will do any good?'

'All my life people have lied to me. And now you, Chauncey. You're no better than anyone else.' She attempted to brush past me.

My outstretched arm barred the way. 'Do you want to go back to that sanitarium?'

She shuddered and went back to the bed. I joined the gentlemen in the hall. 'Apparently she's gone out,' I said blithely.

'Where would she go?' her father asked.

'The only place is Mrs Royce's. And as you say she's not there.' A shrug demonstrated ignorance.

'You think she'll come back?' asked Dr Hyde.

Another shrug was my answer.

'We'll wait,' said Mr Dixon and marched into the library. 'Hope we're not disturbing you,' he added, unctuous as in a speech to constituents. 'Nice house you've got here. Handsome rooms. I must compliment you on your choice of antiques.'

'I didn't choose them. They've been in the Greenleaf family for generations.'

'You're lucky.' Leaning back in the wing chair in the attitude of being quite at home he asked, in a kindly way, how well I knew Gloria. I might have been a suitor seeking permission to wed the gentleman's daughter.

I considered the reply before saying, 'She's told me a great deal about herself and,' I added wryly, 'her parents.'

'I don't doubt it. But I wouldn't advise you to believe her. The poor child's a bit—' He looked to Dr Hyde for assistance in stating a painful fact.

'Schizophrenic. More than a bit.'

'It's a great sorrow to a father, believe me. It was with a heavy heart I consigned my beloved daughter to the care of this good doctor.'

'We've done our best for her,' the doctor said with a grateful nod, 'and believed we'd made progress, but I'm afraid this escapade will set her back.' A heavy professional sigh accompanied these words.

I had no faith in Dr Hyde and little liking for the Congressman, but I could not help being troubled by what they said. A man does not commit his daughter to an insane asylum without reason. (And if, as Elizabeth had hinted, the reason was to prove insanity, if she were ever to be accused of murder, the situation was equally deplorable.) Nevertheless I assumed an air of scepticism remarking that Dixon's daughter had always behaved normally with me and that I had observed no slight sign of derangement.

'Quite so,' said the doctor. 'The girl's clever, many patients cover their condition, and Miss Dixon has great charm when it suits her. A well-brought-up young woman.' A deferential glance was directed at the patient's sire. 'But unreliable. One must be constantly on guard with her. When she's crossed she's likely to become violent. Even—' An oblique glance at Dixon sought permission to go further. A subtle nodded assented. 'I might say dangerous.'

I sniffed contemptuously.

'Believe me, Mr Greenleaf, it's true. For your own sake we're warning you,' Dixon said with a sob in his voice. 'I beg you to trust me. A father doesn't speak lightly of his child's affliction. I still love my little girl in spite—' he paused to blow his nose—'of the trouble she's caused, the terrible sin, the crime.' He blew again and touched his handkerchief to the edges of his eyes.

I was caught by the word. 'Crime?'

'I shall have to tell you. My daughter killed a man.'

'True, true,' muttered Dr Hyde. 'In a sudden inexplicable fit of temper.'

'Not at all inexplicable, Doctor. She was trying, poor

child, to defend her honour.' Dixon turned to me, moist eyes begging sympathy. 'Try to understand. The man had attacked her, a man she trusted, a cousin.'

'Her cousin Hugh?'

'She's told you? What has she told you?' Appeal had turned to demand. Dixon sprang up to place himself before me as solid and stony as a pillar. 'Out with it, sir. What has she told you?'

'Does it matter?' asked the doctor in a voice trained to soothe unruly madmen. 'Professor Greenleaf knows she's not to be believed.'

'That's right, Doctor. Thank you for reminding me. She has probably woven a number of fantasies about the incident. Which did she tell you?'

'The truth, Daddy, I told him the truth about what happened.' And there she was, disobedient to me, defiant of her father, scornful of the doctor, beautiful in challenge. She had donned the white dress, bound her dark hair with a white ribbon. With the dark shadows behind her she seemed, although not a large woman, classic in dignity. Iphigenia came to my mind although it was incongruous at a moment of immediate drama to think of Greek tragedy; relief, perhaps, from the contemporary drama taking place before my eyes.

'Gloria!' gasped her father.

The doctor adjusted spectacles so that his accusing glance could pierce the liar more painfully. 'So she was here.'

'She must have come in the back way.' I waited anxiously for Elizabeth to contradict the lie. She did not protest but avoided my eyes. That she had been listening to our conversation was obvious.

'You're wrong, Daddy. Hugh didn't attack me. I seduced him.'

As poised as a veteran orator speaking from a platform, Dixon said, 'You may think that's the way it was, dear, but Daddy knows you'd never do such a wicked thing. My pure girl, sweet and fresh as a flower, would not—'

'Daddy,' she cut in, 'you're not talking to your idiot public. So don't tell me what I did because you don't know. You weren't there, you didn't come in till we were making love on the couch and Hugh was about to fuck me.'

Her father winced. Elizabeth noted and enjoyed his distress. Obscenity had been used, as in the scene with Hildebrandt, as a weapon of revenge. Dr Hyde gave no sign of having heard, but kept rigid watch on Dixon, awaiting instruction. I was disconcerted; not that the word was unfamiliar; my students use it freely as a verb, a noun, an adjective. But from Elizabeth, today as yesterday, it was a painful shock.

Dixon's ruddy flesh darkened to carmine. The jut of his jaw showed an intense effort at self-control. He breathed as though he were practising yoga exercises. 'Would you interpret that as a symptom, Doctor?'

'Indeed, indeed. A most significant symptom.' He addressed me. 'You see, Professor, how she twists the truth to fit her needs.'

Choked with anger, Elizabeth declared, 'He twists the truth,' a forefinger accused her father. 'He twists everything for his purposes. Like saying I killed Hughie when he did it, he's the killer.'

'A delusion, Professor. She's had it the whole time, poor girl.'

She whirled around to face the doctor. 'What do you know about it? You weren't there to see him pull Hugh off me. And throw him down and bang his head against the

245

floor. I saw him do it, I screamed for him to stop but he kept on banging and banging. Poor Hughie never had a chance.'

Dixon's flush faded from crimson to the dead white of a clown's make-up, and on his cheekbones a clown's red circles glowed. Yet he retained the outward composure to say sadly, 'No wonder she has these delusions. To keep from remembering that she hit him on the head with . . .'

'That's a filthy lie.'

'. . . the bronze urn.'

'I did not, I did not, I did not,' screamed Elizabeth.

'It was you, child, you. You were beating him on the head when I came in. Remember, dear, I took the bronze from your hand—'

'What I remember is you banging his head on the floor, banging and banging and—'

While Dixon and his daughter continued to shout their assertions, Dr Hyde leaned close to me and said, 'Temporary amnesia was, no doubt, the unconscious desire to forget the crime, although it may be possible that it was a ruse. In case her guilt was discovered.'

'Was it?' At once I realised the significance of my question and hurried to add, 'Was anyone else accused of the murder?'

'Hugh Dixon died at home. In his own bed,' the doctor said, but was diverted from further explanation by a growl from Dixon who had hold of Elizabeth's wrist and was pulling her towards him.

'Don't you ever say that again. Never say it,' roared the Congressman.

Taunting him, she said, 'I'll say it whenever I like. You were glad Hughie died, you were afraid of what he knew, wanted him dead.'

'Shut up.' He raised a clenched fist and would have smashed it into her face had the doctor and I not hastened to prevent brutality. Dr Hyde had seized the upraised arm.

'Easy, Claude. You don't want any more trouble.'

Having placed myself in front of Elizabeth, I was rewarded for my gallantry by a great fist smashing into my eyes, but was so intent upon rescuing Elizabeth that I did not immediately recognise pain. As Dixon freed her, I tried to take her in my arms. She pulled away from me and stood on her own, glaring at us as though all males were enemies.

Neither she nor her father was content with the cease-fire. Their feud was as yet unfinished. 'It's all in your mind,' he said. 'You're mad, Gloria, crazy as a loon, you make up these things and believe them.'

'You know they're true, Daddy. You're scared. It wasn't only that Hughie was ruining your little flower, it was what he knew about your lies and cheating and taking bribes and the filthy sex things you—'

He sprang towards her, his hands circled and taut, so that we, the doctor and I, thought he meant to choke her. Once again we attempted rescue, but Elizabeth would have none of us. She stepped up to him, raised her head in defiance, looked into his face and declared, 'You're a liar, Daddy, and a hypocrite and a white sepulchre.'

I laughed. The Biblical phrase out of place in this scene, at this time. In every human tragedy, however, exists the contradictory element of comedy. Would Iphigenia have called Agamemnon the Greek equivalent of Daddy? The doctor regarded my laughter as a symptom of some delusion which should place me in his sanitarium. Untimely as it was, mirth relieved tension. We became self-conscious, drew into ourselves, not knowing whether to relax or prepare for another battle. My eye had become painful. I held my hand to it and Elizabeth asked if I was hurt.

'Now look what you've done to him, Daddy.'

'Raw steak is the best thing,' Dixon said.

'Ice is cheaper. Excuse me, gentlemen.'

In the kitchen, emptying an ice tray and wrapping the cubes in a towel, I listened for sounds of renewed battle, but heard only the hum of voices. Elizabeth hurried into the kitchen. 'How's your eye? Does it hurt much? He's such a brute. They're going.'

'Good.'

'They expect to take me with them. Back to that place. Don't let them, Chauncey.'

She looked at me trustingly. Although I had no power over the dragons in the library, her faith in my strength clad me in armour. Yet I was not the dauntless knight who will rush into battle without good reason. I wanted just cause before I risked the other eye. 'Both stories are hard to believe, yours as well as your father's. Who did kill Hughie? And who was accused? I want the truth.'

'You've got to believe me, Chauncey. Hughie didn't die that night. He passed out for a few minutes and then he got up and insisted that he was all right and could drive himself home. He told his mother he had a headache and went to bed. In the morning he was dead.'

She seemed to think this answered all questions, but I was not satisfied and demanded further information. 'Wasn't the cause investigated? Didn't anyone ask why?'

'Oh, yes. Yes. There was an autopsy and they said it was a brain haemorrhage caused by a fall or blow, his skull was fractured. Daddy said he must have fallen when he was drunk, he said Hughie was an alcoholic like his father.

Which wasn't true. But Daddy had a lot of influence, friends in city offices so, of course, they believed him. And then a few nights later, three or four maybe, Daddy and I had this awful fight.'

'Weren't you to fly to France the next day?'

'Oh, oh yes,' she sounded vague. 'I forgot that. I changed my reservations after Hughie died. We had to appear at the inquest, Daddy and I. Aunt Estelle, that's Hughie's mother, said he'd been at our house that night. So I changed my booking till the day after the funeral.'

'What was the awful fight about?'

Dixon had been calling, 'Gloria, Gloria, come along.' He strode into the kitchen. 'How long does it take you to say goodbye?' He caught hold of her arm.

'I'm not coming with you.' She shook herself free of him and came to stand beside me.

'The hell you aren't.'

'I'll die before I go back to that hell.' This was directed at Dr Hyde who stood at the kitchen door stroking his beard while assuming the attitude of a god looking down from Olympus upon the antics of unworthy mortals.

'You needn't if you don't want to,' I told Elizabeth.

'I'm her father and she's got to obey me.'

Often, when we are least sure of our arguments, we put on the bravest show of confidence. 'She's over twenty-one and free to make her own decisions. You can stay here if you want to, Elizabeth.'

'Here? With you? A single man. How will that look?'

'Will she look better in an insane asylum?'

The doctor resented the crude name I gave his 'home for disturbed adults'. He addressed me in the voice trained to soothe refractory patients. 'May I call it to your attention,

Professor, that this young woman was placed in my care as a psychotic patient suffering a mammoth delusion. She believes she did not commit a murder which was witnessed by a responsible citizen.' He nodded deferentially to the Congressman. 'I believe that the police will respect her father's authority and mine. Where is your telephone?'

I recognised the bluff and called it with the urbanity of a poker player holding a royal flush. 'The phone's in the library and the number of the police station is in the front page of the directory.' Elizabeth regarded me with astonishment. The sight of her stricken face so affected me that I turned my back. 'But wait,' I said as Dr Hyde started towards the library, 'let me warn you—'

'The police will co-operate with us,' he interrupted. 'It's the law that fugitives be returned to mental institutions.'

'I am sure that if it is the law, Chief Potts will obey it. My warning.' I stumbled before an uncertain argument. Elizabeth had come around to stand before me so that I was disconcerted by the reproach in her lovely eyes.

'What's the use of all this shilly-shallying? Make your call, Doctor, so we can get out,' Dixon commanded.

'Yes, do, Doctor. Take her with you, lock her up, but let me warn you that my attorney will start suit tomorrow.'

'On what grounds?'

'Detention of a normal woman in your asylum.' I had no knowledge of the law, had made no preparation for the accusation, but allowed the threat to erupt from the lower depths of tangled emotions. Elizabeth had been tugging at my arm, trying to tell me something privately. I had not deigned to notice. She had retreated then, and with bowed head, eyes on the floor, leaned against the refrigerator for support. Her posture suggested disillusionment and defeat; betrayal by the one person she could trust. At my threat of a law suit she brightened, raised her head, regarded me with faint hope.

With the solemnity of a prosecuting attorney, Dixon said, 'Your argument would be valid, Professor, if she were of a sound mind, but as she is not, the court would rule that she must accept the decisions of her legal guardian.' His smug smile left no doubt as to the identity of her legal guardian.

'Mr Dixon,' I said with as much dignity as possible for a man with an icebag held to his face, 'by what authority do you claim that your daughter is not of sound mind?'

'His.' This time Mr Dixon showed deference to the doctor.

'And what is your authority, Dr Hyde, for asserting that Miss Dixon is not of sound mind?'

'The authority of my training as a doctor of psychology, by my reputation, and by the fact that the patient has been confined in my sanitarium.' With *hauteur* the doctor added, 'And by this authority I demand that you return her to my custody at once.'

'Come along, Gloria. We've had enough talk,' her father said.

'Just a moment,' I said, playing desperately for time, 'let's consider the fact that Dr Hyde's authority can be questioned. If the case should come to court, we could call in an expert witness who would, and has already, declared Miss Dixon to be of sound mind.'

It was Hyde's turn in the game. 'Who is this expert and by what tests has he come to this decision?'

'Surely you've heard of Dr Phoebe Tisch.'

'Of course, of course,' said the doctor. In his haste and aggressiveness I detected a shade of alarm. But he played the game shrewdly. 'Can you tell me what tests were given to the patient?'

'The most common, you must know them, Doctor.' I could see on his face the gathering clouds of disbelief and quickly, as though I were lecturing to graduate students, produced a string of names: 'The Milton, the Donne, the Goldsmith, the Beaumont-Fletcher,' then fearing he might recognise the literary character of my authority, hurried to add, 'and of course the Rasminsky.' It was irrational to think that a layman should be familiar with the names of tests known only to his profession, but Hyde could not admit ignorance, my impromptu fictions were received as solid authority. From his next remark it was apparent that he did not care to tangle in court with Phoebe Tisch.

He addressed Mr Dixon. 'I do not think I should care to be involved in a lawsuit. I am far too busy to spare the time. I suggest that you place your daughter in some other institution.'

Dixon was not readily defeated. Jaw shot forward, fist punishing the kitchen table, he first addressed Dr Hyde. 'Don't worry, Doc, he'll never bring a suit.' And to me, speaking as to an antagonist in political debate, 'By what right, sir, do you propose to bring suit in a case that concerns a man and his daughter and has no relation to your interests?' He strode towards me, forefinger aimed like a gun. 'As a lawyer I doubt that your case would hold water. In all probability it would be thrown out of court. Answer me, Professor, tell me what gives you authority to sue me.'

Elizabeth looked at me expectantly. I had no reply.

Her father repeated the challenge. 'Can't you answer a simple question? What right have you to sue me?'

'The right of a man to protect his wife,' said Elizabeth.

'Huh!' snorted her father. 'Is this true?' he asked me.

I was stunned; speechless; confused; embarrassed by the

look of tender confidence the minx directed at me. 'Tell him,' she prompted in a bland voice. But since I was still in shock, she answered for me. 'Do you think we'd say we were married if we weren't?'

'You mean to say you married *him*.' Emphasis on the pronoun suggested that she had wedded a felon, a convict, a rogue of the blackest reputation. 'Married without my permission?'

I had recovered sufficiently to retort, 'Your permission was hardly necessary. Your daughter is of legal age.'

'After what you've done to me, do you think your permission means anything?' Elizabeth said scornfully.

A few more bitter words were exchanged. How easily she backed up her falsehood; how impertinently she mocked the pompous defences of the errant parent. In the manner of a Victorian father, Dixon threatened to disinherit his unworthy child. She ridiculed him with laughter as she reminded him that he had never supported her. Her mother had paid for her keep until she had come into control of the trust fund from her grandmother. 'Besides,' she added pertly, 'my husband is quite capable of taking care of me.'

The quarrel would have lasted longer if a man called Dearborn, Dixon's pilot and assistant, had not telephoned to remind him that he was to speak that night at a banquet in Wichita, and as there was an hour's drive to the airport where he'd left the plane they had no time to waste. So our kitchen melodrama ended.

After I'd shown my unwelcome guests to the door, I returned to the kitchen to find Elizabeth chopping ice for the treatment of my black eye. She winced as she examined the gorgeous blues and purples of the bruise. 'I'm going to tie the compress on so you won't have to keep on holding it.' As she tied a dry towel over the compress so that I looked like a soldier wounded on the Crimean front, she asked what I thought of her skill as a liar.

'I thought you despised liars. You've always been so vehement about your devotion to the truth.'

'It's different lying to a liar. Besides, this was a convenient lie.' She laughed too merrily. 'You should have seen your face.'

Marriage was not mentioned again. The subject was avoided as though its very name were sinful. Still of a divided mind, I became increasingly aware of the absurdity of a man of forty-nine believing that a girl in her early twenties would consent to marry him. Yet this very obstacle, along with the cosiness of supper in the kitchen, awakened in my heart a protest against the loneliness of bachelor life. I needed a woman but still wondered if the woman I loved was not mad and whether she was guilty of murder. I tried to still my doubts but was plagued by unanswered questions.

What had been the real cause of her cousin's sudden death? Could the Congressman's reputation and influence have prevented a thorough investigation? Why had she been confined in Dr Hyde's snake pit? How had she escaped? The question most vital to my interests I could not ask. Was she in love with Richard Shannon?

Her answers came slowly, sometimes painfully as though memory was an unbearable burden, while long, abstracted pauses hinted of evasion and, perhaps, fictions contrived to mask unwelcome truth. In this domestic atmosphere with the refrigerator humming and water singing in the percolator, our talk of murder and conspiracy seemed no more real than the contrivances of television drama. But there was no lack of salt in Elizabeth's tears, nor artifice in the colour that flamed and died in her cheeks. In the hope of communicating its mood, I shall attempt to re-create the scene in the kitchen.

# 5

She repeated in greater detail the account of her father's fight with Hughie. Her lover had been seized from behind, unaware, thrown down and his head banged again and again on the uncarpeted oak floor. 'Poor Hughie never had a chance.'

'What about the bronze urn that you were supposed to have wielded?'

'There was no bronze urn.' A dark flush rose from the neck of her white dress to the roots of her hair. 'That is,' she faltered, 'the urn was in another room. Anyway there was no reason for me to hit him with it or anything else. You read what I wrote. I wanted to be ruined. Why are you laughing?'

'That word, ruined. It was out of date in my mother's day.'

She spoke quietly of her lover's death, of the postponement of her trip to Europe and of the funeral, but when recalling her father's testimony at the inquest, grew shrill. 'Daddy said he'd come home unexpectedly and found Hughie attacking me after having imbibed freely of the best Bourbon. That's how Daddy said it, "imbibed freely of the best Bourbon". Which isn't true; we'd been drinking champagne. And Daddy said like father, like son, that Hughie's late father had been a drunk and he, Daddy, had kept his late brother in a famous sanitarium in Connecticut. And then,' she raised her fists high in frustrated anger, 'Daddy said Hughie had staggered out and when he was getting into his car, he fell and hit his head on the concrete drive. And how he rushed out to see if the lad was hurt. *Lad*, he said, because it made him sound elderly and sad and fond of his nephew. He said that he'd offered to drive the *lad* home, but Hughie had declared himself unhurt and able to drive.

'The next day when he heard that Hughie was dead, you could have knocked him over with a feather. That's how Daddy said it, "You could have knocked me over with a feather." '

No one had questioned the Congressman's story.

'And what about you, Elizabeth. What did you say when you were questioned?'

'You'll despise me.'

The pause was ominous.

'You lied?'

She had gone to the window and stood looking out at the pale moonlit garden. 'Could I betray my father?' she cried out in anguish.

'After all that had happened? All you had found out about him?'

Still with her back to me she said, 'He wanted so much to be a senator.' Like a mother explaining that her child wanted so much to have a bicycle or a lollipop, she added, 'This was his last chance. He'd failed twice before. He couldn't afford a scandal. In election year.' She turned and came towards me like a penitent, hands clasped under her chin. In a barely audible voice she offered the excuse that grief over Hughie's death had brought her to the slippery edge of a nervous breakdown. At one moment she blamed herself for having seduced him in her father's house and, a minute later, screamed that Daddy had killed her lover. Grief had so weakened her will that she had retreated to the habit of loyalty and supported her father's lies. The succession of shocks compounded by guilt had caused the 'awful fight'.

The night before she was to leave for Europe she had had the vengeful pleasure of seeing him crumple under the threat of exposure. Her aunt Estelle, to whom she had made a farewell visit, was unwilling to believe that her son had been fatally injured in a fall while drunk, and had instructed her lawyer to have the case reopened. A burst of Daddy's famous temper had greeted the news, first with the announcement that such action was ill-conceived, illegal and impossible; then with a sneer and the information that Gloria would have to remain in the country to testify again.

For once in her life she had the upper hand and, returning sneer for sneer, said, 'It's only a few hours' flight and I'll be glad for a chance to tell the truth.'

'What does that mean?' he demanded.

'Just what I said. That I'll tell the truth this time.'

'Haven't you any loyalty?' he thundered.

'I will not lie again. For you or anybody else.'

'You'd deny your evidence at the inquest? Do you know what that would mean for you?'

'A confession of perjury, I guess.'

'A year in jail, my girl. Maybe longer.'

'A life sentence for you, Daddy.'

A stinging slap rewarded the insolence. She had tried to escape up the staircase, but he had caught up with her on the landing, seized her shoulders and shaken her with such fury that her teeth chattered. 'I begged him to let me go and he said he would if I'd swear on the Bible that I'd never betray him. "And if I won't?" I said. He grew absolutely purple in the face and I was afraid he was going to push me down the stairs. It's funny the things you think of at a time like that. You won't believe that I thought of Amy Robsart and how Leicester killed her by throwing her down the stairs. I began to laugh, it was hysteria, I guess, and I went on laughing which made Daddy madder and he yelled, "What's the matter with you? Are you crazy?" So I got this bright idea and asked how it would look if his daughter was killed in his house right after his nephew had had a fatal accident on the driveway.'

His hands had dropped from her shoulders then and she had scurried up to her room, locked herself in and remained there until early morning. In order to avoid another encounter, she had telephoned for a taxi to take her to the airport. With great effort she had carried her heavy bag down the stairs. Her father was waiting in the hall. His mood had changed; as tenderly as when he had cosseted his beloved little girl, he said that he had a surprise for her.

'Let's not part in anger, child. It would hurt me sorely if my sweet girl left without a goodbye kiss for Daddy.'

She recognised his political voice but, since there would soon be half a continent and an ocean between them, decided to humour him in this trivial matter. 'After all he was my father.'

I noted that she spoke of the living man in the past tense.

He drove her to the airport where the pilot, Dearborn, waited beside the hired plane. This was the surprise. Instead of having to endure the delays and discomforts of a commercial plane, she was to be flown to New York in private luxury; there to enjoy a gala farewell lunch with her doting Daddy. 'That's very kind of you, Daddy, but can you spare the time?' She played his game willingly. So great was her desire to return to past innocence that she believed that he was doing penance for last night's brutality. He assured her that the pleasure of his little girl's company was well worth the sacrifice of a few hours; and as it was necessary that he fly to Connecticut this week for a conference with an important political ally, the journey would kill two birds with one stone. Since she was to take a night plane, there would be plenty of time for the detour. Details of the Connecticut visit had been arranged. At the Hartford airport a limousine waited. Dearborn drove them through miles of wooded country to an estate surrounded by stone walls and a gate guarded by a man in uniform.

For a mansion of its size, the house had seemed dreary and ill-furnished. A refined lady, apparently a housekeeper, brought her a glass of cold lemonade. Dr Hyde, introduced as a colleague, asked the lady to entertain her while he conferred with her father. The housekeeper asked if the young lady would not like to wash after the long hot journey. Thinking this a euphemism for a more fundamental need, Elizabeth had followed the woman to the second floor. An overwhelming fatigue had taken possession of her, body and mind. Each step on the tall staircase became an obstacle; her head lodged an impenetrable fog. She yawned frequently, resented the sickly condition, and welcomed the housekeeper's suggestion that she lie down for a nice little nap until her father was ready to leave.

She woke to see darkness descending over the park. According to her wrist watch it was almost nine o'clock. Where was she? Where was her father? Was this a nightmare? Why was the door of her room locked, the window barred?.

# 6

After she had pounded and kicked the door for a while, a nurse in white came to ask if she would like dinner. She raged, demanded freedom, begged to be allowed to telephone, refused to eat. In the weeks that followed she had sent urgent letters to her mother and to the Waterfoot family's lawyers in New York. As these were never answered, she realised that they had not been mailed. Strangest of all she was addressed as Grace; Grace Dearborn. 'Same initials, don't you see? So many of my things were monogrammed. Yes, my bags were brought up to my room with all the things I'd packed. There was no money in my purse, nor my passport or driver's licence and travellers' cheques. Everything that could identify me as *his* daughter. But Grace Dearborn! Imagine having him for a father.' Tightened lips and narrowed nostrils expressed distaste.

'You don't like it here? You'll get used to us in time,' Dr Hyde had said in his most syrupy voice.

She had never got used to the place, never become resigned, never acknowledged the futility of fighting, ate with poor appetite, would take no liquids except water drawn by herself from the tap so that she would not be tricked as she had been by that cool glass of lemonade. When they gave her injections two nurses had to hold her down. Sometimes, after treatments, she would have strange and horrifying visions; would dwell in a fantastic world where flowers were as large as cottages, rats danced to rock music, men beat naked children, lovers throttled or stabbed recumbent women, blood ran down marble stairs. She fought to reject the images, fought harder when Dr Hyde, during his twice weekly treatments, tried to hypnotise her into believing that she had struck the blows that had killed Hughie. To shut out his poisonously sweet voice, to close her mind to the dangerous persuasion, became increasingly difficult. She was not always certain that she was not mad.

Saddest of all, there was no one to share her fears, no one to whom she could talk rationally. A few patients were friendly, but since they were alcoholics nourished on their daily rations, addicts under the influence of various drugs or genuinely crazy, they could not be considered responsible allies. The trained nurses were rigid disciplinarians or ardent admirers of Dr Hyde. In late July, Elizabeth found a friend, a town girl who worked as a nurse's aid, who hated the place and was not afraid to say so. She broke the rule that forbade outside help to communicate with employees by chatting with the only patient she liked. One day the patient asked if the girl considered her insane.

'Why, Miss Dearborn, you're not half as crazy as most of them that work here.'

'You'd better not let anyone hear you say things like that,' the patient had warned.

'So I'll be fired. You think I care. I'm only working here to pay for my trousseau.' She had already confided that she was to be married in October.

The so-called Miss Dearborn thought about this for some time before she asked the girl, 'Would you like to have my clothes?'

The girl gasped. Miss Dearborn's closets and dresser drawers were filled with the contents of the bags Miss Dixon had packed for her journey to Europe: coats and dresses and lingerie with Paris labels, garments that a poor girl dared not dream about.

'You can have everything if you help me get out of here.'

'Won't you need them?'

'I'll buy others,' said the heiress.

For ten days the girls planned, contrived, whispered hopefully. On a Sunday morning with much of the staff off duty and only locked doors to detain the patient, the nurse's aid brought a cup of drugged coffee to the guard in charge of that corridor, pocketed his keys, and when the halls were empty, guided the fugitive patient down the servants' stairs, through a basement passage to an exit close to which she had parked her fiancé's car. For the first few miles the passenger hid in the trunk, for ten more miles sat beside the driver, squatting down whenever a car passed. After another few miles she was let off at a bus stop.

As the bus sped along shady roads she dared dream again of independence. How glorious to be free, how bright the visions of a new life. When the driver came to collect fares, the dream collapsed. In her fervent farewell to the nurse's aid and haste to board the bus, she had forgotten her pocketbook. In it was the ten dollars that was to have paid her bus fare to New York. Penniless, surrounded by strangers, she grew sick with shame. In the life of an heiress no such dilemma had ever been conceived.

'What's the matter, girlie? Lost your pocketbook?'

'Let me off, please.'

'Don't take it so hard. Happens to a lot of people. You can stay on and send the company the fare later. You look honest.'

The passengers stared. A lady asked her destination. She felt like a beggar. 'Let me off, please.'

As she trudged along the sunny road she considered the fundamental lesson of independence. Without money one cannot be free. The situation was so desperate that she could find no solution to her problem. The sensible thing would have been to telephone Pricey, reversing charges, but she hadn't a dime to drop in the slot. There was nothing to do until she got somewhere; to a church where she could ask help of a minister.

A car drew up beside her. She hardly dared look at the driver lest Dr Hyde or some member of his staff had learned the direction of her travels and come after her. A stranger asked if she wanted a lift. When the man asked where she was headed for, she said New York. Sorry that he could not take her all the way, he said he would drop her at the bus station in New Haven.

Burning with embarrassment she confessed that she had lost her pocketbook and had no money for a telephone call. He gave her a dime and bought her a Coca Cola at a roadside diner. She made a person-to-person call to Miss Lucy Price. The operator reported that Miss Price was not in; did she wish to talk to Mr Dixon? She hung up quickly. Instead of telling the kind gentleman that her call had been unsuccessful, she let him take her to New Haven. Feeling like a robber because she had not given him back the dime, she made another phone call to Miss Price. No one answered.

On the hot, dusty road, she was twice given rides: the first by a friendly family on a Sunday afternoon drive to their grandparents' farm. They let her off at a junction with an unpaved back road. She began to walk again, fighting exhaustion but not without hope. She had learned from the movies as well as from the two rides with strangers that hitch-hiking, while slow, was practical. It might be necessary to ride in several cars before she reached New York.

There she would go to the hotel where she had often stayed with her father. No one would demand immediate payment of Miss Dixon, the Congressman's daughter. After a good meal and a long sleep she would telephone her bank and instruct them to send her two or three or five thousand dollars; select a wardrobe at a Fifth Avenue department store where her father had a charge account, apply for a new passport to replace the one taken from her pocketbook, and book a seat on a plane for Nice. The fantasies consoled her, nourished belief in her ability to take care of herself, so that she skipped along blithely at the edge of the road until a car stopped and the driver asked if she needed a lift. That he was going to New York proved beyond doubt that her troubles were over.

Comfortable in the air-conditioned car, soothed by its rhythm, she grew drowsy, barely heard what the driver was saying, indulged in reveries of the future, renewal of old friendships, the furnishing of a flat of her own, a cooking class, delightful dinners prepared by her own hands. The driver droned on, his talk no more to her ears than an accompaniment to the hum of the engine. When he paused for her reply, she muttered brief acquiescence, not knowing what questions her uhs and umhums answered. Once, when he chided her for inattention, she roused herself sufficiently to say that she found his conversation fascinating. She was sleeping soundly when he drove off the highway, and when he woke her, she saw that they were in a dark forest. The hulking brute lifted her out of the front seat and threw her to the ground. She tried to get up, but the weight of his body was upon her and the stench of his breath close to her nose. She tried to fight him off. Tears and entreaties were of no avail. He was determined and angry. The unequal struggle all but forced her to yield. She felt that her bones were breaking under the force of his sweaty embrace.

'It was wild. He tore off . . .' She hesitated, giggling self-consciously and turning from me to stare at a row of Chinese plates on the shelf of the Welsh dresser.

'Go on. What did he tear off?'

'My pants. And I got my leg free and kicked him in the balls.' Her laughter was freer. She faced me again with a smile and the impish look I had admired when I first met the lost girl.

'Good for you.' I blew a kiss.

'While he was swearing and cursing me and holding himself, I jumped up and ran. And hid in the woods. But I had left my overnight bag in the car. I didn't have a single thing, not a pocketbook nor a toothbrush, nor make-up, not even pants.' Now that the danger was over she found comedy in the situation. At the time there was only the desperate sense of being lost.

She started walking again but did not know which direction to take. The woods were quiet, daylight waning. She stumbled on until she was too weary to take another step, sat down to rest under a tree and stretched her aching body on a bed of weeds and moss. 'Like the babes in the woods, only I didn't have a brother to hold my hand.' When she woke it was deep night. Through thick foliage she caught glimpses of the sky and stars. She must surely have tried to go on for she was walking on the forest road when the Royces found her. She remembered nothing except waking in their guest room and not knowing who she was nor how she got there.

# 7

That she had relived the experience in relating the horrify-ing events was clearly shown in the frequent tightening of muscles, the stiffening of a defiant back, the sprinkling of a few untidy tears. When she had no more to relate, she sank back as though giving herself to the kitchen rocker. Her eyes were shadowed, the lids lilac-tinted, drooping of their own weight. She seemed barely able to breathe. Not wishing to disturb her I moved cautiously to the dishwasher with the cups and saucers, returned on tiptoe to peer down at a face that might have been carved in marble. Stillness was total and distressing. I touched a hesitant finger to her cheek, was reassured by its warmth, but perplexed by another problem; remembering Allan's description of the waif who had slept in his arms when he carried her from the car to the guest room. I was both exultant and appalled at the thought of carrying her up the long flight to her room and laying her gently upon the bed, but the rhythm of my heart was not gentle and the heat within my body an irresistible flame.

The lilac-tinted eyelids rose to allow a flood of tears. She made no attempt to dam the stream, but let sobs shake her body, the tears dripping from her chin. Never in my life had I seen, and hope never again to witness, so heartbreaking a torrent. When at last it ended with Elizabeth trembling in my arms, when she looked up at me with eyes lustrous with moisture and said, 'Chauncey dear, there's no one else in the whole world I could have told that to,' my own eyes were wet. I lifted her so that her face was level with mine and kissed her again and again, savouring the salt of her tears. Once more the vision of carrying her up the stairs caused swift and unusual pulsations of my heart. As I was about to carry out this mad resolution, the knocker on the front door had the impudence to exert its tyranny.

'Oh!' exclaimed Elizabeth, 'I forgot to tell you. Rick phoned this morning and I told him he could come over tonight.'

In no mood to offer courtesy to an unwelcome guest, I bade Elizabeth open the door and stamped up the stairs, calling down that she was to make my excuses for retiring early. Into my mind flashed swift and sorry visions that rational discipline could not exorcise, for these subliminal images, like billboards seen from a speeding car, were beyond the threshold of reason. Recollection of the long silence during the fellow's visit on the previous night returned to haunt the jealous mind. I could not remain honourably on the same level of the house without being aroused by the hum of their voices or the excruciating pain of their silence. So that I should not give way to the temptation of eavesdropping I undressed but, as hope was not entirely abandoned, chose my second-best pyjamas.

From the bedroom shelves where I keep favourite nocturnal companions I decided upon *Tale of a Tub* rather than *Gulliver* since the latter might be too familiar to divert me from the restlessness which forbade concentration on any but the drama below my chamber. Dean Swift had never before failed me; the wit, the exuberance, the scorn were to my mind an aphrodisiac, while the richness of his style soothed away the irritations of an ordinary day. Not so on this occasion. I discarded Swift for an essay in the *Saturday Review*, read it through, but if, within the hour, I had been asked its subject, I could not have given the answer. When I heard their voices in the hall and noted the opening and closing of the front door, I lacked the courage to go out and ask the painful question lest its answer compound the agony.

'Chauncey, are you awake?' The minx tapped at my door. 'I saw your light was on so I wasn't afraid of disturbing you.' She came into the circle of light shed by my bedside lamp and, thus illuminated, gave me such a bold sight of glowing cheeks and shining eyes that I held my breath in anticipation of disastrous news.

'I've got something to tell you, Chauncey.'

*Then tell it, minx, instead of keeping me bereft of breath. What is so beguiling about that arrogant young cock? Is it youth, the kinship with your own generation, or do you find that copper hair, the freckled arms, the stocky torso more seductive than this long pallid New England skeleton?*

'And a question to ask you.'

*Ask. Tell. Don't just stand there like a portrait in oil. You are wearing the white dress of the lost Elizabeth X; your dark hair falls about your face with the same enchanting carelessness. Yet the portrait is not of the lost child whose unformed mind a man hoped to mould in the shape of his vanity, but a woman capable and unafraid of decision. I see in your face that the decision has been made. So strike me with the bad news.*

'Look at this.' She came close to the bed to thrust into my hand eleven duplicate pages of a typescript, the story of the amnesia victim whose identity as the daughter of Congressman Claude Dixon had been discovered by Richard Shannon of the *Weekly*'s staff.

'He promised he wouldn't write about me, and then he did this. He wrote all night and part of the morning and brought it into New York this afternoon. It got him the job he wanted. He came back to Westport to show it to me and expect me to forgive him.'

'Have you read it?'

'It's awful.'

'Will you forgive him?'

'Forgive him!' The look of reproach suggested that I'd struck and mortally wounded her. 'What do you think I am? A spineless ninny?'

Certainly my sympathies were not with the young man, but I needed, for the sake of my self-esteem, to know whether her indignation was more than skin deep. The show of resentment might have been a game of female cunning, a mask donned to prove to me that she would not easily allow the rogue to achieve forgiveness and garner his reward. To test her I said in a tone better suited to a pulpit than a bachelor bedroom, 'To forgive is divine.'

'How would you feel about a person who, in a national magazine, called you an over-sexed virgin?'

As yet unwilling to acknowledge pleasure in my rival's downfall, I made little of her anger, saying, 'So what bothers you is not that he broke his promise not to write about you, but what he wrote. Let me suggest a letter to the editor declaring the humiliating facts untrue, and demanding a retraction. You might threaten a suit for libel if the facts are untrue.'

'Please, Chauncey, don't make fun of me. I've been through so much today, I can't stand any more.' The tone was so humble, the appeal so childlike that I was reminded of the lost girl whose winsome charm had won me at first sight. At that time (two weeks ago, was it? Three? The distant past?) I had been enticed by the mystery of the nameless nymph. Yet with the facts known and her person familiar, mystery remained. The 'infinite variety' of Shakespeare's splendid lines can apply to any beguiling woman; she is both child and adult, sinner and saint, judge and criminal, enigma and solution. And so Elizabeth was to me that night, the riddle and the answer.

Uninvited, she perched on the edge of my bed and diffidently said, 'Chauncey dear,' paused, clasped her hands below her chin, 'Chauncey . . .'

'Have you something more to tell me?' To stem the rise of desire, I became stern, but contradicted the severity by taking off my reading glasses.

'Do you remember something you said to me?'

'I've said a good many things to you.'

'You said you'd marry me.'

Against the protest of my heart my conscience nagged. 'For your protection I said. But now you no longer need to be protected.'

'But I do, I do.' She moved closer on the bed. 'You don't know Daddy if you think he's through. He never stops.'

'He will if you take my advice.' I spoke dryly as though I were lecturing to a class on Ruskin's steamy raptures or the fad for obscurity in contemporary prose. 'You must write a letter, Elizabeth.'

'To him? I couldn't. I couldn't even write *Dear Daddy*.'

'Write *Dear Father* or just *Father*, and say that you will never betray him, never tell anyone of the secret matters that could destroy his public image. And don't neglect to say you've sworn this on the Bible.'

She laughed. 'You really do know Daddy.'

'And another thing, Elizabeth. Tell him that you are leaving for France as soon as you get a new passport, and that you will not be coming back to America for several years.'

Laughter died. 'That wouldn't be true.'

'Indeed it would. To be safe you must go.'

'And what about you? Will you come with me?' She moved closer on the bed. The scent of heliotrope assailed my nostrils. It had been my wife's favourite perfume and there were still, after these years of separation, boxes of soap in the guest-room cupboard. 'Don't you want to marry me?' Her lower lip quivered, her eyes widened with appealing sweetness. A hand as smooth and flawless as an infant's plucked at threads of the old quilted counterpane. Good God, I thought, is she going to cry again? Had there been another rush of tears, I would have taken her in my arms and promised to marry her the next day. It was the sight of that childish hand on the old quilt that caused me to see the room and myself as she would see them, if not then, at some future time when she would grow weary of life among the antiques.

'Let's be honest with ourselves, child. Remember, I'm twenty-six years older than you.' In a few months it would be twenty-seven years, but my conscience did not command such precision.

'I like older men better. I always have. Boys have never attracted me.'

'Stop pulling at the quilt. It's almost a hundred years old.' I had not intended to sound harsh. She looked at me in amazement. Liked older men better, did she? Aware of it or not, she craved a surrogate for the lost father. To play my role properly, I put on my spectacles to become the elderly counsellor. Neither soft nor stern, but in a manner I believed to be both kindly and objective, I said, 'You . . . we . . . are tired, dear. It's been a difficult day and you . . . we . . . are both overwrought. This is no time to make a serious decision.'

Silence followed, persisted, unnerved me. I tried to

measure her response by looking into her eyes, but she kept her head lowered as her forefinger traced the intricate pattern of roses stitched into the quilt. More minutes passed. I grew edgier. At last she raised her head and with a look both direct and challenging, said, 'I've made my decision.' Before I could ask the nature of the decision, the determined young woman lay beside me under the quilt. Although it may be indecorous, I shall state for the benefit of inexperienced readers that it is not unpleasant to bed a willing virgin.

I have not seen her since. She was not in my bed when I woke, nor in the guest room when I peeped in there before I hurried to catch the early train. The room was as tidy as though it had never been occupied and her few possessions had been removed. Where could the foolish girl have gone without money, without a passport, without proper clothing? Why had she left so abruptly? Had I done something to offend her? True, I had balked at the idea of marriage, but my arguments had been reasonable and I had not definitely rejected her—immediately afterwards she had come to my bed without invitation. We had made love rapturously and she had vowed never to stop loving me.

The Royces were also puzzled by the defection while Dr Tisch explained in incomprehensible language that, although cured of temporary amnesia, Elizabeth was deeply disturbed, and that the habit of running away from different situations was symptomatic of her particular type of derangement. Richard Shannon earned further profit by writing another article about the (now) senator's elusive daughter. *Where is She Now?* demanded the caption under a full-page picture. I pursued whatever clues might have led to her; to no avail. She was neither at the Shady

Oaks Refuge for Disturbed Adults nor, as I was informed by a silky voice on a long-distance call to Topeka, in her father's house. The silky voice, no doubt belonging to Miss Price, regretted that it had no idea of Miss Dixon's whereabouts.

In a roundabout way I learned from Pop Potter who had it from Dr Hyde that Gordon Hildebrandt had visited the sanitarium to ask if a Grace Dearborn had been treated there and if, as Elizabeth had said, she was an incurable schizophrenic. Dr Hyde had said it was quite true that Miss Dearborn had been lodged there as a patient, that she was schizophrenic but he would not swear that the condition was incurable. Mr Hildebrandt was not seen again in our neighbourhood. And recently I received a marked copy of *The Weekly* with a story by Richard Shannon reporting that the former Claire Foster of Pasadena, kidnapped three days before her wedding to the tycoon, Gordon Hildebrandt II, had been discovered living in Monterey, Mexico, with her husband, Raimondo Mendez, a painter. I wondered how Gordon Hildebrandt II digested the information. A recent photograph of Mrs Mendez posing for her husband bore a marked resemblance to Elizabeth.

Some eight or ten weeks after Elizabeth's disappearance I was summoned to the local post office to pay duty on a package from Paris. It was from the Hermes shop on the Rue Faubourg St Honoré and contained a large crocodile travelling bag bearing my monogram in gold, and fitted with an assortment of brushes, combs, gold-topped jars and crystal bottles; a typical gift of the rich, costly and far too heavy to be carried on a plane, thus utterly useless. There was no card. Nevertheless I sent a note of thanks to Miss Gloria Dixon in care of Lady Harrington-Clark, Cap Ferrat, Department of the Var, France. I did not receive the acknowledgement I asked for.

There are times when I wonder if all of this actually happened or if Elizabeth was not the creation of a lonely man's imagination. Yet the useless travelling case is evidence of her stay in my house, and there are other solid souvenirs; the notebook she left in her bedroom at the Royce house, her confession (eccentrically typed) of inhibitions, the *Weekly Magazine* with Richard Shannon's articles; and the infant born nine months to the night that Kate and Allan took a lost girl into their home. As the child's godfather I held her in my arms when she was christened Elizabeth.

Our recollections differ widely. To each of us Elizabeth is an intensely personal symbol, the shadow of an unacknowledged need. We seldom speak of her nowadays, perhaps because she was dearest to us as a mystery.

# Help us make the next generation of readers

We – both author and publisher – hope you enjoyed this book. We believe that you can become a reader at any time in your life, but we'd love your help to give the next generation a head start.

Did you know that 9 per cent of children don't have a book of their own in their home, rising to 13 per cent in disadvantaged families*? We'd like to try to change that by asking you to consider the role you could play in helping to build readers of the future.

We'd love you to think of sharing, borrowing, reading, buying or talking about a book with a child in your life and spreading the love of reading. We want to make sure the next generation continue to have access to books, wherever they come from.

And if you would like to consider donating to charities that help fund literacy projects, find out more at **www.literacytrust.org.uk** and **www.booktrust.org.uk**.

## THANK YOU

*As reported by the National Literacy Trust